What the critics are saying:

Icy Hot

"If you like an intelligent erotic sci-fi read, this is for you." - *Sensual Romance*

"I would love to own the gown Aaxis gives to Tayra." - *Sensual Romance*

"ICY HOT is definitely on the hotter side of Romantica." – *A Romance Review*

Deep Heat

"I recommend this book to anyone who wants to read a sensual, futuristic, true love story." – *Jill, Fallen Angel Reviews*

"A book full of intense sex and hot sex scenes will have you running for a cold shower." - *Angel Brewer, The Romance Studio*

"This story grabbed my attention and never let it go from the first page." - *Julie Bryan, Just Erotic Romance Reviews*

THE AKTARIAN CHRONICLES 1: ICY HOT & DEEP HEAT
An Ellora's Cave Publication, July 2004

Ellora's Cave Publishing, Inc.
PO Box 787
Hudson, OH 44236-0787

ISBN #1-84360-948-7

ICY HOT© 2002 B.J. McCall

ISBN MS Reader (Lit) ISBN#1-84360-299-7
Other available formats ISBN#1-84360-401-9
Adobe (PDF), Robketbook (RB), Mobipocket (PRC) & HTML

DEEP HEAT © 2004 B.J. MCCALL

ISBN MS Reader (LIT) ISBN #1-84360-817-0
Other available formats (no ISBNs are assigned):
Adobe (PDF), Rocketbook (RB), Mobipocket (PRC) & HTML

Edited by *Sheri Ross Carucci.*
Cover art by *Syneca.*

THE AKTARIAN CHRONICLES 1:

ICY HOT
&
DEEP HEAT

B.J. MCCALL

ICY HOT

For my husband, Rick.

CHAPTER ONE

Tayra, Princess of Glacid, darted through a narrow fissure in the ice wall, then motioned her trusted assistant, Bae, to follow. Within seconds the fissure closed, severing the women from the guards sworn to protect them. Pulling the hood of her silver-mank cloak over her head to ward off the cold wind, Tayra raced along the massive ice walls. Hearing the faint, but distinctive hum of a Sarkian rover, Tayra stopped in her tracks.

"Is it them, my Lady?" Bae managed. Her breath escaped in clouded puffs as it collided with the frigid air. "What if-how can you trust the Sark?"

Beneath the thick fur of her cloak, Tayra shivered in anticipation. The cold she ignored. So much depended upon her actions, her decisions and resolve. So many lives hung in the balance. She could not fail. "I must go. Without the shield our guards will be overwhelmed."

Bae cried out. No doubt her thoughts were for the handsome guard she'd taken to her bed during the long months of imprisonment Tayra and her assistant had been forced to endure.

Protective custody, her uncle said. Tayra knew better.

Since her father's mysterious disappearance, the warlords, led by her uncle, had risen to power once again and her people had been thrust into a conflict ending years of peaceful, but less than congenial, coexistence with the Sark.

Tayra spotted several glowing orbs moving silently toward them. "I cannot elude them. They've released search probes."

Bae pulled a curved ice blade from her boot. "I'd rather die here and now with you, Your Highness, than warm the bed of a Sarkian warrior."

"That's no ordinary rover. Only one man would challenge this storm. Aaxis."

"Your Highness, please reconsider. What if he kills you?"

"If Aaxis intended to harm me the entire palace would have been laid to waste."

"What if you fail? The Sarks hate us. They do not want peace. The Lord Chancellor could hold you hostage for years."

"I will not fail. I cannot."

Bae grabbed Tayra's hand and held fast. "Please, my lady. Let us return to safety."

"The probes would find me. Remain here and you'll be safe."

Tears rolled down Bae's plump cheeks. Tayra managed to free her hand from her loyal assistant's grip. "You must survive, Bae. My people must know the truth. Should my uncle make an attempt to contact me, make sure he knows I have been captured and by whom."

Without hesitation, Tayra lifted her chin and walked into the icy wind toward her sworn enemy.

* * * * *

Aaxis searched the orb's monitors and swore. The Glacidians had returned fire and the laser exchange had destroyed a large portion of the palace, yet his target had eluded him.

"Land this thing," he roared to the pilot as he scanned several screens. Then his gaze caught on one monitor and held as his prey strolled proudly into the open. Aaxis could swear she looked right into the orb, directly at him.

"You're mine, Princess," he whispered.

Aaxis swiveled around and faced his pilot. "Bring our guest aboard." The young man, fresh out of academy, responded without hesitation. Aaxis noticed the trickle of sweat running down the pilot's temple as his fingers moved over the helm control panel. Glacid's ice storms were a challenge to experienced pilots and keeping a vessel under control was next to impossible. Aaxis prayed the wind wouldn't shift. If he lost the Princess now…

Buffeted by the icy wind, the rover shuddered, then dropped slowly to the surface. "Once Princess Tayra is safe and we are free of this planet, return to Phabes," Aaxis ordered. "Light speed."

As the thick door slid open, the shrieking wind drowned out the rover's familiar hum. Aaxis stepped forward and held out his hand. Wrapped from head-to-toe in priceless ice mank, the Ice Princess, as he'd come to think of Tayra, bowed her head, but not in deference to his position or in submission. Her lips moved silently in what he presumed was prayer.

Although the frigid wind sliced through the fabric of his uniform and tiny ice crystals stung his face and hands, Aaxis waited. Without so much as a nod of acknowledgment, the Princess walked past him. Once inside she approached his senior advisor, Drath.

"The Princess demands to be taken to the Imperial Palace," Drath announced after a brief exchange in her native tongue.

Ignoring Tayra's royal snub, Aaxis refused. Although he spoke her language, he let his counselor translate. Drath had his orders and would allow her to make her protests. He closed the short distance to stand beside Drath.

"You dare to imprison a member of the Glacidian royal family?"

Again she'd spoken to Drath instead of him. Aaxis resisted the urge to force her to face him. "Consider yourself my guest," he responded, deliberately refusing to address her by her royal title. "My counselor will escort you to the visitor's quarters." *And scan you for weapons.* The portal scans were useless against ice weapons. The Glacidians had advanced the science of molecular bonding to an art form. To survive the harsh conditions on Glacid they had modified the basic structure of ice and could mold it into any shape or form. Ice that could withstand heat and most lasers made formidable weapons. An ice blade could cut a man in half. Unsure of Tayra's abilities with weapons, Aaxis could take no chances.

When Tayra removed her fur hood and walked past him to follow Drath, Aaxis sucked in a breath. Although he had seen her in dozens of digital images, in the flesh the Ice Princess was nothing less than striking.

Silver-blonde hair worn in the traditional, short, Glacidian style complimented her delicate features. Her close-cropped, military hairstyle only served to enhance the fine bones of her face. Her eyes shimmered like ice crystals struck by the distant sun. She looked nothing like the dark-haired beauties of Sark, or the golden nymphs of Aktares.

Her beauty was legendary and Aaxis was far from disappointed. A sudden heat surged through him: a perfectly natural reaction after months of abstinence.

War was hell, but that was about to change.

She could snub him now, but once on Phabes, her Highness would have no choice but to deal with him in the flesh.

* * * * *

Hours later, Aaxis flipped on a viewing screen that allowed him visual and auditory access to the visitor's quarters. Princess Tayra, naked and utterly breathtaking, slept peacefully as his rover raced toward the secluded outpost of Phabes. Despite his years and experience, Aaxis had difficulty ignoring his prisoner. Her pale perfection fascinated him. Lying in a bed of thick silver furs, she turned, altering her position in a series of slow, sensual, mesmerizing movements.

"At least your sacrifice should be pleasant."

Aaxis glanced at Drath, his friend and advisor since childhood and grinned. Despite his advanced years, Drath still had an impish gleam in his translucent eyes. Aaxis touched the screen and the picture disappeared to a tiny blip of light. "Not all duties should be painful. How is our guest?"

"Physically, she's fine."

"Emotionally?"

"Mad as hell. She called you a Sarkian dog."

Aaxis chuckled. "I like a woman with spirit."

"That's good. She'd prefer to slit your throat than-"

"Is she coming into cycle?" Aaxis asked suddenly impatient to get to the difficult, yet challenging task awaiting him.

After a Sarkian merchant fleet had inadvertently infected the inhabitants of a large Glacidian port city with a deadly virus initiating a series of armed confrontation between the planets, Aaxis had no expectation that Tayra would willingly accept him as her lover. He'd do anything to stop this foolish war. Even impregnate an enemy princess.

His father's failures strengthened his resolve to bring peace to the solar system. Enemies outside the system threatened. Attack was inevitable if he did not. He needed the Glacidians and their weapons to help him defeat the Sutiumi.

Drath nodded. "She'll sleep for several hours. By the time the two of you are ensconced in your love nest, she'll be climbing the walls."

Aaxis glanced back at the dark screen. "It's rumored her kind make the best love slaves."

"Any man who calls a Glacidian female a love slave is a fool. You don't know what you're getting into my boy."

"You challenge me old friend. I'm not about to fall prey to this Glacidian no matter how beautiful or royal she is. Besides those stories are fables."

"As you say."

Drath's expression belied his words.

After Drath left, Aaxis thought about his friend's dire warnings. Surely Glacidian women couldn't enslave a man unless he was a fool. A willing, lovesick fool. No woman, especially a virgin, could make him so weak with need and wanting he couldn't perform with other females, especially the hand-picked harem awaiting him on Sark.

The Princess would produce an heir, a male child who would bring the planets together. One day his son would rule Aktares, Sark and Glacid.

Hopefully, her Royal Highness had the wisdom to understand the necessity of their union and the same commitment to duty as himself.

If not, he would use her physical state as his weapon. Without her powerful crystals to control her urges and no other male available, she'd be the one demanding his body and his seed.

This was war. She was the enemy. Aaxis intended to win.

The future decided Aaxis touched the screen. Again he was struck by Tayra's beauty.

As she rolled onto her back, the Princess rubbed her thighs together and grasped her rounded breast. After several months in the company of his elite, all male, unit, Aaxis couldn't prevent his immediate, physical reaction as her pink nipple budded beneath the manipulation of her fingers and turned a deep rose. If she responded so readily to her own stimulation, what would happen when he teased her soft flesh with his mouth, lips and tongue? The reports of Glacidian mating habits told of natural breast swelling and elongated nipples to attract males during annual breeding cycles. Were the reports true?

Aaxis certainly hoped so. His fingers curled as he imagined her lush breasts cupped in his hands. Eager to begin his campaign, Aaxis sprang to his feet and paced. Unable to keep his eyes off Tayra's naked image, he tugged at the collar of his uniform. Now wasn't the time to indulge his needs.

Aaxis turned away from the screen and considered Drath's warning. He refused to consider the stories about the secretions from a Glacidian female's orgasm penetrating the male system and enslaving a man for life.

He balled his hands into fists. His father had succumbed to a Glacidian temptress called Zara. For her, Antar had deserted his family and his duty.

Would Tayra test his resolve?

Shaking his head to clear his thoughts, Aaxis reminded himself why he was sacrificing his future and hers. Still, he needed to touch Tayra's alabaster curves and experience her cool beauty in every way. It was his duty to melt the ice in her heart and bring her to the heated climax necessary for conception.

What would their child look like? Would his coloring match the silver-white of his mother, the tawny-gold of his Aktarian ancestors or the dark countenance of the Sarks? Despite the differences of their worlds, their cultures, Aaxis wanted this female. He turned from the viewing screen, strolled to the console next to his sleeping space and checked the rover's progress. Within the hour, the crew would begin docking preparations. Only members of his elite unit knew of Phabes, the outpost built deep inside the solid rock of an asteroid circling Glacid. For years he had escaped Glacidian patrols by slipping into the dangerous asteroid belt. For months he'd waited for Tayra's annual breeding cycle.

Aaxis smiled, pleased he had penetrated Glacid's defenses once again, and not only escaped the patrols, but had captured their royal prize, the Ice Princess. The mission had gone smoothly. Almost too smoothly to his thinking. It was if the Princess had been waiting for him.

To kill him? A royal assassin?

Was she waiting for him now? Given her physical state, perhaps she would fuck him to death. If he had to die in combat, what better way!

Aaxis shook his head. He would not die. The enemy would be his, conquered and carrying his heir apparent.

* * * * *

Tayra shook off the effects of her drugged slumber. Looking about the unfamiliar chamber, she remembered the attack and her capture. Was she still on the Sarkian rover?

She recalled protesting her capture as she was escorted down a narrow passageway with Drath at her side and Aaxis right on her heels. The pain to the base of her skull had been laser sharp, far too swift to ward off. Her knees had buckled beneath her, right before she was scooped up and held against a broad expanse of muscle.

A chest as broad and muscled as that of the man now entering her quarters without permission and certainly uninvited.

Taller than most Glacidian males and dressed in a loose fitting white shirt and pants instead of the black commander's uniform he'd worn before, her rival stood before her, then bowed. Long, sun-streaked hair flowed to his shoulders and his skin was as golden as the endless desert sands of Sark.

Aaxis Thrane: Lord Chancellor of Sark, Supreme ruler of the ringed planet of Aktares and sworn enemy of Glacid. At least he wasn't a full-blooded Sarkian male. His Aktarian blood, inherited from his father, diluted the usual dark, forbidding Sarkian features.

His eyes, almost translucent, yet tinted with bright, golden shards locked with hers. Mesmerized by his golden countenance, Tayra remained motionless as his gaze moved slowly to her mouth, then dropped to her bare breasts. That golden gaze touched her, his mind exploring her, slipping over her like a lover's stroking fingers, heating her skin. His scent, potent and male, filled her nostrils, triggering her receptive senses.

The tempo of her breathing increased, her lips tingled, her breasts suddenly ached and her womb contracted in anticipation. Once her breeding cycle began, her blatant physical reactions were impossible to control, but his desire confused her.

Since the Sarks had introduced a killer virus to Glacid, mating between their people was forbidden by order of both governments. Yet here the Lord Chancellor of Sark stood before her thinking the unthinkable, his desire blatantly displayed. Resisting the urge to cover her nakedness with the soft, sleeping furs, Tayra remained kneeling on the elevated sleeping pallet and waited for him to speak.

When he welcomed her and introduced himself, the rich timbre of his voice wrought another flush of heat. Tayra expected him to speak her tongue, but his command of her language, his ease with the softer, harmonic tones, contrary to his native guttural articulation, flowed over her, drawing her to accept him. It would be far easier for her to resist this enemy should he demonstrate the usual, stern Sarkian behavior.

"I hope you find the furs acceptable?"

Her fingers spread, sliding deep into the thick, silvery pelts. "The taking of ice mank is prohibited by Sarks, Lord Chancellor."

"These pelts were taken long before your ban. I moved them from my quarters."

As he'd spoken, he'd approached her pallet. Instead of the ruthless Sark warrior her armies had faced in battle, Aaxis presented himself as a sun-prince emanating a powerful, erotic musk.

"Ice mank is the best way to stay warm on cold, Glacidian nights."

"We are still in the Glacidian trigon?" she asked trying to focus on her location and her mission instead of the tantalizing male scent clinging to the sleeping furs. His scent? That would explain her erotic dreams. Had he given her a potion, or ejaculated on the furs making his allure all the more potent?

"I was thinking only of your comfort," he said, ignoring her question. "You were restless-"

So he had undressed her and had lain her in his furs. Had he rubbed her bare skin with the scented mank and began the mating process while she slept, powerless and vulnerable? Had the hands caressing her been his?

"Do you always spy on your guests?"

"As your host, your satisfaction is my primary objective. I can help you sleep."

Tayra did not need to ask how he proposed to help her sleep. It was reported Aaxis used many weapons.

He reached out and ran his fingers through the thick furs. Long, supple fingers, golden from his powerful sun, skimmed over her hand and slid slowly up her arm.

Urges insistent and essential thrummed deep in her womb. Attuned to her base needs, Tayra's mind filled with images. Sensual images of she and Aaxis entwined upon the soft furs of her pallet, their bodies coupling, and becoming one. Whether she liked it or not he had won the first salvo: she wanted him. Now.

Innocent, Tayra had no means to compare Aaxis as a lover, but once they joined, climaxed together, conceived together, he would be her mate for life. His scent forever clinging to her skin and warding off any other amorous males.

She must resist or she would belong to this man whose gaze devoured her, within the hour. She had much to negotiate before giving her body and bonding, forever, with this powerful male.

"Do I frighten you?" His voice was a bare whisper, much like that of a coaxing lover. "Your Highness has no reason to fear me."

He leaned toward her and his scent enveloped her.

"I do not fear you, Lord Chancellor," she managed.

"Then why is your heart racing, your breath shallow and your breasts quivering in anticipation?"

Before she could answer he dipped his head and licked her nipple. The touch of his tongue sent shivers of need right to her center. She throbbed. His eyes narrowed as their gazes met and held. He took a deep breath and waited for her to react.

Despite his cool control, he hadn't been immune to the contact. Did Aaxis understand, realize the consequences of his erotic desires? Should she warn him? Would he believe her or think she was refusing him because of his race?

All her life she'd counted on the natural bond created by her own mating secretions. Like any female she wanted her lifemate's love along with his fidelity. Since birth Tayra had accepted this unbreakable bond as her due.

Would the Lord Chancellor of Sark become her lifemate?

Tayra glanced at his hand resting upon her bare arm, then looked into his fascinating eyes. "Why me? What possible value could a female, even a royal one, be to you?"

His fingers caressed her, then slid away. He forced his arms behind his back and clasped his hands. Tayra understood his need to touch her. Few males could resist the aura surrounding her. The flare of his nostrils assured her Aaxis wasn't unaffected. He wanted her, but instead of rubbing his face in the furs to communicate his desire, as was customary Glacidian foreplay, he held himself aloof.

Why had he captured her?

"You are free to leave. However, my ship will not return to this outpost until your cycle has passed."

She needed to concentrate, but having him so close was driving her wild. Resisting the temptation to run her fingers through her hair to search for the crystals she had secreted there, Tayra dug her fingers into the furs.

"If I cannot return to Glacid, then I am not free. You have simply exchanged ice for..." Tayra looked around. "Walls still surround me."

"There are no guards. Only you and me." He cupped her face in his hand, his fingers slid over her cheek, his fingertips touched her hair. His voice had deepened. "I mean you no harm."

She pushed his hand away and prayed her crystals weren't discovered. All captives were searched. Tayra recalled hands, strong and sure, touching, probing as she drifted in and out of consciousness. Had those hands belonged to Aaxis?

"You attacked my palace. Killed my guards. Searched me."

Again his gaze drifted to her breasts. "Your soldiers fired upon my ship."

"Why did you capture me? What do you hope to achieve?" She gathered a fur, held it before her, shielding her nakedness. The fur sliding across skin was as tantalizing as his touch. Almost. "My uncle will use this incident to incite my people against you."

Aaxis leaned forward, his face mere inches from her, bracing his weight with his arms. Although his hands clutched the edge of her pallet, his fingertips slid into the furs. "Will they hate our child?"

Tayra grasped. His musky scent assailed her nostrils. His desire wrapped around her like a cloak. The idea of breeding with this powerful male sent a flash of heat, hot and molten, through her middle.

She rubbed the soft furs against her swelling nipples. She wanted to stimulate her clit, bring a fast, necessary climax and end the delicious pain building between her legs, but she dare not. Aaxis watched her, aware of her need, waiting. Despite his Sarkian blood, the Lord Chancellor was handsome as sin and his scent...

He's the enemy. His purpose in abducting her was to conquer Glacid and rule all that she loved.

"I am pledged to Kyth-"

"And he is yet to claim you, to give you a child."

"He is young-"

Aaxis accepted her insult. He'd pondered Tayra's youth. She was no child, but he was older and thankfully much wiser than Kyth.

Typical Glacidian thinking, to mate her with the highest-ranking warrior. Except Kyth cared for no one but himself. The young warrior planned to rule Glacid for his own personal glory. Bringing peace was the last thing on his agenda.

"I understand he enjoys a promiscuous life." Aaxis doubted Tayra knew about Kyth's active sex life.

"Which will cease the day of our marriage."

"What makes you think Kyth will change his behavior?"

Tayra lifted her chin a fraction. "Once we have mated, *my* husband will seek no other."

Aaxis discounted her confident words, but couldn't ignore the sultry gleam in her brilliant eyes. This woman intrigued him. She had from the moment she'd surrendered. "Kyth will not be your husband."

"Neither will you."

"I said nothing about marriage, but the only child *you* will bear will be *my* son."

"A Sarkian bastard. Never!"

If her remark was meant to sting, it did. Aaxis intended to marry Tayra. Only a formal union would placate the powerful lords of her world or the council leaders of Sark, but her immediate thought of the young warrior, Kyth, had triggered something akin to jealousy.

Did Tayra see him as old? Too old to be her lover or simply as the enemy?

The challenge in her shimmering eyes brought forth his warrior instincts. Only a good fight could heat his blood more than a beautiful woman-the combination was irresistible. Aaxis leaned forward and brushed her lips with his. The fleeting contact seared like a hot brand. His demand for her total submission caught in his throat as he threaded his fingers into her short, silky hair and covered her mouth with his.

She would surrender. All his enemies surrendered. Eventually.

His thoughts gave way to the lush warmth of her mouth. Their tongues warred, entwining, daring the other to break the searing contact.

Her scent, primal and sweet, replaced the air in his lungs, forced all thought from his brain, except the desire to have her and make her his forever.

She wrenched her mouth from his. The contact of her hand across his cheek brought him back to reality. He grasped her by the neck, shoved his thumb beneath her chin exposing her throat. His battle honed instincts demanded he fight back, force her into submission as he would any other enemy, but his purpose managed to keep his reaction to her assault in check.

This battle would be fought in the luxury of the furs, between her milky white thighs. And he would win.

One day she would kneel before him, submissive and ready to please.

Slowly he eased his grip. He leaned down and touched his tongue to the throbbing pulse at the base of her neck just below her Glacidian pleasure node. A current as sharp as a laser lashed through him. Clasping one hand about her narrow waist, he lifted her, bringing a firm breast to meet his lips. He suckled, drawing on the taut nipple like a ravenous infant seeking nourishment.

A tingling, like none he'd experienced before, began in his balls. His shaft stretched, tightened, heated until he ached. Great Gods, he ached. Seeking relief, Aaxis pressed her back into the soft furs, climbed onto the sleeping platform and settled himself between her beckoning thighs. He needed her warmth, her slick moisture to ease the wonderful pain, but if his intelligence reports were correct Tayra remained a virgin. He wanted to strip off his clothes and drive his cock deep inside her wet warmth, but held back. He wanted her to beg for him and demand he end her anguish.

Primal moans, his and hers, mingled as he licked her breast. Her nipple reddened, hardened as he suckled. Beneath his weight she bucked. His balls contracted. The need to taste her, penetrate her overwhelmed him. He drew a slow, wet trail down to the indentation of her navel, then lower to the soft, silver-blonde curls surrounding her sex.

Levering his shoulders beneath her thighs, he knelt between her legs and licked the moist slit. Her hips arched, urging him to thrust his tongue deep into the center of her heat to taste her sweet nectar. Her breath quickened, her sex quivered and she cried out as she climaxed.

With her orgasm, Aaxis shuddered. An odd ripple flashed through every nerve and muscle, searing heat raced through his veins, leaving him momentarily immobile.

Her feet connected with his shoulders, forcing him up then drove into his chest, the impact taking him by surprise. Off balance, he fell backward, off the platform, suspended for a split second before he hit the hard floor. Landing with a thud, he gasped, his lungs screaming for air like a swimmer fighting to reach the surface. Finally, he caught air.

He'd been knocked on his ass before, but never by a woman! Few men would dare.

"I do not mate with Sarks."

Looking up, Aaxis locked gazes with Tayra. Arms akimbo, she knelt on the platform, her knees slightly apart for balance. His gaze fell to the display of silver-blonde curls.

Fearing he was falling irrevocably into some sensual mindnet. Aaxis struggled to clear his brain. He should be angry, but all he wanted to do was crawl back upon the platform and immerse himself in the hot folds of Tayra's sex.

Drath had been correct. Aaxis couldn't see Tayra as any man's slave. Tasting her had nearly overpowered him. What would it be like when he joined with her?

He'd walked into her quarters, cocky and sure of himself, believing she would capitulate, if not to him, then to reason. He'd been wrong to approach her in her quarters. While naked, she had the advantage. He didn't want to negotiate or convince her of anything. He wanted to fuck her. Gathering what little control he had left, Aaxis pushed himself off the floor and left the room.

This was war.

Aaxis had to admit he'd lost the first skirmish. He didn't like it.

CHAPTER TWO

As the portal silently closed behind Aaxis, Tayra forced herself from the sleeping platform. Legs trembling, she dropped to her hands and knees. The cool floor was a welcome change from the warm, male-scented furs. After several slow, cleansing breaths, she began humming an ancient chant designed to clear the mind and ease the physical cravings.

Never before had a male's intimate touch electrified her senses to this intense fevered pitch. Well chaperoned until she reached her majority, Tayra's sexual experience was limited, but as with all Glacidian females her training in the art of pleasure was exceptional. Taught how to pleasure by monitored instruction, she fondled and manipulated chosen male subjects who were blindfolded and unaware the pleasing female was a royal princess. Mutual pleasure between lifemates was an accepted part of a long-term marital relationship. Satisfying sex strengthened life bonds.

Damn Kyth for publicly claiming her as his future mate. His presumption had threatened her timetable, forced her actions. Fortunately, Aaxis had seized the opportunity she had created.

Aaxis. Her skin still shivered from his touch. How was she supposed to think of him as the enemy when the memory of his tongue buried inside of her made her muscles clench with need? She wanted to give in, needed him utterly, completely. Thank goodness she'd managed another option. Tayra grinned. He'd even looked good landing on his backside.

The shocked look on his face was as pleasurable as his kisses. Almost. Kyth could use a few lessons in seduction.

Mindful that all her actions were monitored, Tayra rubbed her temples then slid her fingers along her scalp to the top of her skull. Her fingertips touched the four tiny beads affixed to her scalp. Each bead represented critical control of her urges, used only when her resistance would falter. Without them she would surrender, tie her future to his without negotiated powers and leave her people to his mercy. She needed time to seduce him, to bond with love. If Aaxis loved her, Tayra would retain governmental control and Glacid would survive.

Thankfully, Aaxis hadn't discovered the beads.

Until then she must concentrate, perform the ancient dance her mother had taught her when she'd confronted her first cycle, until her skin no longer tingled from his touch and her womb ceased its minute, intense fluttering.

"The urges within us are strong, but you must be stronger. Our people will look to you one day for leadership," her mother had warned. *"Your cyclemate will be your lifemate. By tradition your lifemate will command the military while you head the Chamber of Lords. Choose well."*

Kyth was her betrothed, but not the man her father had selected nor the man she wanted. Her uncle had chosen the young warlord who, as Aaxis had reminded her, preferred war and women to marriage and her.

She had no intention of marrying Kyth, much less giving him sons to plague future worlds with mayhem. But Tayra wasn't about to aid the enemy with this information. Aaxis had gone to a great deal of trouble to isolate her, leaving her no choice but him as a mate. Obviously the man had no idea of the long-term consequences. Had his advisor, Drath, not warned him?

There were rumors that the Sarks had developed an antidote, but Tayra had received no evidence to support the claim. If an antidote was available to Aaxis that would explain his dismissal of her ability to physically bind him for life. Or had the Lord Chancellor begun to believe the songs and stories that had made him a legend?

The latter seemed the more reasonable conclusion as she rose and walked around the wide sleeping platform centered in the room. Her quarters were utilitarian at best. Other than her pallet, the room had only a tiny table and one chair. The walls, devoid of paintings or decoration of any kind, were perfectly smooth except for a small control panel. She touched a disc. Beneath her fingers, the disc glowed, bright yellow and a panel slid open to an empty closet. She had expected Aaxis to search her clothing and destroy her weapons so Bae had affixed the crystals to her body.

Curious, Tayra touched the next disc. Another door slid open and she crossed the room to peer inside. Before her stood a cylindrical tube for cleansing, next to that a sun tube and the necessary facilities: all as austere and cold as the men who designed them. Instead of a relaxing, hot steamy bath, she'd have to settle for a short, sonic shower. Her quarters were as expected. What did the Sarks know of comfort or beauty?

At least Aaxis had provided his precious white mank. But even that kind gesture had purpose. He must know his scent would cling to the furs, reaching her subconscious as she slept, making her susceptible even in her dreams.

If he came to her while she slept, could she resist?

Tayra pondered the long night ahead and the feasibility of sleeping on the hard floor as she touched another disc. To her left a panel slid upward revealing a communication center. A large screen filled the wall and a series of discs lighted. Uncertain as to how the system worked, Tayra touched a green disk.

"Have you changed your mind?"

Aaxis. His handsome faced filled the screen and his voice sent a ripple of desire through her chest down to…

She swallowed. "I would like my clothing returned immediately."

The lowering of his gaze told her his view was of more than her face. His eyes gleamed as they focused on her chest. Aware her nipples were hard and erect, Tayra remained still. Sexual titillation could work for her as well as against her.

His lips twisted into a sexy grin. "Your wish is my command."

His mouth drew her gaze, reminding Tayra of the delicious sensations he'd inflicted upon her eager flesh. Were his actions a miscalculation or did he realize her secretions would penetrate his system through his tongue? She hadn't expected permanent bonding to begin on their first private encounter.

She lifted her gaze and met his. "I wish to be released."

"The moment my ship returns you will be. You may even choose your destination."

"Then summon your ship."

"Ask for something I can give you."

Tayra hadn't missed the underlying sensuality of his words. "I wish to bathe. I wish to erase the scent of Sark from my skin."

"I have a bathing vessel in my quarters," he said, ignoring her insult. "You are welcome to use it."

"You are determined to detain me against my will."

"You and I have unfinished business. Your clothes will be returned and I will summon you when appropriate."

The screen went black. Isolate and conquer. How many battles had Aaxis won using the strategy? Isolate and impregnate. Same tactic, but with an erotic twist.

The thought of joining with him heated Tayra's already simmering blood.

Did he want peace? Or did he intend to use her to capture Glacid?

She must concentrate, keep her wits about her. She mustn't succumb to her own natural urges, but how was she to fight them with the stimuli of the most powerful warrior in the star system confronting her on the most primal level? Unless the Sarks had found a way to fool her olfactory senses, he was an extremely healthy specimen with an equally high sperm count.

Had she the strength? He was the enemy. This was war. The fate of her planet, her people, lay within the soft folds of Aaxis's furs.

Despite her desperate situation a needy urge remained coiled inside her, warming her sex. She wanted Aaxis. Hungered for his touch and for the act that would end her virginal life and bind them for eternity.

The desire to breed with a healthy male would only grow stronger as her cycle progressed. Aaxis would do anything and everything to exploit her state for his own needs, both physical and political.

Could she beat him at his own game?

Lifting her arms, Tayra poised her weight on one foot and began to dance. She circled the fur-strewn platform and performed the ancient movements. The complicated dance, designed to drive away the demons of lust, drilled the mind with a series of intricate movements. Combined with her crystals the dance was the only weapon, beyond her strength of will, in her arsenal.

* * * * *

Stepping out of the shower, Aaxis reached for one of the unlighted disks on the station's control panel. From his private quarters he could monitor everything from the room temperature to the lethal rays protecting the main entrance. His trembling fingers hovered over the disk as his mind fought to resist Tayra's erotic pull. Drawing in a breath, he assured himself this unusual, overwhelming physical reaction was due to the lack of female companionship, the months of abstinence. He thought of the women waiting for him at home. All hand-picked, each one a familiar source of pleasure. He couldn't bring a single feature to mind.

The disk glowed beneath his fingertips as a screen flickered to life.

She danced. Naked and exquisite, the Ice Princess performed the most erotic dance he'd witnessed in the cosmos. Her hips undulated to a silent tempo. Her breasts quivered as she swayed to music he could not hear, but sensed in the acceleration of his heartbeat. His pulse leaped. His heart drummed. A pleasant, insistent thrum began in his nether regions, a natural response to the vision on his screen. As she moved, stretched every muscle, revealed curves and angles he longed to touch and explore, he throbbed. Blood rushed and pooled.

The dance ended and the Princess, oblivious to his state strolled into the cleansing room to remove the slick sheen of perspiration from her perfect skin.

A disk at the opposite end of the panel glowed. The bluish light alerted him the communication came from Drath.

He touched the disk and his counselor appeared on the screen to his left. Drath's eyebrow rose a fraction. "Your mission?"

"I've barely begun."

"That would explain your flushed face and breathing pattern."

Drath's observations didn't embarrass Aaxis. The man knew him well and had been his mentor far too long. "She...If the Glacidians had any sense they'd send their women into battle. We'd lose within hours."

"They are magnificent creatures." Drath's mouth curved into a slow smile. "During their breeding cycles, irresistible. Have you...?"

Aaxis shook his head. "It's going to get worse?"

"Much worse. Now do you understand?"

"I still can't believe the part about forever."

"You will. Your father understood."

Aaxis welcomed the conversation, anything to distract him from the insistent, near painful, throb in his groin. "The reason for my mother's hate?"

"Your mother had her choice of consorts. She loved your father and when she became Chancellor Regent she placed her world at his feet. He rewarded her by breaking her heart."

"She never told me she loved him. Only that he betrayed the Sarks."

"She sent him to Glacid as her representative. Your birth inspired her quest for peace, but he became involved with Zara, the negotiator assigned to our delegation. She came into cycle while we were there."

"A female in cycle as a negotiator! I never realized the significance. No wonder his mission failed and he was banished to Aktares." For the first time in his life Aaxis empathized with the father he'd never known. "I guess the Glacidians have sent their women to war."

"He didn't dare bring Zara and their child to Sark. If it weren't for you and your claim to the throne, your mother would have destroyed Aktares. The council wisely prevented a strike against Glacid."

"Did she destroy his ship?"

"I don't know."

"You must know. You're the one person she trusted."

"I never asked. But if she did, it was to protect you."

Aaxis clenched his hands. He loved his mother, but he'd wanted to know the Aktarian prince who had given him life. "My memories of him are vague. I would have liked to have spoken with him, heard his side of the situation."

"She feared she'd lose you. Your father could be persuasive."

"So she killed him and his concubine. She should have allowed me the chance to make my own decision."

"You don't know what your father's betrayal did to her."

Drath's expression hadn't changed, but anger simmered beneath his words. Ever the protector. "Yes, I did. I lived with it every day of my life until you insisted I attend academy. Did he love Zara?"

"I think he loved them both, but in very different ways. He couldn't leave Zara. He was bound to her."

"And her child?"

"Yes, but he loved you. I know he did. When you were born, he held you with pride. He begged your mother to let you come to Aktares to visit. He wanted your forgiveness."

"If you think Tayra will have the same power over me that Zara had over my father, you're wrong."

"Will you use your son the way your parents used you?"

"I want peace."

"So did your father."

Aaxis ignored Drath's declaration. "I need the antidote."

Drath's eyes narrowed. "What antidote?"

"I know about my mother's experiments. My position gives me access even to her secrets."

"Did you read about the failures? The impotent soldiers."

"That was years ago."

"Its purpose is to prevent conception."

"I am aware of the cover story cooked up by my mother. She wasn't content with killing Zara. She wanted to break the power of all Glacidian females. The serum prevents the female's ability to bind her mate for life. Mother's revenge works to my advantage."

"The antidote is dangerous, far more dangerous to you, to Sark, than a full strike on Glacid. If you have a negative reaction the consequences could leave you sterile."

"I want her, Drath. I want the child, but I can't take the chance I'll become a victim like my father. Otherwise I might as well resign now and live out my life on Aktares."

"What of your mother?"

"She'd prefer a fatal strike, but I can't destroy a world, a whole civilization because my father bedded another woman."

"Her price for betrayal can be high," Drath warned.

"I know."

Silence fell between them. Aaxis understood the internal conflict Drath had. If this mission failed, they both would be tried for high treason and branded as traitors. Drath would lose his life. Tayra and the child would share that fate. But he would live with his failure. His mother would see to that.

The price was too high to fail. "I need the antidote."

"In your safe. Pre-measured to avoid miscalculation."

"Why didn't you inform me?"

"Would a lifetime with Tayra be so ill a fate?"

"I prefer choice to surrender."

Drath bowed and the screen went black.

Sighing, Aaxis leaned back. The throbbing in his groin had ceased. Maybe he should think of his mother when he was with the Princess. Great Gods, that thought was alarming.

A woman like Tayra made a man forget everything. If he had given into his mother's wishes and married a Sarkian woman, could Tayra turn him from his duty?

This test of duty was more than enough to plague Aaxis. His father had failed. He would not.

He touched a series of discs in rapid succession. Nearby a panel slid open. He rose and withdrew a small pistol-like object, then retrieved a tiny pellet from a long vacuum tube. He placed the pellet on a small depression on the top of the unit and instantly the antidote disappeared. A faint hiss informed him the pellet had been absorbed and transformed into liquid. Drawing a deep breath, he pointed the nozzle on the pulsing artery in his neck and injected the finite stream.

Slowly, Aaxis exhaled. The microscopic particles raced up the artery and spread throughout his system. Determined to win what he hoped would be his last battle with Glacid, Aaxis sealed the safe and left his quarters.

* * * * *

Tayra fastened the row of jeweled clasps decorating her left shoulder. The prized clasps held ancient stones, hard and clear as ice, rare and worn only by royalty. Aaxis had summoned her to join him in the station lounge. He had called it neutral ground. If there was such a thing here…wherever here was.

He had refused to tell Tayra the location of this private prison.

Her display of official ornamentation and dress should remind the Lord Chancellor of her status. The shimmering material of her silver skinsuit covered her from neck to toe and provided the illusion of protection. At least this time, she wouldn't be naked and vulnerable to his touch.

She prayed he'd wear his black, commander's uniform. It would remind her that beneath his beauty, he was a Sark. Nothing like that hated uniform to keep her urges in check and her resistance firm.

The short distance to the meeting gave her a brief moment to prepare herself. On her third, silent repetition of the Glacidian oath, she reached the lounge.

The large room was filled with plump, colorful pillows in various shapes and sizes surrounding several low tables. Lounging against a golden pillow bearing the Aktarian royal crest, Aaxis appeared at ease, a man without the weight of two worlds, three if he conquered Glacid, upon his shoulders. He looked nothing like a Sarkian warrior prepared for battle.

Or was this master of seduction prepared for an entirely different kind of confrontation? Having only will and nerve for weapons Tayra understood her disadvantage. She must strike first. Victory lay in the terms of their final negotiation.

On the table before him stood two glasses and a bottle, distinctly Glacidian in form and labeling. At least he was a knowledgeable host. The wine was her favorite.

He rose as she approached. Beneath her bare feet the thick, maroon-colored carpet was warmed by a heating system built into the floor. He bowed in deference to her status as was demanded by her choice of her official trappings. Was he disappointed she had not chosen to wear the beautiful but revealing gown of shimmering silver-blue she'd discovered in her quarters?

His own dress was casual, far too casual for a formal meeting. His pale yellow shirt enhanced the color of his eyes and the loose white pants favored by the easy-going Aktarians softened his appearance. His open shirt exposed a generous amount of golden skin. With every movement he subjected her to flexing muscles and masculine grace. Obviously Aaxis intended to seduce, not negotiate.

"I wish to welcome you, officially."

"Our earlier meeting?" she asked, far too aware of the huskiness of his voice.

"Forgive my eagerness, your Highness. Please, be seated."

"What one should expect from a man who maintains a harem." Despite his Aktarian ancestry, Aaxis practiced a decidedly Sark tradition. "At last report, the number was five. Or was it six?"

She eased herself to the floor and folded her legs beneath her to sit, her spine straight. He resumed his relaxed position and gazed at her across the short length of polished wood.

"And why would your Highness care?"

"It is rumored you have captured a Siluko."

"I did not capture Sy." His tone was low and even. "I discovered her chained. Her captor accepted coin from any male who wished to best her in a wresting contest. Few did."

"But you did not grant her freedom?"

"Her tribe had been massacred. She had no place to go and chose to remain in my service."

"So she was given a place in your harem?"

His lips twisted into a grin. "Actually she's in security."

"She does not share your bed?"

"Let's talk about you."

"I abhor slavery." Tayra seized on this topic. It reminded her why her people must never give in to the Sarks and helped to keep her thoughts on something other than his sculpted torso. "Why *you* allow it is beyond reason."

"If you know anything about me and I think the Glacidian spy network is somewhat efficient, you'd know I have spoken often against the concept."

"Still you house sex slaves in your palace? Your actions speak for you."

"None of my women were forced. None are captives."

Despite the truth of his words, Tayra refused to condone maintaining a harem. She tugged at the high collar of her skinsuit. "A benevolent master. But tell me, how does a merchant's daughter say no to the Lord Chancellor?"

"A man knows when a woman is unwilling. I choose for mutual pleasure–"

"Not to conquer? Then why am I here?"

"I do not wish to conquer you, only to impregnate you."

His voice, husky and low, penetrated her too sensitive receptors. "And how would that benefit me or my people?"

"Our son will rule–"

"That my child will rule Glacid is a given."

He leaned forward and her nostrils flared in response to his scent. Male musk: potent and far too healthy for her to ignore. Her womb fluttered. No wonder the Aktarian species had survived every possible disaster.

"Your son, the son we would conceive, the son you will carry, could rule Sark."

She touched the clasp of her collar. Her fingertips grazed the hard stones. "He'd never live to walk, much less rule."

"I will protect him. My unit is sworn only to me."

"Will they stand with you when your mother declares you a traitor?"

"You choose to commit your son to war, rather than *our* son to peace?"

"Our mating is forbidden."

"Laws become outdated. Times change."

"Perhaps you can choose your laws at will. Aktarian laws must be far easier to live with than those of your mother's, but I have but one law."

"You'd prefer to mate with a man who makes a mockery of your laws for his own benefit?"

He had her there. Kyth had proved he wanted power more than duty. Unable to defend Kyth, Tayra remained silent.

"Our son could rule under all our laws. Is it not our duty to save our peoples' lives, to bring them peace through our union, through our child? A son to bind us together for life? Would our mating not bring us both pleasure? Could we not share the joy of raising our child, or if we are blessed, children?"

How could he make duty sound so enticing? "Your solution is to lose the purity of our races?" she asked reiterating the premise her uncle had used to wrest the crown from her father.

"I honor the best in both my worlds. The separatism celebrated by Glacid and Sark will be the downfall of both. Since when did you agree with your Uncle Brac? I would think your father's death would have severed that connection forever."

His statement slammed into her heart. "My father is under house arrest. Ill I fear, but very much alive."

He moved around the table, kneeled beside her and placed a hand on her shoulder. "You have spoken to him?"

His touch was comforting. "No. But I would know here," she said, pointing to her heart. "If he is dead."

"Once Brac seized power he couldn't take the risk and you know it."

"You lie! I will die before I submit to you."

"Why do you think you were imprisoned? Your father never would have chosen Kyth."

"I don't believe you." A sob formed in her throat. Deep inside Tayra knew Aaxis told the truth. Since her uncle had placed her in protective custody, she understood her father's life was in jeopardy. She hadn't wanted to face the truth. The fact that her people would revolt and Kyth had yet to claim her had given her a glimmer of hope. Alone, she had clung to that slender thread.

"Kyth is an acceptable suitor-"

"As were many. He's Brac's choice, not your father's. Nor should he be yours. He hasn't claimed you, but he will as soon as the army is secure. Haven't you questioned why so many of the leaders your father appointed are dying? Can anyone believe in so many accidents or fatal battle wounds?"

His grip tightened on her shoulder. His golden gaze bored into hers.

"Your father's supporters are dwindling. Most are dead. Those who have refused to join Brac are being executed. Those that have fled are being hunted. Your uncle needs Kyth in full command before he announces your father's death. Only then will Kyth claim you. He needs you as his wife to legitimize his position. That time is drawing near. That is why I had to act."

Aaxis had no need to instruct her in the current events of Glacid. She was well aware of the forces at work...and also why she must act. "You think by taking me, you'll force Kyth to surrender?"

"I wish it were so simple."

Why his statement should insult her so, Tayra didn't know. She didn't love Kyth, but still his lack of commitment stung. Maybe it was because in her heart she feared she would have to marry for duty instead of love and her lifemate would desire power far more than he would his wife. All Tayra could count on was her mate's fidelity.

If she couldn't count on that then she'd be nothing more than a pawn in a powerful game of interplanetary dominance.

"Your father would see the rationality of our union. I think if he were alive he would support it."

A tool for the man whose fingertips were tracing the line of her jaw far too tenderly? "You say he is dead."

He smoothed her cheek. "I have no reason to lie."

She shoved his hand, his comforting gesture, aside. "You have every reason to lie."

"By telling the worst possible news, I will gain your trust?"

She hated the silkiness of his voice, the compassion in his eyes. "By destroying my hope, you draw me into your scheme, make me a traitor to all I hold dear."

"I could have tied you down naked the first day and taken you."

"Conception without climax is impossible. Our scientists perfected that protection in the last millennium, otherwise the pure Glacian race would have been wiped out long ago. The Sarks tried that ancient method to destroy us once. Rape will not achieve your goals."

"I said nothing of rape. I understand that without the nectar of your pleasure mingling with mine..."

Again his voice held a coaxing tone. Tayra thought of her father, then of Brac's betrayal. She welcomed the anger. "What do you intend to do?"

"I could restrain you with silken cords and pleasure you with my tongue, my touch until you demand I end your agony. Then I would enter you gently, as one should when introducing a virgin to the joys of love."

He didn't need cords, only his silken voice to hold her. "How can restraint be pleasurable?"

A smile teased the corners of his mouth. His fingertips skated along the curve of her jaw, pausing beneath her chin. He leaned close and grasped her wrists. He levered her down onto her back. "It can be quite pleasing. If you would allow..."

"I do not lie with Sarkian dogs!"

Within seconds Aaxis flipped her onto her stomach and pinned her to the floor. His battle-honed body anchored her firmly. She tried to rise, to lever his weight, but failed. Extending her arm he slipped a fur-lined restraint about her wrist. He'd hidden restraints beneath the pillows.

He licked her neck tasting her as a beast would its prey.

"Rough foreplay does excite the blood."

Again, Tayra tried to throw him off. Locking his legs about hers he rolled her onto her side. He fastened her free wrist. His legs still wrapped about her thighs Aaxis grasped her by the waist and levered her onto her back. He rested on her thighs and smiled down at her.

"As I see it, conception is merely a matter of mutual climax. Some women like playing captive, enjoy the foreplay of restraint."

"Force is the only way you'll have me, Sark."

He slid down her legs, keeping them immobilized until he pinned one ankle with a knee and the other in his hands. He bound each ankle by the fur-lined restraints and kneeled between her spread legs.

"I must teach you how to wrestle. Or at the very least to enjoy restraint."

Leaning forward, he licked her nipple through the thin material of her skinsuit. Her reaction was immediate. Again he teased the taut bud with a flick of his tongue.

"You like that?"

She arched her back, pulling at her restraints. Seizing the opportunity, he slipped an arm about her back and held her as his mouth covered her nipple. Although he had her completely at his mercy, he drew slowly, gently, leaving her aching for more. Tayra closed her eyes and willed away the delicious sensation, refused to arch her breast and communicate her need.

He lifted his head, leaving the thin material wet and slick. Then he blew a soft breath over the area. A tremor of need thrummed between her legs.

"Conception while restrained is not a victory. You gain nothing."

Again his breath caressed her nipple. "Nothing except attainment of my goals."

"I thought your goal was peace. Cannot the great Lord Chancellor think of something more gallant than rape?"

Slipping his fingertip along the shoulder seam of her skinsuit, Aaxis separated the overlapping layers, exposing her neck. "I have no intention of raping you. Seduction is far more enjoyable."

His tongue encircled the nodule beneath her ear. No warrior would dare play with what could result in instant death for his captive. The Lord Chancellor must know he played with fire.

To Tayra's relief, Aaxis moved away from her nodule and kissed her. He kneaded her breasts, explored her body with his hands, learning her curves and hollows. Ripples of need raced beneath her skin.

"I haven't been home in months. You tempt me to take my pleasure."

"You are self-serving my Lord Chancellor. Have you forgotten your peace mission?"

He cupped her sex and massaged her swollen labia, his fingers branding her through the thin fabric of her skinsuit.

"Although you speak as an enemy, your body sends another message."

"Perhaps if you were another man."

His head snapped up and he held her sex in his powerful hand. "I have days to fill you with my seed. Can you resist your owns needs? Your womb is fertile and wanting. Eventually you will succumb and you will conceive."

"Neither council will accept a child conceived under these conditions."

"There is truth to your words, but our councils are far away and I have a beautiful captive with which to take my pleasure."

He lowered his head and laved his tongue along the crease of her sex, back and forth, slow and fast, pressing, teasing and playing. Her skin heated and burned. Her resistance melting with each sensual stroke.

The wet material rasped against her needy clit. Tayra bit her lip to keep from shuddering. She failed.

He raised his head. Eyes blazing Aaxis rubbed her mons with the heel of his hand, pressed a fingertip along the crease of her sex, creating an unbearable heat beneath the fabric of her skinsuit.

A smile teased his lips as Aaxis leaned close bringing his lips but a mere breath away from hers. He continued to tease and touch, bringing forth a delicious throb.

"As I suspected, your veins run hot, not with ice, but with fire."

His deep kiss forced her to swallow her retort and accept the invasion of his tongue. His tongue teased at her determination to resist. Tayra succumbed, an unwilling participant to the firm touch of his lips and the erotic exploration of his tongue.

The rhythm of his breath increased as his mouth moved along her neck to the swell of her breasts. He suckled each nipple in turn until her skinsuit was soaked. Again he licked her neck, leaving a trail of aching flesh in his wake.

Although his kisses, his licking and his now ardent caress of her sex, were meant to seduce, Tayra knew he was as much her captive as she was his. With each skin-to-skin, fluid-to-fluid contact they would bond. She doubted he knew the long-term effects and wisely Tayra wasn't about to tell. Instead she climaxed.

Once his luscious licking had ceased, she opened her eyes.

"You would enjoy it more if I were deep inside you."

"As long as I am restrained, access is impossible."

"It seems I found an ice blade. I can use it to remove this most inconvenient barrier."

His threat struck fear in her heart. If she conceived now Aaxis would have no reason to negotiate. She had to convince him to remove her bonds.

"I had other wishes for my first time."

"What did you wish for?"

"A great warrior with a gentle touch. A man of honor to instruct. A lover to hold in my arms."

"Then you will reconsider your refusal to mate?"

"Not as long as I am in bondage."

"One day I will school you in the pleasure of bondage."

"I would enjoy it, if you are the one bound."

"Then you would ride me or..." He released the bindings about her wrists. "Or would you take me in your mouth?"

Once her ankles were free, Tayra sprang to her feet and moved out of his reach. She needed distance from his enticing touch and coaxing words. Everything about Aaxis, the sheer maleness he exuded, his ability to make her sizzle, the ease with which he brought her to pleasure.

"Is that a preference, Lord Chancellor?"

CHAPTER THREE

"Only a wish to give you pleasure."

Tayra drew a deep calming breath. He couldn't possibly be expecting her to drop to her knees and suckle him. He did and her mouth watered at the thought.

"I should think you would be the one receiving pleasure."

"Do you not wish to feel me shudder as you shuddered?"

She licked her lips, teasing him with a deliberate slow movement of her tongue. "What erotic fantasy drives the Lord Chancellor of Sark to have his women bind him then bring him to pleasure?"

Still on his knees he grinned. "One fantasy and only one woman."

"What purpose would this fantasy serve?"

"You expressed an interest in bondage. For your pleasure I will make an exception. A capitulation never before made to any female. I ask only that you give the same pleasure you received. I cannot impregnate you in such a humble position."

Taking him into her mouth and drawing his seed would continue to bind them closer as lovers without the possibility of conception. Did Aaxis realize his request would serve her goals far more than her supposed supplication would serve his?

"You agree to be bound?"

He held out arms. "I am at your mercy, Princess."

If his erection hadn't been so obvious, Tayra would have doubts about his motives. Wary and ready to react should he lunge toward her, Tayra approached him slowly. Aaxis stretched out on the floor. The man was far too eager.

She bound one ankle and moved to the other. He made no move to stop her. She quickly bound his wrists.

"Do with me what you will, but first kiss me."

Lowering her mouth to his, Tayra kissed him and he let her take command. He complied with the sensual demands of her lips and tongue, never tried to wrest control of the kiss.

Heady with power, Tayra treated him as a pleasure toy, exploring the contours of his sun-kissed chest, licking and kissing his face, running her fingers through his long, golden hair.

Holding the drawstring of his pants, Tayra met his gaze.

He lifted his hips off the floor giving her permission to undress him. She pulled the string and slid the loose pants down his hips. His cock, rigid and thick, jerked beneath her cautious touch. She encircled him with her fingers.

"So the rumors are true?"

Every muscle in his body contracted. "Rumors?"

"It is said you are well endowed...for a Sark."

His answering grin was charming and sexy. A soft chuckle rumbled in his chest. "How many men, Sark or otherwise, have you fondled?"

Tayra released his penis and prayed her burning cheeks would not display her embarrassment. Despite her schooling in the art of sex, nothing in her personal experience prepared her for the impact of caressing him. He wasn't a blindfolded subject chosen for her education. He was the most powerful male in the star system and he would belong to her: lover, lifemate, husband and father of her children.

Every delicious inch of him, hers. She licked his lips, his nipples and the tip of his penis. He groaned. She touched him, pinched his nipples, tugged lightly on the dark gold hairs surrounding his cock while kissing and fondling his length and thickness.

"You tease me."

"Do you like it?"

His cock jerked in her hand. "What do you think?"

Again she ran her hands over his chest and down to his belly, caressing, memorizing his body with her fingertips. She'd reviewed many photos of Aaxis in the course of her research, but her favorite was one in a scant bathing costume taken at his palace on Aktares. The photo had prepared her for the muscled contours of his warrior's body, for the potential hidden beneath the thin material, but not for the feel and taste of him.

The man could kill an opponent without breaking a sweat, but the gentleness of his touch, the sweet seduction in his kiss and his willingness to let her take control seduced Tayra.

She'd read every tidbit of information available about him. His exploits, both political and romantic, were news. Despite the interplanetary conflicts, gossip spread freely at trading ports and informants sold their wares as well as merchants. Aaxis's conquests were complimentary as well as graphic. She needed to please him. Never did she wish to leave him wanting. Glacidian wives took great pride in their lovemaking.

Closing her fingers about his erection, Tayra moved her hand slowly up and down his length. She covered the broad tip of his cock and suckled, letting her fingers continue their lover's rhythm. The skin-to-skin contact caused a deep thrumming in her womb.

Her lips followed her fingers, down to the base and back again. Heat emanated from his body and Tayra ached to remove her skinsuit. She wanted to rub her skin against his, take him deep inside her and claim him.

Instead she suckled, her mouth wet, his cock so hot she wanted to touch herself. She cupped his balls, caressing and fondling the tight sac. Shifting her weight Tayra pressed her mons against his hard thigh. Stroking, rubbing, teasing she brought them both to climax.

Aaxis bucked beneath her and semen, hot and salty, touched her tongue. As part of the bonding ritual Glacidian wives drained their grooms, swallowing their semen. Although he had yet to propose, Tayra accepted his semen.

She barely caught her breath when he asked her to release his bonds. No sooner had she untied him then he caught her about the waist and rolled on top of her. "Open those royal thighs and let me love you. I must have you."

Handsome, hard and almost naked, he tempted Tayra, but to succumb now would gain nothing. Aaxis must see her as more than an easy conquest; a women to be used than banished to some remote region of Aktares when Glacid surrendered.

"Begging, my Lord?"

Aaxis chuckled. "If it will serve to ease this ache to have you, I will beg."

Tayra pushed his shoulders and he rolled off of her. She rose to her knees as Aaxis pulled up his pants and tied the drawstring.

"The time will come when you will beg for release and I shall be generous."

Noting the change in his voice, Tayra stood. "I cannot comply with your request."

He rose to stand before her. "You play with me."

"I gave you pleasure." She stepped back several steps. "I promised nothing more."

With slow, purposeful steps, he approached. "I only want your submission." He reached out and touched her cheek. His fingers fanned over her ear and neck.

She raised her chin. "Never."

Before she could move, he pressed his thumb to the tiny nodule at the base of her left ear. Rendered immobile, Tayra cursed herself as he caught her in his arms and lowered her to the plush carpet. He'd managed to mask his intent with his words and coaxing voice. He knew exactly how to apply the proper amount of pressure to this most vulnerable spot. Too much pressure brought a rush of super strength, but the correct amount of pressure rendered one immobile. If held too long the nervous system shut down all involuntary functions. Breathing ceased and the heart stopped pumping.

Unable to move, Tayra's mind raced. Had she misjudged him? Did he intend to kill her? Was this his true purpose in capturing her? He had restrained her once, would he again?

His eyes said *no* and his slow smile let her know he enjoyed taking her by surprise. When had he acquired this skill and how did he plan to use it to his advantage?

Proper manipulation of the node during copulation intensified the orgasm. Improperly used, death was certain, quick and painless: the final ecstasy.

How had Aaxis perfected this skill? If he didn't ease the pressure soon...

Using his weight to hold her down he lifted his thumb. Her heart rate accelerated as much from the rush of her awakened nerve endings as the sudden pressure of Aaxis's solid chest and muscled thighs.

"You are far too beautiful to be a martyr."

Trapped beneath him she had only words for weapons. "You are far too skilled to be a man of peace."

B. J. McCall

"You have yet to test my skills." He shifted his position, levering his torso between her thighs, balancing his weight on his arms. The bulge of his genitals pressed against her center. He'd studied Glacidian anatomy well. A surge of desire heightened by the recent deprivation of the pressure hold nearly consumed her. Not until she regained full feeling in her arms and legs could she challenge him physically.

Tayra remained relaxed, focusing on the chore at hand, ignoring the heat building between her legs. His *I'll-have-you* grin offset the deliberate, teasing brush of his erection. He liked to win. He expected to win.

She intended to disappoint him.

Tayra wished she had the advantage. Unfortunately, he'd maneuvered her onto the floor, demonstrated once again his superior strength and taken away any chance and the pleasure of landing him onto his backside. Instead she had to challenge him to a wrestling match in which he'd already won the first count.

The muscles of his arms relaxed, his weight sagged against her. "Give me a child, Tayra and he will bring peace."

"A bastard to be exiled on Aktares until you need him to enforce your control of Glacid. Never."

Her knee thrust up to connect with his groin. He recoiled, sucking up his knees, pushing his weight up. Rolling, Tayra took advantage of his momentum. He landed squarely on his back, she hard on his chest.

"If you wanted to be on top," he said wrapping a hand about the nape of her neck and pulling her so close her lips were a breath away from his. "All you had to do was ask."

"Call your rover. I wish to return to Glacid. Once I deal with my uncle, we can end this war."

"Kyth will claim you the moment you land. That's never going to happen. You belong to me. Get used to it."

Before she could argue the point, Aaxis kissed her. His lips demanded she surrender. His tongue commanded her resignation. Her rights were of little concern to this warrior.

Despite his assertion of his needs and wants, Tayra responded to his potency. She admired his strength, his ability to control and lead two diverse worlds. Even his kiss was masterful.

Taking each of her hands in his, Aaxis rolled her onto her back. He forced her arms over her head, locking both her wrists with one hand.

42

The weight of his thighs held hers immobile. Understanding she had enjoyed their kiss, his gaze dared her to try and throw him.

"Do you surrender?"

"Not in this life."

His eyes narrowed and his lips thinned. "I will have you, Princess. You can fight and resist, but the result is clear. You will surrender."

"One day I will yield to a man of honor, but not today and not to you, Lord Chancellor."

To demonstrate his dominance, Aaxis caressed the vulnerable bead at the base of her ear with his tongue. The deliberate, controlled pressure sent shock waves of desire racing down each nerve path, firing every synapse. The delicate balance between pain and pleasure made her cry out. She hadn't counted on Aaxis using this dangerous, but intense method of bringing her to climax and into submission. His tongue stilled.

"You will take my seed and your belly will swell with my son." His labored breath fanned her neck. "You will enjoy it."

She smiled at him, a slow sexy grin, meant to provoke. "It's more likely your technical skill will kill me."

He didn't take the insult well. The pressure on her wrists increased and his nostrils flared.

If a female was in cycle, her vulnerability to death was as heightened as the intensity of her pleasure was enhanced. No alien male had ever completely mastered the skill, except perhaps his father. Zara had excelled in the art. The challenge to Aaxis's ego, his manhood, was undeniable.

Had she signed her own death warrant?

He flicked his tongue across the sensitive bead. "Then you'll die happy."

"I doubt it." The lie came so easy. Despite the situation she enjoyed the dangerous game they played. The winner influenced the future of three worlds. The loser had to live with their failure. Aaxis was a worthy opponent.

"You refuse to mate with me?"

"I refuse to surrender."

Aaxis touched his lips to hers, then flicked the tip of his tongue across her nodule. The brief, potent contact sent tremors rocketing through her middle. "Can you not see the wisdom of our union?"

"You call it a union. I see it as an invasion. You want me to give you a child of royal blood so you can rule Glacid and control our star system. Is it no secret that the Sarks wish to enslave the entire galaxy."

"Are all Glacidian females so difficult? No wonder your numbers are dwindling."

"Our people are dying because your army attacks our outposts and trading vessels. You kill our men. You are murderers."

He ignored the insult. "You will give me a child. It is the only solution for peace."

"A Sarkian peace means Sarkian rule. I cannot exist under your rule. I will not."

Aaxis smiled. "You will be quite alive under me, your Highness. More alive then you have ever dreamed possible and before your cycle is completed you will climax. You will conceive. You will scream in pleasure while I have you again and again."

"You believe your skill can defeat my will?"

"I shall prove it." Aaxis shifted his weight to emphasize his words. As if she needed a reminder that he was rock hard and he had her at a disadvantage.

"You're willing to give up your harem and be bound to only one female for the rest of your life?"

He shifted again. "That won't happen."

"If you manage to impregnate me you will be bound to me forever."

"I don't believe in that fable. My will is too strong for you to control or conquer."

"Then I accept your challenge."

The huskiness in his voice danced along her spine. His golden eyes narrowed. "Challenge?"

"You say you will plant a child in my belly by the end of my cycle."

He slid his hand along the slick contours of her skinsuit, exploring the curve of her hip, then back to her breast. "I will. Your ice against my heat. Your resistance against my skill."

44

She shivered as his fingers began the campaign his challenge promised. "And I say if you succeed you will be bound to me and only me for life."

"I won't."

"Succeed?"

"I'll not be bound by anything but my own will."

"Then I accept your challenge. And when I win?"

He laughed. A short explosion of air telling her how ridiculous he found her statement. "I will melt the ice in your veins and it is you who will be bound to me."

He'd eased his hold on her hands, letting himself relax, but Tayra had no intention of moving. Her position served her purposes at the moment. He wanted her. She could see the excitement in his eyes and hear the tension in his voice. His erection pressed her belly, urgent and needy.

She brushed her breasts against his bare chest. "Surely there's a prize for the winner?"

"The winner gets what *he* wants."

It didn't surprise her that Aaxis expected to win. Any warrior of his reputation breathed confidence. That he would banter, tease and cajole her into his bed and take the time to gain her support for his ambitious plan was a beguiling notion. That he believed her power to bind him as mere fable was his miscalculation.

Was his confidence based upon fact? Had the Sarks an antidote or was his bravado pure bluff?

She shifted beneath Aaxis; a subtle movement signaling her own determined campaign. His eyes widened in acknowledgment.

"And if you lose, Lord Chancellor?"

"I'll return you to Kyth. Willingly."

"And you will cease all military action against Glacid and withdraw your warships. You will not interfere in our trade routes."

"Agreed." Aaxis slid his hand between their bodies and covered her belly. Deliberately he brushed the sensitive rounded hill of her mons with his fingertips. She sucked in a breath. "Don't be discouraged when you lose. You'll have a child and a—"

"Position in your harem?"

45

He was about to say husband, but her interest in his harem stilled his words. Was his icy hot Princess jealous? "I was going to say an estate on Aktares. The barren, polar region should keep you comfortable and our child safe, but if you insist, I could reinforce my palace and keep a soft pallet at the foot of my bed."

"Wouldn't that interfere with your love life?"

"I don't love them." His admission surprised him: not the truth of his statement, but the need to inform Tayra of his feelings. He wanted her, now. He wanted to plunder her silken depths, lose himself in her heat. He considered licking her pleasure bead to test her reaction. What a woman! Two nodes of passion on one amazing body, each capable of intense gratification.

In her current state she couldn't resist for long. His heart hammered at the thought. Never before had a virgin enticed him. Tayra was unlike any female in this star system and several others he had visited. She challenged him on every level, far more than any other woman.

His blood pounded, but he held himself in check. He needed her submission, he needed her to cry beneath him in joy. She must never ache for her betrothed, for what might have been. Most of all he wanted her to love him and their son.

"The rules of engagement?"

Since when did seduction, lovemaking, have rules? "Rules?"

"No weapons."

"I am not armed, except with semen." Pushing off on his hands and toes, he raised his body above her. "You can search me."

She placed a fingertip on the nodule. "Give me my ice blade so the odds are equal."

Her fears weren't unwarranted. An eager misstep could kill her. Aaxis lowered himself until he once again was positioned between her legs. "No blades. Will against will."

"And the terms of surrender?"

"If you win I return you to Glacid and pray you can gain control and hold onto it. If I win you will have my child to love, peace for your people and my forces to protect you."

"Only a fool would think so simply."

"What are your terms, your Highness?"

"If you win…"

That she was negotiating the terms of her surrender to him came as a shock. So she doubted her ability to resist him. "You agree that I will win?"

"Since our people's future is at stake, negotiating the terms of our surrender is prudent."

The possibility of her winning was remote at best, but she was right. He had to protect Sark and Aktares and she had an obligation to protect Glacid. Again Tayra stirred his curiosity among other things. "What do you have in mind?"

"We discuss the terms of surrender and the rules of play."

Her rules of play intrigued him, but he needed to break the heated contact of their bodies to discuss terms. Right now he was ready to surrender all to slip between her slick folds and ease his painful erection. "Shall we discuss this over a glass of wine, your Highness?"

"I'd like that."

What else would she like? The thought of all the techniques he might use to excite her made his cock throb all the more. An exquisite pain eased by the myriad positions he could introduce? Which would bring her the most pleasure?

He stood and held out his hand to her. She placed her hand in his and rose to her knees. Her gaze rested on the obvious bulge before her. She'd enjoyed taking him in her sweet mouth. Would she find pleasure indulging him again once the rules of the game were set?

She lifted her gaze and ran the tip of her tongue along her upper lip. Of course she would. She'd attempt to drain his semen and seek a safe climax for herself. Aaxis grinned as she stood. In this war he intended to enjoy each skirmish, every battle and then wallow in victory among mank furs redolent with the perfume of their mating.

He led her back to the table and they sat on opposite sides. He poured each of them a glass of wine and offered a toast.

"To the victor."

She bowed her head slightly, then drank. This was one contest Aaxis planned to enjoy. Victory would be sweet and satisfying.

"The rules?"

"I must have a weapon to equalize your use of the pressure hold. A miscalculation and you could end my life."

"You have a powerful weapon or so you say. My complete fidelity would be the end of my free will for life would it not?"

"It would only control your physical appetite, not obliterate your mind. I cannot control whom you love."

"Just whom I make love with?"

Tayra nodded. "I am willing to die for Glacid, but you must also to be willing to give the ultimate sacrifice."

"Your death at my hands would serve no purpose. I have no intention or desire to kill you." *Just take you until one of us dies of pleasure.*

She peered at him over the rim of her drinking vessel as if she had heard his unspoken thought. Her eyes sparkled like the multifaceted clear stones she wore on her shoulders. Rare and beautiful.

"Then your use of the hold must be limited." Limitations were no problem as long as Aaxis could experience the ultimate orgasm. Glacidian males were notorious for their loyalty to their women. Their skilled manipulation of the pressure node while a female was in her fertile cycle was legendary. Another Glacidian fable? He hoped not.

"I will not use the hold to restrain you or to win physical advantage. I will use it only when making love and only after I have breached your virginal shield."

"Agreed. You may not harm me."

"Nor you me. No more knees to the groin."

Thankfully she agreed. His never-ending erections were painful enough. The mere thought of a shot to the balls made Aaxis shudder.

"You're still a virgin?"

"You know that I am."

"You must swear. I need your oath that you are not bound to another. Otherwise this negotiation is pointless."

That she had duped him and was already bound to Kyth wasn't an acceptable option. The idea of Tayra with another man… Aaxis had to know.

"I swear by all I hold dear, upon my father's honor that I have never accepted another male, that I am bound to no man, that I am pure."

The tension of his muscles eased. The realization that within days she would belong solely to him brought instant relief and joy. The depth of his joy came as a shock. He had intended to please himself and

Tayra while they negotiated the treaty necessary to end a useless war. Her position and status were necessary to the mission of peace. Given her training and lineage he could ask for no better female to carry his child and stand at his side.

When had she become essential to his heart?

Or was he so caught up in the challenge as to believe he stepped across some invisible line between passion and love?

He poured them each another draught of wine.

"Shall we decide the terms of your defeat, Lord Chancellor?"

"Are we finished with the rules?" he asked.

"We are. Upon your defeat you must cease all aggression against Glacid. You will return all prisoners. You will allow all trade vessels to move freely. Glacid will not breach Sark's atmosphere and I will expect the same of you. Aktares is open. Lastly, you will dissolve your harem."

By the Gods her audacity piqued him. None of his women would dare to think they could defeat him. Except perhaps the aggressive Siluko.

"Pray tell why would my harem be part of your terms? I thought you had no interest in my sex life."

"I don't," she declared with a shake of her head. "I am compelled to see these women freed."

At least the conversation and drink had eased his painful erection. "And if they choose to stay with me, to share my bed."

"You must transport each female back to her people and remain separated for a period of 100 days. If they should wish to return to you, it is their choice, not yours."

He smiled. "They will return."

"Then they are fools."

"You haven't shared my bed, Princess. Perhaps after tonight you can understand their loyalty."

"Tonight?"

His cock stirred in anticipation. "We will share my furs."

"I am not ready."

"The rules of engagement are cast. You are only allowed to resist my lovemaking, not refuse my attempts. Now for the terms of your surrender."

She raised her glass and drank deeply, then asked, "What will you demand of me?"

"You will support my peace plan, protect our son and afford to me all the rights you would your chosen lifemate. You will take the Sarkian wife oath."

"You cannot be serious," she said, placing her empty glass upon the table. "I will agree to be your equal, never your handmaiden."

"I must know you will never seek to denounce me or join any effort or conspiracy to usurp my authority as leader."

"To do so would endanger our child. I will not kneel at your feet, but stand by your side. We will lead together. To that union and our son I will so swear my total fealty."

He refilled her glass. "If this Glacidian bond is as you believe, would I not have your complete loyalty from the moment you conceive?"

"I would be bound to you physically and it would be my duty..." She unfolded her legs and relaxed against a large pillow. "I would not have to love or respect you."

He reached out and caressed her cheek with the back of his hand. "Could you love me or does Kyth hold your heart?"

"Do you care who holds my heart as long as you achieve your purpose?"

He finished his wine and set the empty glass upon the table then leaned toward her. "A female with divided loyalties is dangerous."

"You expect your women to love you while you love them not?"

Touching her made him hard as stone. "My women have nothing to do with my duties, only my pleasure."

"So I am part of your duty?"

"You could be my pleasure, too." To prove his words, Aaxis brushed his lips to hers. The mere taste of her caused his heart to hammer. Tayra's lips were soft and pliant beneath his.

He had expected resistance. Instead her mouth clung to his for a brief, but enticing moment.

In that moment Aaxis believed she wanted him as much as he wanted her. Duty bound her as surely as it bound him, yet her resistance melted with every encounter and every kiss they shared.

By the Gods, Tayra would be his wife. Would she also be his love?

Aaxis had counted on his skill as a leader to persuade Tayra to accept his plan and depended upon his skill as a lover to seduce her into his bed, but never had he expected the need to win her devotion.

He had fought many battles, but none as personally important as this war of the heart. Beyond her commitment to galactic peace, he wanted Tayra to say those simple, yet powerful words.

CHAPTER FOUR

Desire mingled in the exchange of breaths. If he kissed her again…

"Battling you is quite painful."

His rich, coaxing voice sent shivers rippling across her skin. "It is my duty to inflict pain upon my enemies."

He covered her hand with his and guided it to his erection. As her hand cupped him, he moaned.

"While your hand remains there I am your prisoner, completely at your mercy."

"I can imagine the mercy you wish to be shown, Lord Chancellor." As she spoke, Tayra brushed him with her hand. His balls were tight and his cock hard.

His fingers slid along the seam of her skinsuit exposing her breasts. "I too can be merciful, my lady."

Aaxis lowered his head and kissed her breasts. She fell back against the soft pillows. Fierce streams of molten hot need shot through as he nursed first one breast than the other. He circled her areola with his tongue, licking the tip to an engorged point. He suckled, drawing deeply, lustily on her aching flesh, filling his mouth with her. He cupped her other breast, rolled her swollen nipple between his thumb and finger.

From one to the other and back again, seducing, tormenting her. She rubbed her thighs together seeking release.

She wanted his hard cock inside her, filling her. Tormented by the need to join, to mate with him, Tayra grabbed two fistfuls of golden hair. Aaxis lifted his head. His gaze remained on her swollen breasts. Her nipples were elongated and deep rose in color. He flicked one plump nipple with the tip of his tongue as if testing its rigidity.

Her sex fluttered in response.

"Your nipples are magnificent. Is it true Glacidian females climax while breast feeding?"

Icy Hot

"Yes, it's true." Tayra had never experienced a climax from just breast stimulation. Her married friends loved nursing their babies. The extraordinary climaxes they experienced were sensual bonuses. Right now she wanted Aaxis to ease the ache he'd wrought. "Nurse me."

His eyes gleamed as he lowered his head and captured a rosy nipple. He drew deeply, purposely, suckling her. Fire raced through her veins, heating her blood, pooling heavy and hot between her legs. He cupped her breasts kneading her wanting flesh, suckling one and flicking the sensitive tip of the other with his thumb.

Tayra shuddered, surrendered, and came. Her juices flowed, hot and wanton, soaking her skinsuit. Aaxis reached down and slid his fingertips suggestively along the thin, wet barrier covering her sex. She rolled onto her side to face him and snaked her arms about his neck. Needing contact she scraped her nipples against his bare chest.

He untied the drawstring of his pants and slipped his cock between her legs. Holding her hips Aaxis moved back-and-forth increasing his tempo and teaching her the act of love with each tantalizing stroke. Her labia plumped as his heat penetrated the thin, wet material.

He kissed her hard, thrusting his tongue, deeply, possessively. He wanted her to know how it would feel to have him inside her.

Another thrust and another. She squeezed her thighs tight and cried out as she came. Aaxis shuddered in her arms and stilled. For a moment neither of them moved. Breathing hard Aaxis rolled onto his back. A creamy bead slid over the tip of his penis. Tayra reached out and scooped up the bead. Without hesitation she sucked his climax from her fingertip.

Their gazes met and held.

"Come to my bed, Tayra. My furs are soft and waiting."

His use of the traditional Glacidian invitation to lovemaking shouldn't have shaken her. He'd studied her culture, spoke her language, but did he understand the meaning of those words? When a woman was in her cycle the invitation was tantamount to a marriage proposal.

"At the moment I'm far more in need of a meal than a lover."

Finally Tayra understood why her friends went into seclusion during their mating cycles and returned exhausted, but very happy. No wonder they couldn't explain the utter joy of lovemaking.

"And I thought Glacidian females preferred love to all else."

Tayra covered her bare breasts. "We prefer our chosen lifemate to all else. His pleasure is our duty."

"Then I shall provide sustenance in every possible form."

He tied the drawstrings of his pants, stood and held out his hand. Once on her feet Tayra excused herself to prepare for their meal. The wet skinsuit clung to her sex as she walked, reminding Tayra how much she wanted Aaxis and how very close she'd come to surrendering all.

After a shower Tayra washed her hands in cold water then removed one of the tiny beads affixed to her scalp. Carefully, she washed the nearly invisible bead, then swallowed it. Warm digestive juices would do what cold water did not. The crystal would mute the effects of her cycle, allow her to control the urges Aaxis activated.

The crystal had worked wonders on her physical condition during her previous cycles, but Tayra had never tested it when confronted with a virile male. For years she had remained in seclusion during her annual cycles and last year Kyth had not chosen to challenge that ritual. This year Aaxis had seized the opportunity. Tonight and the three nights to come would test the crystals and her will to resist. But what of her heart?

Could the crystals compensate for love? Yes, she loved Aaxis. Part of her had fallen for the handsome warrior months ago when all she had was a collection of photos, volumes of research and juicy gossip.

Eventually, her meager supply of crystals would run out and Tayra doubted her will or desire to resist Aaxis could continue beyond the fourth day. With each touch, each kiss, her surrender became inevitable. Aaxis would not leave her side until she belonged to him. But somewhere between her losing and Aaxis winning lay compromise. She vowed to win certain concessions and surely Aaxis would be reasonable.

Despite his ability as a soldier and his warrior history, Aaxis had shown mercy to those he conquered. His rule was strict, but compassionate. She must convince him to let her rule Glacid as regent. Otherwise peace was impossible.

Tonight she must show him mercy. On her terms. Sensual contact served her purposes as well as his.

Unwilling to sit through a meal in her well-used skinsuit, Tayra decided to wear the silver-blue sheath and matching cloak she'd discovered earlier in the day. The material was gossamer thin and unlike any she'd ever seen.

The shimmering sheath was a meager bit of material in an intricate featherlike pattern. As Tayra slipped on the sheath her breath caught. The material molded to her skin, conforming to the contours of her breasts, buttocks and sex as if fingers held them in a gentle embrace.

When she moved the fingers stimulated her clit, her nipples and caressed the cleft between her buttocks. Walking created a virtual firestorm between her legs.

Tayra had little doubt who had designed the gown and its purpose. Every time she moved his hands caressed her. His cells lived in the fabric of the gown.

Curious about the full-length cloak, Tayra drew it about her shoulders. She closed her eyes and thought of Aaxis. She imagined them naked and entwined.

The inner gown came alive rubbing and caressing her as if his hands were sliding over her skin, teasing her sex, fondling her breasts. Tayra dropped to her knees and spread them wide.

One finger slipped inside her teasing and licking her flesh. Not a finger, but a tongue. Her heart hammered as the tongue thrust inside her, slid over her clit and dipped inside of her again and again. In-and-out, stirring, arousing every cell until nothing existed except pleasure. Tayra panted as she came. Hot nectar gushed over the fingers. The tongue lapped the juices from her sex and absorbed them.

No matter the results of her negotiations with Aaxis, Tayra would keep the magical gown.

* * * * *

Aaxis's heart skipped a full beat as Tayra glided into the galley, a vision in pale blue. She'd worn his gown. Had she experienced its full effect?

"Princess, you flatter me."

"Your, ahhh gift has some unusual properties."

So she had experienced the tactile sensations, but had she climaxed? "My pleasure, I assure you," he said, holding out his hand.

"And I thought my pleasure was the objective."

As their hands touched the gown shimmered, reminding him of sunlight striking blue ice. Aaxis lifted her palm to his lips and stroked his tongue across her sensitive flesh. Her knees momentarily gave way.

"Something wrong, your Highness?"

"Nothing I can't handle."

Her confident smile told him the chase had begun. He knew she was certain she could deal with any challenge he might devise. Aaxis smiled. He knew he would breach her fortifications, defeat her defenses...one by exquisite one.

Aaxis leaned toward her and touched his lips briefly to hers. Her mouth was a perfect place to start his campaign.

"I shall be your master."

She narrowed her eyes in alarm. Now that she had touched him, intimately stroked him, experienced the delicious effects of his gift, did she expect him to act aggressively? Demonstrate Sarkian mating behavior?

One day he would. He would teach her the joy of wild sex. Perhaps even the fierce mating he had enjoyed with his Siluko female, but not today.

Today he would introduce Tayra to lovemaking. Gentle passion was best for wooing a neophyte. Her Highness had a lot to learn about his Aktarian traits. The first lesson was his love of kissing.

"The master of your pleasure," he said. "Only your pleasure."

Again he touched his lips to hers. Instead of turning away, she responded, molded her mouth to his. Her arms snaked about his neck. Aaxis coaxed her lips apart, explored Tayra's moist, hot mouth. Her sensual scent filled his nostrils. She was primed and fertile, ready to receive him.

He wanted to tear off his clothes and hers. He needed her nakedness against his chest, belly, and thighs. The urge to fill his hands with her soft breasts and to suckle on her taut nipples overwhelmed him. Aaxis forced those desires aside and concentrated on the kiss.

The intimacy of a gentle kiss meant far more than a primal joining. A kiss could bind a man and woman and join their hearts in ways mere sex did not.

A man could not woo a woman by fucking her. He touched her heart with words. Love words. Sex words. Words that made their hearts pound in unison. For the first time in his life Aaxis wanted to say those words, whisper them as they touched and fondled one another, scream them as they climaxed. They clung to the tip of his tongue, but Aaxis suppressed the urge. Instead he reached out and drew Tayra to him.

When Tayra moaned, Aaxis managed to hold his passion in check. She gasped as he slid his tongue along her lower lip and sucked in a breath as he traced a lazy trail along the shell of her ear. He captured her lobe and drew softly. She trembled.

"Now I understand why they call you the Seducer."

Aaxis had learned about the nickname from Drath, but no one else had had the temerity to bring it to his attention. But then Tayra wasn't one of his subjects. He raised his head and looked her in the eye. Best to address her concern head on. "They?"

She dropped her arms, but Aaxis caught her hands in his.

"Gael of the outer lands. Jadda of Siits. Mae of Nepof. Lav-"

"You shouldn't listen to gossip."

"I guess I should be honored. Such an illustrious list of females! You're lucky to be alive. It's rumored Lav's father wanted to behead you."

"He wouldn't dare." An explanation seemed prudent. "Lav came to me late in the night and presented herself as a willing gift from the king. It wasn't until morning I discovered the truth."

"At sword point if I recall the story correctly."

He lifted her hand to his lips and licked it. Again she trembled. "Are you jealous, Tayra? Or do you wish to add to my reputation?"

"Neither, but you do kiss well."

Latching onto her compliment rather than his brush with death, Aaxis curled an arm about her waist. "I do many things well. I can make you tremble with the touch of my tongue. I can cause your breath to catch by the gentle caress of my forefinger. I will give you pleasure so intense your heart will stop beating-"

"What of your heart, Lord Chancellor?"

"Mine? My heart is strong. I've heard the rumors. I can handle anything you deliver."

Heart attacks had become a medical memory except when Sarkian males mated with Glacidian females, but that had not happened since his father's time.

"I've read of the deaths," he admitted. "But most of the men were well beyond their prime. Could be the stories are rumors spread by Glacidian females?"

Tayra shrugged a delicate shoulder.

"If you plan to kill me with pleasure I cannot wait until your next assault. First, we shall share a meal."

She laughed at his jest. Aaxis liked this woman. When he had chosen Tayra as the bearer of his children and the woman who would stand beside him as a wife, Aaxis had considered her royal bloodlines, her education, virginal state and beauty as the primary reasons.

Now, as Aaxis guided Tayra to the galley he found himself enthralled. Her laughter pleased him. Her voice settled softly on his ears. Her eyes held mystery and mischief as if he had been the one snared in the ice storm.

Her touch made him tremble.

Not once since he had captured her had Tayra resorted to tears or tantrums, nor acted the victim. Instead she had taken the offensive and challenged him.

She would lose this sensual game they played, but in the end his wife would be the final victor. She'd have a lifemate who loved her. War between their planets would cease and with the full weight of his support behind her, Tayra would rule Glacid.

The wisdom of Tayra as regent would have repercussions: the Sarkian Council would balk, but hopefully the Glacidians would rally behind her and their son. Aaxis understood the Chamber of Lords would never accept him. From the moment he had conceived this marriage-for-peace-plan, Tayra's rule had been the cornerstone.

The mantle of war lifted from Aaxis's shoulders. With Tayra as his lifemate, peace between their worlds was assured. If any advisor would have suggested he might enjoy marriage, prefer monogamy and actually fall in love, Aaxis would have scoffed and dismissed the man from his duties.

He had accepted that this marriage would have a life altering affect, but Aaxis had never suspected the decision to touch his heart.

As a wedding gift he would dismiss his harem. Not only because their services would no longer be required, but out of respect for his bride.

He offered her a chair. Unable to resist, Aaxis leaned down and brushed his lips to hers before taking his seat.

"The fish is not to your liking?"

In her absence, he'd prepared an intimate dinner. Tayra's stomach fluttered more in anticipation than in hunger, but a light meal would help activate the crystal.

"Do you usually prepare Glacidian delicacies at Sarkian outposts?"

"It is said that Glashark is an aphrodisiac."

While Tayra chose to eat in measured bites Aaxis had consumed his generous portion of fish. "Surely if you are in need of a stimulant-"

"A beautiful woman is all the stimulant I require. I simply wondered if your reason for liking the delicacy has to do with its properties or its taste?"

Glashark wasn't Tayra's favorite dish, but releasing the information was a test of his information sources. That this false peculiarity had reached him and he had acquired the rare fish and her favorite wines exposed the depth of his interest. Her capture hadn't been mere opportunity. Aaxis had planned her surrender to minute detail. The gown she wore proved his abilities as a creative tactician. Aaxis would have her. Losing wasn't an option.

He poured two glasses of wine, offered one to her. He toasted her health, the future birth of their son to remind her of his intentions, then rose from the table. "Join me."

Intrigued, Tayra placed her hand in his. He guided her down a long corridor to the last door. As she had suspected he'd escorted her to his private quarters. He touched the lock panel palm down and the heavy door slid silently open.

The door, built to sustain assault, closed behind her. Tayra suspected an exit or escape pod was hidden within the walls of his chamber.

Although the room was as austere as the quarters assigned to her, Tayra noted the fur-covered bed would accommodate a man of Aaxis's size with ease.

Soon the time would come and she would share this warrior prince's bed, hopefully for the rest of her life.

Aaxis crossed the room and touched his palm to another lock. Two panels separated revealing a deep circular bath with crystal knobs. The pale aqua tub was a duplicate of the one she enjoyed at her father's official residence. Her heart lurched as she stepped inside the enclosure. She longed for home and for her father. Had she now lost her father, too?

Her mother's sudden death during an ice storm ten years earlier still hurt.

Aaxis brushed the tears from her cheek. "I wished to make you comfortable and at ease."

His thoughtfulness soothed her pain. "Thank you, Aaxis. I've missed home these many months."

"I wanted to give you a small part of it. I understood you enjoyed your bath."

Tayra nodded. It was all she could manage at the moment. Again, she was struck by the gentleness of this warrior prince.

He moved to stand behind her and wrapped his arms about her waist. For the first time in months Tayra trusted. She could believe Aaxis. Although he'd led a carefree love life, his word was solid. Never had he broken a treaty with an enemy or betrayed a friend. Secure, she leaned back and reveled in the gentle caress of the gown's multitude of fingers.

"I shall enjoy watching you bathe. I wish to lave you with scented soaps and rinse your delicate skin with waters from the well of Hammar," he whispered.

Although they were alone, Aaxis understood the power of a husky whisper, rich with desire, in a woman's ear. Tayra trembled. The waters of Hammar were sacred to Sark. Few were so honored.

"Do all your thoughts revolve around pleasure?"

"When you are in the room, yes. I have plotted many methods of ridding you of your clothing."

"You do not wish me to wear your gift?"

"Only when we are parted. I assure you the garment is a poor substitute."

His words, his coaxing voice made her wet. The tongue lapped at her center. She resisted her desire to capitulate. "How long have you been planning my abduction?"

"Since you disappeared."

Given his experience in strategic planning, the depth and scope of his plotting shouldn't surprise her. Had it been directed at another subject it wouldn't have, but his admission that she was the object of his thoughts for the many hours necessary to abduct her and then seduce her emboldened Tayra. Aaxis needed her. She turned in his arms intending to ensure his need on many levels.

He seized the opportunity and drew her pelvis tight to his groin.

"Our joining is inevitable."

"Despite what I may want?"

His gaze narrowed. "Peace is more important than a whim of the heart. I counted on your intelligence and reason."

"Not on your charm?"

"So you admit I am charming."

"I admit nothing, Lord Chancellor, or should I call you Lord Seducer?"

He slid the cloak from her shoulders and scooped her up in his arms. Tayra suppressed a smile as he carried her to his bed. Although Aaxis was now grinning, he had definitely revealed a jealous streak. She could use this.

He dropped her onto the furs, but did not join her. "I could restrain you again," he said. "Bring you to the brink of ecstasy again and again until you beg for release."

Tayra relaxed, slowly stretching out on his furs. "Or I could restrain you again. This time I'd prefer you naked."

"You don't have to restrain me. Ask me to join you."

How could you resist a man who asked so politely when his need protruded so prominently it was impossible to ignore? You didn't. You simply gave him a taste of what could be his. Tayra patted the furs and within seconds Aaxis had stripped off his clothes and lay naked beside her.

She should have known he'd view her subtle invitation as a total surrender to his desire.

"Kiss me." His soft command matched the burning gaze in his eyes. "I've kissed you. Now I want you to kiss me. Then I want you to touch me, anywhere, everywhere until my flesh is as familiar to you as your own."

Ever since she'd looked at the photo of Aaxis dressed only in a scanty bathing costume, Tayra had dreamed of touching him, loving him. Was this one of the Seducer's techniques or a Sarkian tradition?

Aaxis wanted sex and a son, but for Tayra sharing her husband with another female, or females, wasn't an option. She wanted a faithful husband, but more than that Tayra wanted to capture Aaxis's heart. In the game of love, it was all or nothing.

"You grant complete access?"

"Yes."

"I may do anything I wish."

"Yes."

Permission granted, Tayra leaned toward Aaxis, intending to take full advantage of the opportunity to make love to him on her own terms. She touched her lips to his, skimmed her tongue along the seam.

Although he didn't touch her, his lips clung to hers, inviting her to deepen the kiss while letting her know he wouldn't remain passive however limited the contact. When she eased her tongue into his mouth, he seized her offering, drawing her inside. Breathless, she explored the hot depths, played a sensual game with his tongue.

Her dress came alive. The tip of its tongue slid deep inside her center.

A deep moan escaped his throat as she broke the kiss and traced a slow trail down his throat along the pulsing artery in his neck. She rubbed her cheeks against his chest unable to resist the ancient Glacidian mating ritual, then flicked her tongue over each flat nipple.

The tongue flicked her clit. The fingers pinched her nipples. Her turn to moan.

Running her fingers across his chest, she teased his nipples and explored the taut curves of his pectorals. His eyes danced with excitement and promise. Next time it would be his turn and she would endure his sweet torture.

"Now who is the seducer?" he demanded, his stomach muscles flexed as she stroked his belly.

She answered by kissing a meandering course down his torso, pausing to circle his navel with her tongue. She licked a lazy path below his navel. He shuddered.

Tayra stroked his straining erection. The tongue lapped at her sex.

"Suck me."

Instead of taking his cock in her mouth, Tayra placed her lips beneath his balls and suckled the root of him. Aaxis cried out as his fists curled deep into the furs. His breath came in harsh gasps.

"Don't stop."

His ragged request moved her. She loved kissing him, touching him, feeling his struggle for control.

She stroked his cock, pressing, releasing him. She moved to his balls, kissing and licking them, drawing one into her mouth. Gently, she suckled the delicate orb.

The tongue lapped furiously at her drenched sex. Rivers of heat radiated from her center, thrilling her, consuming her. Unable to resist, she came. Rendered momentarily immobile she released Aaxis. Her head flung back, Tayra gasped for air. Her once busy hand stilled as the powerful orgasm rolled through her.

"Great Gods, help me."

Perspiration broke out on his brow and his skin glowed with a slick sheen. His swollen cock jerked as he spoke beckoning her to impale herself or at the very least touch him.

"Tayra, please. End this."

"I can ease your suffering."

"What is it you want?"

She wrapped her fingers around his throbbing penis. "Bathing privileges."

"Done."

Tayra slid her fingers along his length, squeezing and releasing his flesh. "Alone."

He swallowed. "I wish to serve you wine and fetch warmed towels, to feast upon your naked beauty. To gaze upon your lush breasts and enticing pussy."

Although Tayra hated to remove the dress, she needed control. With deliberate slowness she peeled the dress from her breasts, down her torso and thighs. His gaze followed the slow descent, lingering on her thatch of pale curls.

His cock jerked and his fingers dug deeper into the furs.

"You'll serve at my will?"

"Yes."

Kneeling beside him on the furs she spread her knees wide. He groaned, but still he did not reach for her. A bead of semen appeared on the tip of his swollen cock. Tayra leaned down and brushed his groin with her breasts as she licked his pleasure.

Again, she stroked his eager flesh. Eyes closed, he lifted his hips, urging her to increase the tempo. Tayra squeezed, sliding skin against skin, creating a heated friction until his breath came in harsh puffs. She blew gently on his balls and took one gently in her mouth.

His groans of pleasure ceased and his muscles tensed. Beneath Tayra's fingers and mouth the pulse of life undulated and released.

The heavy, heart-stopping waves brought an unexpected ecstasy of pain coupled with extreme pleasure. Aaxis resisted the urge to clutch his chest and reveal to the Princess the amazing affect she had on him. Great Gods! If she could bring him to such pinnacles with her hands and mouth…

She sucked his balls.

The desire to love her, fuck her overwhelmed him.

Between gulps of air Aaxis vowed never to remain abstinent for so long a period again. His reaction must have more to do with anticipation and need than her expertise at manual manipulation of the male organ. His balls still hummed and his breathing remained ragged. He was too young to die from sexual exertion.

"You're scowling, Lord Chancellor. Were you not pleased?" Her sweet lips curled into a knowing smile as she rubbed his semen between her palms.

Perhaps Tayra's plan was to kill him. Of course she'd choose to do it in small measure. A far more exquisite way to die than at the wrong end of her ice blade.

Aaxis wanted to live for many reasons, but the most urgent was her fingers wrapped around his cock. Her massage increased his heart rate and pumped his blood back into the necessary veins. Her tongue teased his balls, the length of his cock, and the too sensitive head. Her finger slipped along the crease of his buttocks.

That knowledge that he would be her one and only sexual partner pleased him. Having no predilection for virgins that realization came as a surprise. Right along with his second climax.

She scooped up his semen and rubbed her hands together as if washing them then touched her palms to his sweat-drenched skin. Ever so slowly she massaged his chest.

Was she performing a Glacidian ritual? A binding ritual? Was she giving her permission for mating?

The thought of entering Tayra's tight, virginal vessel excited him. When Aaxis took her hand and licked her palm, she closed her eyes and moaned.

He licked her other palm and again she moaned. Her nipples beaded and Aaxis's cock jumped in response. No woman had ever kept him so hard or so excited for so long.

Aaxis laved each of her palms. "You will choose me, Tayra."

She did not moan as he wanted, but merely shrugged one shoulder. "Will I?"

No wonder Drath had laughed when he mentioned having a Glacidian sex slave. As if any man could enslave Tayra! Already she had him willing to settle for the pleasure of her untutored hand and sweet mouth instead of proceeding with the necessary deflowering.

Impregnating her was his duty, but her challenge had presented an enticing pursuit. A chase to stimulate him both physically and mentally. A hard won victory was far more satisfying than an easy conquest. He preferred a worthy opponent to an unskilled enemy. He was a trained soldier, a diplomat not a barbarian invader.

He'd taken his warrior skills to the negotiation table, but never to the bedroom. Tayra's challenge would force him to reign in his desires, test his ability to restrain his impulses and use every weapon as a lover to woo her.

"You are welcome to share my furs," Aaxis said as he touched a panel beside the bed. The chamber door slid open.

"But should you choose to return to your quarters, think upon my plan. Not only for your people, but for you," he whispered, despite the fact they were the only occupants of the large room on an orbiting rock at the edge of a vast asteroid belt.

Tayra kissed him, her lips soft and pliant. She rose and strolled to the door. He hadn't expected her to leave him not after…

Right before she disappeared from view, Tayra glanced at him. Was regret shimmering in her eyes? Or was she pining for home and her betrothed?

CHAPTER FIVE

Her weight supported with one hand, Tayra made slow progress along the corridor. Her skin burned. Her needs raged. The rapid quick-fire flutters in her womb threatened to bring her to her knees. She had willed herself to leave Aaxis and had managed to control the fierce battle raging within her. Each step away from Aaxis brought her closer to her goal.

Once inside her room, Tayra climbed into the scented furs. With each breath, she drew his scent. Mindless with need, Tayra rubbed her breasts and mons against the soft mank. She regretted leaving his gift behind. She couldn't sleep. Her whole being hummed. She placed a fingertip against the sensitive nodule at the base of her ear. Her practiced manipulations brought instant relief.

At the onset of puberty, Glacidian girls were taught the art of self-pleasure. Along with the virginal dance, sexual release provided a means of self-control. Heightened sexual need was not an excuse for promiscuity, especially for a royal. Tayra expected to employ Glacidian control methods often in the next few hours.

She wriggled in the soft furs, loving the feel of them against her skin, then closed her eyes to dream of her warrior prince.

* * * * *

That Aaxis would awaken as hard as steel wasn't unusual. That he would remain in this state for hours was likely. His hunger for Tayra gripped him like a man deprived of food and drink. Had he lost all control?

Aaxis rose, showered and spent the required time in the sun tube. He tried to turn his thoughts away from his guest to fulfill his duties. Despite the flood of messages, some urgent, most not, requiring his attention he failed. Tayra had manipulated him well. So well he swelled at the memory of her touch, the stroke of her hands on his cock. He craved the feel of her lips and mouth on his balls.

When Drath contacted him, Aaxis welcomed the distraction.

"The Sutiumi?"

"We've detected probes in the Glacidian trigon."

Aaxis balled his hands into fists. The Sutiumi threatened the entire system. Alone, Glacid couldn't repel them. At best the Glacidians would offer time to reinforce the Sutiumi's next target, Aktares. Defeat of this formidable foe lay in the unification of Glacid, Aktares and Sark. Together, their armies could defeat the Sutiumi.

His mission to bring peace and unite the three planets before the Sutiumi attacked hinged on Tayra. Future peace and cohesion would lie with their son. If only the Glacidians would look forward. Instead of seeing the benefits of peace, Brac would view the Sutiumi as an opportunity to seize power. His brief reign would end with Glacid's obliteration.

"You should inform the Princess."

"I intend to."

He did. He would. Aaxis had to reassure himself that she wanted him and not Kyth. His whole life he had put duty before his own wants and desires. His heart had belonged to Aktares and Sark. Now Aaxis faced a new choice. Could he choose between duty and Tayra? Could he send her back to Kyth? Could he live without her?

"You're struggling. Is it Tayra?"

"She overwhelms me, consumes my every thought."

"Your father faced similar conflicts. Losing you nearly destroyed him."

"How do I choose?"

"Convince her. Marry her. The vows of marriage are sacred to her people. Together the two of you can bring peace and thwart the Sutiumi."

"How long before they strike?"

"A few weeks at most. If nothing else, the Sutiumi are unpredictable."

"Then I have only hours to complete this mission."

Given her affect upon him, Tayra was far more than a mission. She twisted his insides into knots.

"Trust Tayra. Her father trained her well."

"She demands the position of Regent."

Drath's eyebrow rose a fraction, but the counselor remained silent.

Aaxis expelled a breath. "Actually, she challenged me to win it?"

"Challenged?"

"She doesn't think I can seduce her. Even in her current state, Tayra believes her will is stronger."

Drath smiled. "I will speak with you tomorrow."

The screen went black. Shaking his head, Aaxis touched a series of discs to open the secret panel. As he loaded the injection pistol, he pondered the question Drath had confronted him with yesterday. Although ready for commitment and children and despite his growing feelings for Tayra, the cost was far too high. He couldn't afford the chance that Tayra could bind him as Zara had bound his father. To lose his political influence at this juncture could destroy any chance for peace. He injected the antidote.

Emboldened, Aaxis left his chamber to seek the enemy. His balls hummed at the thought of seeing her.

* * * * *

Tayra turned. Although Aaxis moved with the grace of the white saber, she knew the moment he entered the galley. His dress was casual: a loose fitting pair of sand-colored pants and a matching long-sleeve shirt. His feet were bare.

"Tea?"

He murmured a thank you and took the steaming cup she held out to him. He tasted the brew. "Just the way I like it. I'm impressed. You'll make-Thank you."

What would she make? Would he see her as nothing more than another pleasing addition to his harem? Did his women serve him? She couldn't envision his Siluko brewing tea.

"I'm pleased with your choice of dress."

"My choices are limited." Although the white desert caftan common to the Sarks was comfortable, Tayra would make no such admission to Aaxis.

"Next time I abduct you, I'll make sure to secure your wardrobe."

"Next time?"

He moved closer. "If you ever think of leaving me, be advised I'll come after you."

Tayra stood her ground. "You said none of your women were slaves."

Aaxis set his cup aside and reached out. His fingertips grazed her cheek. "You have yet to become my woman."

His primal male scent teased her senses. Her mating response grew stronger with each passing hour in his presence. How could it not when confronted with the erection tenting his pants? Her womb fluttered and her nipples peaked in anticipation.

Aaxis's gaze locked onto the hard points obvious beneath the thin material. "Why do you fight me?

She scooped up his empty cup and refilled it. "Any news?"

His golden eyebrows drew together as she handed him the steaming cup. "I have spoken with Drath."

She trailed her fingertips along his forearm. She needed to touch him.

"How do you do it? You pleasure me with your hands and mouth. You lick my semen. Yet, you deny the obvious. You want me."

His gaze bored into hers, challenging her to admit her needs, daring her to make the first move. Silence stretched between them. She glanced at his erection and licked her lips to tease him.

"You refuse me?"

She remained silent. "This must end, Tayra."

"You concede, Lord Chancellor?"

"Politics is a poor substitute for lovemaking especially when one is in pain."

Tayra glanced at his cock. "Begging again, my Lord?"

"Will it help?"

"News first, then I'll play with you."

Aaxis expelled a slow breath. "Will you always be so difficult?"

She smiled at him. "Probably."

"Brac has disbanded your father's cabinet."

Tayra had expected this move by her uncle, but the information Aaxis chose to share surprised her. Aaxis's briefing reflected the brilliant intelligence network of the Sarks. Her house arrest and removal from the capital city had limited her information. Discussing current events with Aaxis was reminiscent of the private council she had shared with her father.

She brewed more tea as they discussed Brac's intentions. "My Uncle hates you. He placed a bounty on your head."

"If Brac thinks my death would guarantee victory, he is sadly mistaken."

"Your death would serve as a rallying point. Without my father to speak against him many would follow."

"He's counting on Kyth's marriage to you to consolidate his power. Don't allow him to use you for his political agenda."

"And what of your political agenda?"

"My agenda is peace. Your government is fractured. Your armies are scattered and your general's loyalties are divided. I cut your supply lines months ago. Glacid is ready to fall. The only thing holding your people together is their mutual hatred of Sark."

"Why haven't you ordered a strike?"

"I see no purpose in destroying your people and Glacid's resources. The cost to Sark in men and money would be beyond reason. What would Sark gain? Peace is far more profitable."

"Then I must return to Glacid and address the Chamber of Lords."

"Kyth wouldn't let that happen, not without claiming you as his bride. Marrying Kyth will not bring peace. You'll be nothing more than a convenient showpiece."

"Are you not guilty of the same political intentions? At least Kyth honors me with marriage."

"Would you rather have a man who desires you more than any female in the star system, or one who marries you for power and influence?"

"Desire is fleeting. Marriage is total commitment."

He lifted her hand to his lips. "Are you proposing, Tayra?"

"Will you guarantee my position as Regent?"

He led her to the lounge. Again, he relaxed against the large pillow decorated with the Aktarian royal crest. She sat beside him.

"Do you love him?"

Before she formed a response, his mouth closed over hers, hot and demanding. His arm slid about her, pulling her close and tight. Sex tight.

She twined her arms around his neck and answered his kiss. Some things come naturally and given her physical state, kissing Aaxis soothed the persistent ache in her womb while bringing her one step closer to surrender.

When he flicked her pleasure bead with the tip of his tongue, need shot through her, hot and searing.

Tayra covered her nodule with her hand. "You forget the rules, Lord Chancellor."

"So I have. I must admit I am eager to test my skill."

Aaxis cupped one breast, caressed a taut nipple with the pad of his thumb. Tayra stilled an audible gasp. The friction of the fabric combined with Aaxis's skilled touch…

How long could she hold out? How long did she want to?

He pushed the garment off one shoulder and kissed her heated skin. "I went to sleep needing you. I awoke wanting you."

Having awoken in the same state, Tayra had swallowed two precious crystals. Down to one, she had misjudged her dosage. Ten crystals could not curb the need he provoked.

Could any dosage compensate for the intense combination of an annual cycle and falling in love?

He pushed the garment lower and exposed her breast. His warm breath danced over her skin. His lips covered her nipple. She arched as he suckled. An unbearable heat built between her legs.

"My cock aches for you. All I think about is being inside your heat, feeling you surrounding me, hot and wet, making you scream as we climax."

Aaxis slid his hand beneath the caftan. His fingers glided along her leg to her pulsing sex.

"Let me love you, bring you joy."

His words, his voice seduced her. He could talk her into climaxing.

He parted her wet folds and gently touched her clit.

Engulfed in her own needs and his touch, Tayra managed to suck in a breath. His hands, his mouth promised ecstasy. Her heart pounded as her receptors leaped in reply. Using the pad of his forefinger, Aaxis gently rolled her clit. The primal urge to copulate fired in every nerve, heated every muscle and membrane and burned in every cell.

"I throb for you. Only you."

He increased the pressure, gentle yet deliberate. His finger slid inside her sex, stimulating, enticing her to the edge of climax. At fever pitch, Tayra lifted her pelvis to meet his sweet touch, her own delicious oblivion.

Caught in a vortex of pleasure, Tayra struggled to breathe. Air froze in her lungs as Aaxis leaned down and laved her sex with his tongue. Every nerve ending in her pleasure center heeded his entreaty.

His hands stroked her ass and his hair brushed her inner thighs as his tongue delved between her swollen folds. Each thrust brought mindless aching pleasure. One flick of his tongue and Tayra succumbed. Orgasmic spasms, unrelenting and violent, coursed through her.

Eventually, the fierce throbbing between Tayra's legs gave way to a satisfied hum. Her eyes opened.

"There is no substitute for the real thing. Touch me, tell me you want me."

She wanted him, but he'd promised nothing except impregnating her. Once he penetrated her virginal shield would he negotiate or would he dictate?

Lips glistening wet with her climax, Aaxis leaned between her thighs and fastened on her ultra sensitive clit. He suckled. His concentration, intense and relentless, gave no pretense of seduction. His mouth ordered her to another orgasm.

Her will crumbled beneath his erotic demand. Her resistance gave way. Release came in one shuddering wave of heat.

Aaxis raised his head and licked her pleasure from his lips. "Now we're even."

Without another word, he stood and strode out of the lounge leaving her sprawled among the pillows struggling for breath and wanting more. Wanting him.

* * * * *

Once out of Tayra's view, Aaxis dropped to the floor. He sat against the wall thankful she hadn't rendered him immobile like the first time he'd performed oral copulation on her. This time he had managed to walk twenty or so feet before the impact of her climax hit him. He wanted to return to his quarters and recoup in private, but at this point he could only crawl.

No enemy had ever made him crawl.

With each intimate contact he wanted Tayra more. Yet, his ability to handle the effect of her essence on his system grew stronger. One day he would control the situation.

The thought of mastering their copulation promised pleasure in galactic proportions.

He leaned his head against the wall and contemplated the future. Great Gods, Tayra had the ability to stop a lover's heart, literally. But Aaxis saw her as the challenge of a lifetime. Her ability to give, receive, to sustain pleasure, immeasurable.

He sucked in a breath and released it slowly. His cock throbbed in pain. He needed relief.

How to convince her? He'd rather fuck her than negotiate, but the latter seemed a surer course.

She appeared in the hallway. Her loose caftan floated behind her as she approached. Aaxis prayed his pose looked relaxed instead of defeated. Tayra looked down upon him; her ice-blue eyes glittered with the knowledge she had reduced him to her sex slave begging for her favors.

He was the most powerful man in the galaxy: except when he wanted to love her, to fuck her. Yes, he wanted both. Tayra would satisfy all his needs if he could get off his backside.

A smile curled her lush lips, a smug, victorious smile. "We're even. What now, my Lord Chancellor?"

Her challenge to his position, his manhood fired his warrior brain. Damn her. His nostrils flared. Sex perfumed the air.

Aaxis inhaled slowly, deeply. Her sex-laced scent replaced the air in his lungs. His blood heated, surged, thundered into the necessary vessels.

He rose and stripped off his clothes. Her gaze dropped to his cock. He protruded like a brandished sword ready for battle. Determined to end this ache, this insanity, Aaxis scooped her into his arms.

Seduction hadn't worked. The chase was over.

He carried Tayra down the corridor and dropped her onto his furs. Aaxis caught the edge of her caftan, yanked it high, capturing her arms and winding the loose material around his forearm, trapping her beneath him. He wedged his hips between her thighs, rendering her immobile.

Despite his forceful actions she was wet, ready, but her eyes censured rather than invited.

"Don't look at me like that. You're no victim here."

He kissed her as he entered her. Thick, hot essence surrounded the tip of his penis. He shuddered at the contact. His heart pounded, banged against his chest wall. He couldn't describe how she affected him.

"My furs are soft and waiting," he managed.

He pushed deeper expecting to encounter her virginal shield. Instead a thick essence surrounded him, held him in a hot impervious sheath. Again he pushed in, but could not penetrate the thick sheath.

A deep shudder coursed through him. Unable to control the overwhelming need to release, Aaxis ejaculated. Tayra's shield held fast. She rejected him, his love and his child, even peace for her own people.

He'd failed.

Shocked, he withdrew and stumbled from the bed to the communications console. After spiting out orders to Drath, he faced his enemy. Tayra still lay upon his furs, beautiful, beguiling, and unconquered. Her gaze was focused on the open panel displaying the injection gun.

In his haste to see her he'd forgotten to close the panel. So she knew he'd used the antidote. At least he didn't feel like a complete fool.

She discarded the tangled caftan and slid from the furs. Standing before the open panel, her shoulders shook either in mirth or in anger. Unable to see her face, Aaxis couldn't discern her reaction.

"The rumors are true. You've perfected an antidote."

She picked up the injection pistol as if testing its weight and turned to face him.

"Yes." Despite his anger, his utter defeat at her hands, Aaxis wanted her. The urge to touch her washed over him.

"You have made your mother proud, Lord Chancellor."

Her eyes shimmered. Surely, not in sorrow. She had defeated him, humbled him, made him fall in love with her and he still wanted her.

If she knew the depth of his feelings, Aaxis would not survive the humiliation. He'd rather die.

"You should dress, your Highness, unless you plan to greet my guards informally."

Aaxis strode to the sonic shower, praying with each agonizing step, she would remove herself from his quarters as quickly as he cleansed her scent from his skin. His mother's often repeated words now haunted him. *Never fall in love. Love makes you weak. Hate makes you strong.*

✷ ✷ ✷ ✷ ✷

She'd failed.

All her plans had worked to perfection, but Tayra hadn't controlled her own reaction. She had wanted Aaxis to win her, but she had pushed him too far, misjudged the point where the teasing Aktarian prince receded and the Lord Chancellor of Sark surfaced. She hadn't been prepared for the angry fire in his eyes, the transformation of his beautiful face into a determined mask, or how he had manhandled her as if she were as light as a snowflake and a conquered prize for the taking. The fierce warrior he'd loosed in the hallway had frightened her half-to-death. Her defensive systems had reacted.

Tayra understood at great cost to her heart and her people why his enemies quelled before him. Aaxis had one purpose in ordering the rover's return, delivering her into Kyth's hands.

Did Aaxis understand the permanent bonding between them had already begun? Tayra had lost her heart and Kyth would know. He'd accuse her of treason, and she'd die a traitor to all she loved, including Aaxis.

What have I done?

She'd gambled with her people's future for self-gain. Now all she could do was pray for forgiveness. Would Aaxis listen? She deserved his disdain, but the millions of innocents she'd sworn to protect did not. She'd grovel before him if necessary. Do anything to save her people. Fearing Aaxis's retribution upon Glacid, Tayra dressed in her formal skinsuit. Was it too late to lay her heart at his feet?

She found Aaxis at the docking control panel preparing for the rover's return. Dressed in his black uniform Aaxis's transformation was complete. He refused to acknowledge her.

"I must speak with you, my Lord."

He ignored her.

"Please, Aaxis. You must understand I am obligated-"

"You've won, your Highness," he said, without so much as a glance in her direction. "You're going home. That's what you wanted to confirm, wasn't it?"

Although he'd asked her a question, he strode out of the room without waiting for an answer. She followed, calling his name, catching up with him at his quarters.

"You cannot blame my people for my actions. I am responsible. Punish me."

At the door he faced her, barring her access. His golden eyes were penetrating, his jaw firm. "You have nothing to fear from me. I will not invade Glacid, but neither shall I protect it. My ships will hold position surrounding Aktares and Sark. The Sutiumi are probing Glacid defenses as we speak. Time is short. You and your betrothed are on your own."

The Sutiumi! Her father's worst fears had come to pass. The portal began to close. She reached out. "No, Aaxis, please you can't-"

Right before the portal sealed, he said "Good luck, Tayra. You'll need it."

Begging for help, Tayra pounded on his door. Her pleas went unanswered.

Shut out of Aaxis's plans, fear clawed in her heart. The Sutiumi were a far worse threat to Glacid then Sark. Compared to the Sutiumi, the Sarks were friendly rivals.

He couldn't leave Glacid to defend herself. Tayra's forces would fight to the death, but defeat was certain. Alone, Glacid could not withstand or repel an attack.

Aaxis knew. To protect his own, he'd lie in wait and let Glacid buffer the assault. If the reverse were true, she'd do the same.

If Glacid would join with Sark and Aktares, her planet would have a chance. She had to convince Aaxis. Tayra pounded on his door. She wept and pleaded until her arms ached and her voice grew hoarse.

Tayra's only hope in saving her people lay in convincing Drath to reason with Aaxis.

CHAPTER SIX

Drath sat before a console, speaking in his native tongue. Breaking protocol, Tayra walked past the young officer serving as his assistant and approached Aaxis's trusted counselor.

He ceased speaking immediately. The console went black as Drath stood and bowed his head in deference. "How may I be of service, your Highness?"

Tayra had expected Aaxis to deliver her to Glacid immediately. Instead the rover had docked with his flagship. His words were few, his voice clipped when he bothered to remember her presence. Within an hour of arrival, he'd left.

"Honored Counselor, where has Aaxis gone?"

"My Lady, I assure you-"

"Forgive my rudeness, but his rover has departed."

Again Drath bowed his head "I am not at liberty to speak, my Lady."

"We made a bargain," she said, balling her hands into fists to contain her frustration. "He gave his word. No action against Glacid."

Drath folded his hands before him reminding Tayra of the ancient holy men that had once ruled Sark. "My Lord Chancellor seeks peace. If you have learned anything of him during your time together, you must know that is his mission."

"Why is he returning to Glacid without me?"

When Drath remained silent, Tayra reached out and curled her fingers about his hands. His skin felt dry and paper-thin. His eyes widened a fraction at the familiar gesture. Tayra withdrew her hand.

"I must know."

"We were allowed to capture you, my Lady. When we approached your prison, someone lowered the shields."

Fear slammed into her heart. "Aaxis has returned to find the traitor?"

Drath did not speak. His silence was her answer.

Tayra thought of the young soldiers in her guard and the members of her household. Despite what their show of loyalty might cost them, all had remained during her imprisonment. All except Rasf, the commander of her guard, personally selected by her uncle. In spite of their small numbers, they would resist. To the death if necessary.

"You must call him back." Tayra's stomach rolled in fear for her staff, especially for Bae. Aaxis's search for a traitor would lead him straight to her.

"At the very least let me speak with him."

"He has cut off all communication to prevent detection. I doubt he would listen, your Highness."

"I must return to Glacid. You must take me, now."

Although her voice had risen with her concern, Drath remained indifferent.

"You are to remain here until it is safe."

"There is no traitor," she admitted. Tayra prayed Drath believed her. "I lowered the shields."

Drath's translucent eyes narrowed. "You?"

"My father and I discussed a royal marriage as a solution to peace. Once my uncle separated us I had to act on my own. I released the distress signal. I wanted Aaxis to intercept the signal, knowing he would seize the opportunity."

"How could you-"

"I know about the information you secreted to my father. I knew the necessary codes. Capture by anyone other than Aaxis could bring all out war."

"Your father shared our-"

"Drath, we must go now and prevent Aaxis from making a terrible mistake."

Impatient, her heart laced with fear, Tayra stood ready at the portal when the rover landed. Tayra spotted Aaxis storming through the jagged hole in the ice gates toward her. Blue veins spiked along the edges of the rent shield that had once protected the gates of her prison. Aaxis had ordered a full laser blast. As expected, her guard had refused to cooperate.

Tayra ran toward the gaping hole, her heart in her throat. "Are any dead?"

Aaxis caught her by the arm as she tried to hurry past him. "What are you doing here? It's dangerous here."

"No one here is a threat to you."

His eyes blazed in anger. "You were betrayed. Someone here is your enemy."

"Order your men to stand down, now." Tayra wrenched herself free of his hold. Within a few steps, he caught up with her.

"My people are loyal," she declared. "Come and I shall prove it."

Just inside the blown gates her guards stood huddled together, surrounded by Aaxis's elite troops. Upon spotting her, each dropped to a knee and bowed. She approached the group with Aaxis at her side.

"Do not fear. I am not a prisoner and neither shall you be."

The commander of her guard picked up the hem of her mank fur coat and brought it to his face as a sign of respect and loyalty. Rasf inhaled then slowly raised his gaze to her. Realization froze his war-hardened features.

Rasf glanced at Aaxis. His nostrils flared and his eyes burned with hate. Aaxis stepped toward the soldier, but Tayra raised her arm to halt his progress.

"Do not lose heart, Rasf. All is well. You'll be briefed within the hour. What of Bae?"

"The Sarks have her."

Tayra turned toward Aaxis. "I must visit my quarters. Accompany me and you shall understand."

As they walked away, Aaxis took her arm. "That soldier may have betrayed you. His is not the look of a loyal supporter."

"Rasf is loyal. He has served my family well. He believes as others do that Brac's leadership is temporary while my father recovers. When he learns my father is dead by Brac's hand, he will turn against my uncle."

"I saw his reaction. He wanted to kill me, perhaps you."

"What can you expect when I have your scent upon my furs and skin."

"My scent? But we haven't-"

"Rasf knows I am in cycle and Sarkian scents are strong, especially yours, Lord Chancellor."

"You're saying I smell?"

"Your scent isn't pure Sarkian or Aktarian, but a strong mixture and as you are in your breeding prime and have recently been active-"

He stopped, halting her hasty progress toward her quarters. "My sent lingers upon you?"

"May we proceed?"

His lengthening stride forced Tayra to quicken her pace to a near run down the wide corridors of ice. Finally, she reached her quarters. Two Sarkian soldiers loomed over Bae. She was bound by a force field unable to move.

"My Lady," she whispered.

"Release her at once," Tayra ordered. "Leave us."

The soldiers looked at Aaxis. "As the Princess commands. Return to the gates and await my orders."

Bae was freed and fell into Tayra's arms as the soldiers took their leave. The assistant tried to stand.

"Are you well, Highness?"

Tayra guided Bae to a lounging chair. "It is you I am worried about."

Bae rubbed her arms. "I am unharmed, my Lady. Did your plan succeed?"

"No, I failed." Tayra removed her cloak and draped the fur over her assistant.

Bae started to rise, but Tayra stilled her with a restraining hand. "It is not Aaxis we should fear. Rest. I'll gather our belongings, then we must leave."

Her thoughts centered on warning her government of the impending Sutiumi invasion, Tayra rushed into her bedchamber. Aaxis followed. No guard, not even Rasf would dare enter her private chamber without permission.

Aaxis halted inside the chamber. "Kyth kept you here?"

Tayra ignored his question as she tossed clothing into a traveling case. She needed no reminders of Kyth's care. After seeing her prison could Aaxis still believe she loved Kyth?

"Of what plan did your servant speak, Princess?"

Feet slightly apart, his arms folded before him, Aaxis barred the door. Now, finally, he was ready to listen.

"There was no traitor. I lowered the shields."

He scoffed. "You couldn't possibly know I planned to abduct you."

Tayra reached out and touched her open palm to the ice wall. The shield forming the ice walls shifted and a small portal opened. She stepped inside. "I've studied you in depth, Lord Chancellor," she said as Aaxis dipped his head to enter the small secret room. "My father thought it wise for me to know the-"

"Enemy?"

Although that wasn't the word Tayra had intended to say, she remained silent as Aaxis's gaze searched the myriad of images adorning the walls. All were of him. Tayra had spent hours pondering the possibilities, both political and personal of their union.

"I have underestimated your intelligence network as well as your determination."

Now that she had his undivided attention, could she convince Aaxis to reevaluate their future? "The day would come when you and I would face one another. When you came I had to be ready."

Tayra touched her palm to the wall and a small screen appeared along with a communication module and a series of diamond-shaped crystal spheres. Selecting one, Tayra placed the sphere in a slot beneath the screen. A view of Aaxis taking his oath as Lord Chancellor appeared.

For a long moment, Aaxis stared at her. His eyes sparkled then darkened with suspicion. "You wanted to be captured?"

"Yes."

"You used me to win your freedom."

She had, but not in the way he thought. "I wished to win peace by marriage and giving birth to a son or daughter to bind our people together."

His gaze flicked from the photos on the wall to her and back. Aaxis winced when he spotted the photo of him in a bathing costume. "You wanted a child?"

"It was the logical way to end the war."

"*My* child?"

"Yes." She had wanted his child, but much more. "My father planned to approach you about a royal union."

He leveled a typical Sarkian look, stern and implacable, at her. Marriage wasn't any more palatable now then before.

"Had your father succeeded he would still be alive," he said. "I would have protected him, and you."

"Unfortunately, Brac seized power before..." She swallowed the sudden lump in her throat. "When your rover entered this quadrant, I decided to carry out the plan on my own. I sent out the encrypted distress beacon."

"That was meant for me to intercept?"

Tayra nodded.

"How could you know it was my unit and not a reconnoitering rover?"

Tayra retrieved another sphere and exchanged it. The screen filled with the plans of Aaxis's rover along with its distinctive signal.

His gaze hardened. "How did you get these plans?"

If she told him he wouldn't believe her. Drath must admit his complicity in her plan. "My father received them from a source who supported our plan for unification."

"So it is I who have a traitor."

His voice sent chills down her spine. "My father assured me this source had no ill intent toward you or your people. The plans show nothing of the rover's weapons or defensive capabilities only enough information so I could detect your ship from others."

"Kyth does not know this room exists?"

Tayra shook her head. Had Kyth discovered her plans, he would have branded her a traitor.

"You had no intention of marrying Kyth, did you?"

"Never. Glacid would suffer greatly under his command."

"Your plan almost worked, Princess. It's been a long time since I walked into an ambush."

"I intended no harm-"

"Gather your people, your belongings and report to the rover in ten minutes."

He turned away and strode out the door. Tayra caught up with him. "What do you plan to do, Aaxis?"

The look in his eyes froze her heart. "Destroy this place and everything in it."

Defeated, Tayra set to work. She didn't doubt for a moment Aaxis would leave the tardy behind.

He remained aloof and thoughtful during the journey to his flagship. Upon arrival her soldiers and staff were housed. Bae was escorted to a separate section of the ship while Tayra was sequestered in Aaxis's private quarters. He ordered her to sit. She complied, selecting one of four chairs surrounding a vast desk. He paced.

Tayra waited and worried. What did Aaxis plan to do with her? She had approached Drath upon arrival, advised him of her desire to reach Cryss, Glacid's capital city, via an Aktarian trading vessel. She had to address the Chamber of Lords and warn them of the Sutiumi threat.

Aaxis stopped behind her and rotated her chair until she faced him. He leaned down, clamped a hand on each arm, trapping her.

"If you wanted what I wanted, why didn't you tell me the first day? Why did you make things so difficult? Your conception could have been achieved within hours. I would be challenging the Sutiumi, not looking for a phantom traitor in your guard."

The truth of his observation hit home. Anger simmered around him like a shield repelling heat, yet he'd sought out her enemy. He'd wanted to protect her.

"I should have told you. Our union, our child would bring peace, but father wished for a royal marriage and shared leadership."

His gaze settled briefly on her mouth. "What did you wish for?"

Your love. "I wanted the impossible. I wanted—"

He released an audible breath and righted himself. "Control over Glacid? As my bride, irrevocable status under Sarkian laws?"

She did want those things, but the one thing he was unwilling or unable to give her was her personal heartbreak, her burden to bear. Now she had to accept a political union, and save Glacid.

"Without a legal marriage," she began, hoping to salvage the situation. "Obtaining the support of the Lords would prove difficult, if not impossible. An illegitimate child would give cause for those who oppose our plan."

Icy Hot

"Namely your uncle and Kyth."

Aaxis gazed at the gray wall to her right. All the walls were gray without a painting, or sketch to distract one's mind. How many battle plans had been discussed and ordered in this room?

He turned to face her. "Why didn't you suggest marriage?"

She stood. Despite her failure to win his love, she was an equal. "Why didn't you tell me the Sutiumi were poised to invade us?"

"I wanted-" Aaxis hesitated. "I'd hoped our union would be based upon something other than fear and survival," he said.

"I wanted-"

He folded his arms before him. "Fidelity. My total obedience at any cost?"

"Do I have that? Tell me, Aaxis, you have an antidote. You used it on Phabes."

His gaze softened, but he remained silent.

"Since your father mated with Zara your mother has sought revenge on Glacidian females. You have accomplished her mission."

"I can't be bound like my father. His bondage to Zara destroyed any chance he had to bring peace. He deserted the people of Sark, my mother and me for Zara."

Given his feelings, Tayra was amazed he hadn't engaged Glacid in all out war.

"Your father and Zara fell in love, but he was committed to you and to peace."

"Zara trapped him."

"That's your mother's truth. They understood they couldn't bind. Zara had chosen a mate, a political union with Brac."

"Brac!" "His hatred for Sark equals your mother's for Glacid. My father suspected he attacked your father's ship, but could not prove his complicity."

Aaxis said nothing, but his eyes changed. "Continue."

"Zara and your father were caught in an ice storm. They were forced to land and wait it out. She went into cycle. Having no crystals, she was helpless to resist. She truly loved him."

"Unlike you who came prepared?"

"You knew?"

"I like a challenge and you were a worthy opponent. I play to win."

"You aren't bound to me. You have won."

"If I were the Sarkian council and my mother I would never accept us. Since I was a boy I've been trained to put my happiness, my desires aside. I can't destroy a chance for peace to give you personal power."

"I too was raised for one purpose. My duty is to Glacid. Still I wanted-" Tayra had nothing to lose by admitting the truth. Although her virginal shield was intact, she belonged to Aaxis. "I wanted a real marriage, love, companionship…I wanted you, Aaxis."

He stepped toward her. "Love?"

Unable to read his reaction, she stepped away from him. "Yes, love."

He backed her up against the wall. "Do you love me?"

"I do. The first time you kissed me, I knew." she said.

"I loved you the moment you brazened the ice storm and boarded my ship. You chose to ignore me, making it utterly impossible for me to ignore you. I wanted you. I still do."

He loved her? "Then why haven't you proposed?"

"I did. More than once. When I was deep inside you, with every cell in my body on fire, every urge to climax, I asked. You had what you wanted, but you didn't lower your shield then."

He had understood the meaning of asking a cycling female to share furs. Now her cells were on fire. "You frightened me. My defense shield was activated."

"I had no intention of harming you," he said. "I wanted you. You knew it, yet you played a dangerous game keeping me hard, making me wait. You were driving me crazy. What did you expect?"

The rich timber of his voice, the husky eagerness sent shivers of passion down her middle.

"The shield is extremely sensitive when a woman is in cycle. If you recall the first Chancellor of Sark tried to destroy the Glacidian race by raping our women."

"That was long ago. A tragic part of both our histories."

"Once the shield is activated it traps and destroys semen. I shouldn't have challenged you."

His gaze locked on her mouth. "Why did you?"

"I wanted to be more than another convenient female."

A smile teased his lips. "You're anything but convenient. You resisted me from the first moment, fought every advance I made. Why? Did you enjoy making me suffer?"

"You respect those things you fight for, you treasure those things you earn. You hold dear those things you love. I wanted to be one of those things."

"You aren't one of those things. You are *the* thing. I love you, Tayra. To have you I will challenge any man, any army. I will defy my own mother to keep you, but I will not be shackled by you or anyone, ever."

"Aaxis."

"I think we have unfinished business, your Highness."

Despite the demanding nature of his words, Aaxis's eyes glittered. She'd seen that look before and her receptors fluttered in response. He still burned for her. Still wanted her. Need shimmered between them like a force field, drawing them together.

"I must address the Chamber of Lords. My people must be warned."

"Drath is making the arrangements. You will address the Chamber from this ship."

He pulled her close. So close his erection pushed against her belly. He wanted her to feel him.

"Until it is safe, you'll not set foot on Glacid."

The wall behind her parted revealing a large sleeping platform covered with furs.

"The time has come for you to choose your lifemate."

Mind and body, Tayra responded. Her sex tingled in anticipation.

His gaze locked onto hers. "My furs are soft and waiting."

Tayra removed his general's cap and tossed it aside. She twined her arm about his neck and untied the narrow black ribbon binding his golden hair. When she reached for the almost invisible seam of his uniform jacket, Aaxis stilled her hand. Within seconds he had removed his uniform and stood naked before her: his erection more of a passionate invitation than a weapon.

She tore at the collar of her skinsuit. As she worked the ornate clasps, Aaxis bent his head and wet her lips with the tip of his tongue.

Her insides quivered as his lips fastened on her mouth, claiming, demanding her surrender. He eased the tight suit off her shoulders. Her breasts ached for his touch as he bared them, caressed them, teased her nipples to firm, aching points.

Aaxis flicked his tongue against her pleasure bead. Fire shot through her middle as he pressed his tongue against the sensitive node at the base of her ear. Unrestrained, Tayra's mating response flooded her sex. Wet and ready, she wanted him inside her, filling her, breaking her shield, ending her agony.

As soon as she was free of her restrictive skinsuit, Tayra thrust her naked breasts to his chest, rubbing the hard peaks of her nipples back and forth. The combination of his warm skin and rock hard muscles drove her mad.

She licked his neck, nipped his shoulder.

Burning, aching beyond belief, Tayra brushed her belly against his erection as he peeled the tight skinsuit down over her hips.

His hands cupped her buttocks, squeezing them, grinding her pelvis against his. Tayra, eager to shed her suit but unwilling to break the erotic contact with Aaxis, fumbled with the restrictive material.

He kneeled, relieved her of her boots and stripped her naked. Rising, Aaxis ran his tongue along her thigh, his hands over her hips.

He stood, naked and ready. "You aren't frightened?"

Tayra shook her head. He sucked in a breath and his biceps bunched as he reached for her. She throbbed too much to speak, ached so much she threw herself into his arms.

He carried her to his bed and joined her on the furs. His gaze locked with hers as he positioned himself between her thighs. His thighs trembled as he probed her swollen folds in slow, measured strokes. The control he exercised was complimentary, but unnecessary.

Lifting her hips, Tayra demanded his length. She cried out as he penetrated her shield. Wet beyond belief, her womb contracted around him, drawing him deeper and deeper with each thrust. Tayra wrapped her legs about his hips holding him, binding him, accepting him as hers forever.

He arched. Head thrown back Aaxis's hips stilled. Pulses, heavy and throbbing, coursed his length, triggered her pleasure. She released in waves. Together they climaxed, mingled their life nectars, bonded.

A cry tore from his throat. He shuddered.

Tayra drew him close, holding him as he gulped air. Finally, he spoke.

"I'm still hard. How is that possible?"

"The bonding process is incomplete."

"I breached your shield. My legs feel like jelly. I don't think I can stand."

"I wouldn't try right now."

"Will it always be this when you cycle?"

"The first bonding cycle is intense, but during my annual cycles you'll suffer as much as I."

"I'll be hard like this for days?"

"Yes, my love. Even if we are apart when I cycle you will suffer. Your commander's uniform will be most uncomfortable, but with time you will train your body to deal with your affliction."

"Then we must never be apart."

Tayra placed a fingertip to his mouth. Aaxis latched onto her finger. She guided him to her breast, moaned as he licked, then suckled.

Grasping his taut balls, she caressed him, teased the smooth skin beneath his sac with the pad of her finger.

Finding his second wind, Aaxis rose to his knees. Tayra's nipples were distended, her breasts swollen and firm, her sex wet and inviting. His cock strained and ached.

Tayra drew her knees beneath her and positioned herself to receive him. Aaxis caressed her rounded backside, licked her sex before kneeling behind her. His heart lurched as he entered her. Wet and hot, she sheathed him. He couldn't think, only feel. The urge to mate, to procreate surged through him, drove him. Thighs slapping, he thrust again and again, penetrating Tayra's slick core. She matched his primal rhythm; her sex flexing against his cock, demanding his seed.

Every sinew, muscle and cell exploded in pleasure. Brutal, erotic, waves pulled his semen from his balls and hurled it along the length of his cock. He shuddered, joined Tayra in ecstasy. Unable to move, to breathe, Aaxis held onto her undulating hips.

Finally, she stilled. He remained buried inside her, unwilling to withdraw. A half-smile quirked his lips. No wonder Drath had scoffed at the idea of a Glacidian female as a sex slave. Tayra had already taken him to new heights of ecstasy, given him a cosmic climax. And he'd thought he would teach her!

He leaned forward to kiss her back. Without thinking he licked her skin, tasted the salty dew, and rubbed his face against her heated skin. At that moment Aaxis knew he was the one enslaved.

* * * * *

Tayra awoke, hips writhing in needy response, her legs spread wide. She opened her eyes. Aaxis lay between her thighs, licking her moist slit.

"Good morning, my Lord."

He lifted his head, inhaled a deep breath then expelled it slowly.

"You fascinate me."

"You flatter me."

Aaxis curled his hands about her thighs. "Every time I lay eyes on you I think of sex. When we're apart I think of sex. No matter how many showers I take all I have to do is inhale and your sweet scent surrounds me."

His compliment pleased her, but when he rubbed his face against her damn curls Tayra pondered the effectiveness of the Sarkian antidote. Aaxis displayed the usual characteristics of a bonded male. "Are you complaining?"

"About the sex? Never. But you are a distraction. Instead of planning battles I want to seek you out and make love. Sometimes I want you so bad my balls hurt."

"Do they hurt now?"

"Not yet. But they will unless..."

"Unless?"

He lowered his head and plunged his tongue between her folds, in and out, until they were swollen and achy.

"No matter how many times I lick you into a frenzy and feast upon your nectar, I crave you more. Even when we're apart I taste you."

Gently, he separated her folds, exposing her sex. He laved her slit with his tongue, tasting, teasing, probing her willing flesh. He flicked her swollen bud with the tip of his tongue, over and over. She swallowed a cry and dug her fingers into the furs.

He captured her pulsing clit between his lips, drawing her inside his hot mouth and loving her with his lips and tongue until she burned.

She lifted her hips begging for more, seeking sweet release. He gave her heaven.

Aaxis licked her hot juices and rolled her onto her knees. "I need to be inside you."

His cock kissed her ready passage and he plunged. Buried deep, he stroked her hips, her belly with his hands. She flexed her sex, pulling at his hard length, willing him to thrust.

A hand on her belly he lowered her, pressed her breasts and mound to the furs. He withdrew, then entered her, slowly pushing her into the soft furs. He withdrew and entered again.

"Spread your legs, wide."

She complied. With each stroke the soft mank stimulated her breasts, teased her clit. Tayra moaned as the furs slid against her nipples, caressing them, bringing them to aching points of pleasure.

He flicked her pressure bead with his tongue. A fierce heat speared her middle settling in her womb. Aaxis fastened his mouth around her sensual node and using his tongue matched the rhythm of his strokes. Her sex flooded, wet and hot, she clamped around his cock.

He'd mastered in a few short days what some took years to accomplish.

Caught in the rapture of his deep strokes, Tayra's heart hammered, threatened to explode. He drove into her, his thrusts deep and needy.

Their lungs labored. Their hearts pounded in unison. Perspiration beaded between them causing a heated friction. He pushed deep and held. She came, touching ecstasy, drawing his climax, his life-giving semen, mingling their essence.

"I can't get enough of you," he said, before giving in to the physical exhaustion.

* * * * *

Drath's assistant stood at attention and saluted as Aaxis strode into his advisor's office.

The young officer excused himself and closed the door. Aaxis relaxed and dropped into a chair facing Drath.

"Tayra insists on waiting out the war in Cryss."

"Now that Brac and Kyth are under arrest her place is with her people. She must lead if they are to follow. Her coronation will take place as soon as she arrives."

"If the Sutiumi break through my lines, the capital city will be their primary target. Glacid will fall."

"She believes in you and her armies. Her show of complete faith will inspire the troops she places in your hands."

"I will fight to the death to keep her safe."

"A man should be ready to die for what he loves, but Tayra gives you far more to live for."

"I want to marry her. I know I intended to from the beginning, but now I would do so even if the Sutiumi were not a threat and a century of peace between Sark and Glacid were a certainty."

"Your words bring me comfort. All is set for tomorrow's ceremony."

Aaxis rose and paced. "How is my mother taking the news?"

"She understands why you're entering a political marriage, but your choice of brides disappoints her."

Aaxis had recited his reasons for marrying Tayra, except for the one that truly mattered, by encrypted message. He could not afford the time to visit Sark. "I didn't expect her to congratulate me, only accept my decision."

"I assured her you are taking the antidote. As long as you are in control and Sutiumi are defeated there is little she can do to speak against you."

"Thankfully, Tayra's cycle has passed and I will have no further need of it." Aaxis paused in front of Drath's desk. "At times I wonder if its effectiveness or your dosage were miscalculated."

Aaxis waited for a response. Drath remained silent. He didn't expect him to defend his accuracy.

"I'm obsessed with her. My desire for her consumes my thoughts. I don't look at other women. It's unnatural."

"You are in love."

"I admit I do love her, but the need for her grows ever stronger. Perhaps our separation is a good thing."

"There is no antidote for love. Glacidian females are not ordinary women."

"They all can't be like Tayra."

"It is their commitment to their lifemate, their desire to keep their males sexually gratified that makes them unique. Tayra will give her life for you. As for other women, she'll keep you too physically exhausted to be interested."

"I don't want to leave her and I can't take her with me." Aaxis crossed the room and retrieved an ornate bottle from a recessed cabinet. He poured two small glasses and set one before Drath. Often they would share a drink at the end of the day of whatever potent liquor Drath had on hand. Barely noon, Aaxis needed a shot.

"Before deployment I would drink to excess and indulge in the pleasures of several females." Although Aaxis had few secrets from the old man, he needed to talk. With Drath he could speak freely. "I'd take one after another, fucking like an animal, satisfying my every whim until I could no longer perform. The lust in my blood prepared me for battle. By the time I faced the enemy I had shed the pleasures of home and mentally readied myself for war."

"You and Sy raised quite a ruckus during your mating rituals."

Aaxis drained his glass. "Now, I want to remain at my wife's side. I want to watch her belly grow with my child and make love to her each morning."

He slammed the glass down upon Drath's desk. "How do I rally three worlds to face an enemy like the Sutiumi when I have no blood lust in my veins?"

"Do not doubt your ability to face the enemy. You have fought for your homelands, protected the people of Sark and Aktares. Now you have Tayra."

"She's conceived."

"Congratulations, my Lord. You will soon be a husband and a father. Your lust for life has changed. You face the enemy not out of duty, but to keep your family safe."

Drath picked up the bottle. "Shall we have another drink?"

They shared several drinks. Aaxis rose to leave. His balls tingled in anticipation of seeing Tayra. Drath activated the door. As the panel slid open, Aaxis bowed to his advisor.

"Thank you, Drath. Thank you for giving Tayra's father the plans for my rover. As for the antidote, you should fill the injection pistol with the genuine cure. Just in case my mother decides to verify your information."

A slight smile curled Drath's thin lips as Aaxis marched out of his office.

* * * * *

Aaxis stepped out of the sun tube. His skin glowed golden. Although he had recently left their bed, the scent of his heated flesh fired Tayra's receptors. Her cycle had passed, but still her need for Aaxis had not abated. The knowledge that soon he would leave to face the Sutiumi, the fear that he could die in battle kept her sexual need for him at fever pitch. She rubbed her thighs together. His nostrils flared and his penis stretched.

"My cock no longer obeys me," he said, joining her on the bed. "I have other duties my love."

"The Sutiumi?"

He curled an arm about her shoulders. She lay against his broad chest. "Today you will be my wife."

Tayra understood their time together grew very short. His place was at the helm of the newly formed federation and hers restoring order and unity in Glacid.

"I will miss you."

"We'll have a few precious minutes after the ceremony," he said, licking the bead below her ear. No matter how many times they loved, Tayra wanted more. "I demanded time to consummate our union. Nothing will ever part us."

Despite their hours of lovemaking, a needy heat surged through her middle. Tayra rose to her knees and straddled him. From gentle lovemaking to fierce mating she would give him memories to take with him.

Her sex suspended above his face, she leaned down and took his hard length into her mouth.

He grasped her thighs and drew her closer. He slid his tongue deep inside of her, kissing her sex.

Cupping his balls, she squeezing them lightly as he traced the crease of her buttocks with his fingertip. Gently, she drew one delicate orb into her mouth, fondling him with her tongue.

His stomach muscles clenched. "You drive me wild."

Moving to his cock, Tayra suckled the broad tip. Beneath her, Aaxis bucked. Answering his unspoken plea, she swallowed his length. She pulled and tugged bringing them closer to climax. Thrusting her hips, she pumped her sex against his plundering tongue. She arched. Heat seared her pulsing clit, her sex flooded in pleasure. He dug his fingers into her thighs and lifted his hips. Thick hot semen filled her mouth.

He rolled her onto her back and covered her body with his. He ran his fingers through her hair and cupped her head gently in his powerful hands.

"I will miss you," he said. "I will dream of you and ache for this."

He lowered his mouth to hers and kissed her, deeply, longingly, entering her in slow, deliberate strokes. Tayra wrapped her arms and legs about him, holding him close to her heart.

The wildness of last night melted into a deep longing and a sweet loving. Saying they loved one another wasn't enough. Tayra wanted Aaxis to feel it, to know it in every cell.

Aaxis rose from the sleeping platform. Taking Tayra's hand he guided her to stand before him, then he knelt. "Accept me as thy husband, as protector and provider."

Although spoken in Sarkian, Tayra understood his request. "I accept."

"My love is for eternity," he said in the soft melodic tones of Aktares. "Join me in life."

Tears of joy wetting her cheeks, Tayra touched her fingertips to her lips then to his. "For eternity and beyond."

* * * * *

"Bound by commitment to one another and by the laws of Aktares."

Tayra and Aaxis kneeled before the High Prefect of Aktares and he tied together their clasped hands with a golden cord. An ancient Aktarian custom, this symbolic gesture left no doubt to the large audience viewing the ceremony unfolding on Aaxis's starship by broadcast throughout the star system that they were bound for life. The custom no longer practiced except by a few, disallowed any legal form of ending the marriage. Only death remained an option.

Aaxis and Tayra had decided on the ancient custom to convince their people and prospective governments of their peace covenant. The decision was easy for Tayra; her commitment to Aaxis was total.

As the binding ceremonial prayer ended, Tayra opened her eyes and met the gaze of her husband.

"You honor me," she said. Tayra had requested the traditional Glacidian vow as part of the ceremony and Aaxis had agreed.

"You honor me," Aaxis responded and lifted their bound hands for all to see.

Together they rose, naked except for the cord binding their hands, before their people, their governments in the ancient Aktarian wedding tradition. Their lack of clothing symbolic to all that no official trappings, obligations separated them. They were one.

DEEP HEAT

CHAPTER ONE

"We dock on Pyxis in one hour, my Lord."

Gyrr Thrane, Prince of Glacid, Lord Commander of the Outer Regiment, stamped his seal on the last of several official documents. Phase One of his mission, a covert journey to meet with Uyin, a Cheddian rebel leader, would begin the moment he disembarked. Pyxis, one of twelve distant, but busy skyports surrounding the Aktarian system, provided the perfect opportunity for a royal to assume a new identity. From Pyxis, he'd journey on to Zeon, a trading skyport at the edge of the Vidarian system. On Zeon, Portmaster Sy, a trusted ally, would provide security.

The prince rose, the weight of his mission heavy on his broad shoulders. Civil war could throw the Vidarian system into chaos. As Lord Commander his mandate was to maintain peace in the Outer Regions, to protect Aktares and its sister planets, Sark and Glacid. "I must prepare."

Husi, his aide-de-camp, plucked the documents from the prince's desk and secured them in a portable vault. A military attaché would transport them to Aktares. "I'm amazed your father supports this mission."

"Uyin demands the direct ear of my father. If nothing else, we'll finally learn the urgent need for this mission."

"I will pray for your safety. If your true identity were discovered and you were taken as hostage—you must be careful."

Despite Gyrr having attained the age of thirty-five, Husi worried over him as if he were still a boy driving his first rover. "I promise to be careful."

Gyrr inserted special blue contact lenses to disguise his silver-colored eyes while Husi retrieved a packed traveling valise. Gyrr began stripping off his clothes. All royal adornments and any item that identified him as such were discarded.

Removing the signet ring his parents had presented to him at eighteen, Gyrr reluctantly placed it in Husi's palm. Three ancient crystals decorated the ring, each representing the three planets of the Aktarian Federation. The treasured ring was a duplicate of the tiny ring placed on his elder brother's finger on the day of his birth. Gyrr had pledged his life to the Federation.

"If anything should happen to me, the ring is yours."

Husi closed his hand around the ring, holding it tight. "I should be going with you."

"Our friends and our enemies know wherever I am, you are close. I'm depending on you to convince them all I'm taking a meditation furlough. Assure everyone, I will attend the state dinner with the Vidarian Tetrarch as scheduled."

"No one will realize you are gone."

A relative of Gyrr's mother, Husi served as advisor, tutor and mentor from the day of Gyrr's fifth birthday. His Glacidian aide understood the dangers of traveling in the Zeon sector. The outer regions were plagued with enemies.

"So what cover have you and my mother invented? A merchant? A wealthy tourist?"

The plain white shirt, dark trousers and matching jacket Husi withdrew from the closet dismissed both.

"A communications expert? A trading specialist?"

While Gyrr dressed in the simple, but comfortable garments, Husi secured the signet ring in a vault and withdrew an assortment of documents.

"Queen Tayra and your father selected your cover." Husi held out a wallet. "Your Ident card, employment contract, and bank credits. Your name is Conr, Aden Conr."

"Common enough. My profession?"

Husi deposited the traveling valise next to the door. "Perhaps you should familiarize yourself with the documents."

Gyrr flipped through the cards. The embedded photo on his identity card looked nothing like any of his official photos. Husi had dyed Gyrr's platinum-colored hair to the dark gold hue common to Aktarian males. The blue contact lenses he wore were designed to match his eye scan to the identity card bearing his cover name. Of all his siblings, he'd inherited more of his mother's features and could easily pass as a Glacidian warrior. For this mission, he needed to assume Aktarian styles and mannerisms. Aktarians and Sarks were far more common on Zeon than Glacidians. He needed to blend.

"A contract? I don't understand." Gyrr swallowed hard. "I'm indentured?"

"You're indentured to Sy, head of security and customs of the Zeon skyport. She has access to any and all ships and is authorized to land on any planet, moon, and skyport in the Aktarian and Vidarian Systems. Sy will pass any necessary messages to your father. If anything goes amiss during your travels, you'll be protected. Sy will pay well for the return of her property."

"General Sy, the Siluko?"

"Who better than your father's ally?"

"You should have informed me days ago. I could have used the time to reacquaint myself with the trading laws and regulations."

Husi smiled. "You are well versed in the skills required of you."

"Skills?" Gyrr read his profession. "A sex consort! Great Gods, the General is twice my age. My mother would never agree to this. Sy was my father's lover."

"Before your parents' marriage. That is why the cover is perfect. The General may be twice your age, but she contracts annually for sexual consorts. The timing is perfect. Last year's lover is on his way home as we speak."

"I'll never be convincing. When I'm with her, I'll think of my parents."

"I don't believe the General will expect you to fulfill your consort duties. Her proclivity for young, healthy Aktarian males provides a safe method for you to complete your assigned mission. That these young men tend to resemble your father will aid in your cover."

Duty first. Husi's reminder was reminiscent of his training as a youth. At sixteen, girls and sex had provided enough distraction to cause his parents considerable concern.

"At the General's side, you'll have total privacy and complete security for your meeting with the Cheddian. Your father doesn't want you walking into a trap. Certain factions could misconstrue your meeting as official support for the Chedds."

"And when the meeting is over?"

"Sy will express her dissatisfaction with you as a lover and contract with another consort."

"Dissatisfaction! I've never disappointed a woman."

"Remember, you're not Gyrr Thrane. You're Aden. Start thinking like the hired help. "

Gyrr shoved the documents into the inside pocket of his jacket. "I fuck for a living."

"Among other things."

"What things?"

"Consorts perform a myriad of personal duties."

Gyrr sucked in a breath. "Such as?"

"Anything the General demands. Dressing, serving, feeding, driving, dancing, bathing."

"I will not dance and under no circumstances will I *bathe* a General. If my regiment found out—"

Husi grinned.

"You're enjoying this."

"I'm sorry, your Highness, but it does make up for all the times you sneaked out when you were forbidden to leave your quarters."

Now it was Gyrr's turn to smile. "I did get laid, often and well."

"Leaving me to explain to the Queen."

"I apologize. My mother did bend your ear."

Ignoring his half-hearted apology, Husi carried the valise to the door.

"You should exit the ship at the aft door. Join the throng of travelers at customs then… Please, your Highness, be careful."

The banter ended and the seriousness of his mission stood between Gyrr and his aide. Shouldering the valise, he extended his hand to his aide. "Cover my ass, Husi."

"I will pray daily for your safe return, your Highness."

* * * * *

"Do you think his cock is in proportion to his size?"

Captain Ria Torr glanced at the Aktarian sitting two tables over. "You think far too much about sex, Doc."

"That's because I haven't had any in months." The diminutive medic sipped her drink. "The only cocks I see are those displayed on the posters hanging on the walls in sick bay."

"I shouldn't have given in to you. Everywhere you turn, naked men."

"Naked men with erections," Doc corrected. "The crew needs something to perk them up on these long runs."

"The crew goes out and gets laid at every port."

"Everyone except you and me. I'd love to get laid. I miss Pol. We talk, but it's not the same. I'm tired of phone sex. What's your excuse, Captain?"

Ria ignored Doc's question and glanced at the Aktarian.

"He's big. At least six inches taller than Pol. I think he's sexy. Don't you think he's sexy, Captain?"

The Aktarian turned, their gazes caught and held. "He's sexy."

If you like tall, broad-shouldered, blonde, blue-eyed hunks.

The Aktarian smiled. Inside Ria, a spark flared. Shifting in her seat, Ria forced her gaze back to her ship's medic. Damn, why did Doc have to start taking about sex? If she walked over to the hunk, would he invite her to join him? Maybe. He'd probably prefer her Aktarian cargo loaders. No matter where they docked, the twins popularity never ceased to amaze her. With fifty ships docked, undoubtedly, the twins' were fucking the brains out of a ship's officer right now.

If the twins saw the Aktarian, they'd kick themselves for making a too hasty selection.

Ria checked her wrist unit. The compact unit acted as a communicator as well as providing time, date, relevant security and docking codes. Scheduled to undock the *Telum* at midnight, she had a free hour or two. Again, she locked gazes with the Aktarian.

Get up. Go back to the ship. Sex isn't necessary to survival.

"He's coming over. Be home by midnight."

Before Ria could protest, Doc had sprinted for the exit. The hunk stood beside the seat her medic had occupied.

He's interested. Grab him before the twins return looking for a last minute quickie.

"Is there a fire?" he asked, speaking her native tongue without a trace of Aktarian accent.

Only in my pants!

"Doc runs at full throttle."

He extended his hand and introduced himself. Her hand disappeared within his. Calluses, the kind soldiers have from wielding heavy swords, ridged his palm. The Lord Chancellor's Elite Unit practiced the ancient art. She recalled the caress of a similarly callused hand. She pushed the painful memories aside and grew all the more curious about the blue-eyed hunk.

His clothes were simple, but tailored to fit his wide shoulders and narrow waist. Like most Aktarian males, he wore his hair long. The thick golden mass curled gently about his shoulders. Unlike her own, his skin was gently kissed by the sun.

"Have a seat, Aden. I'm Ria."

Setting aside his valise, the hunk punched in an order for another round of drinks, scanned his currency card through the request module in the center of the table then leveled an interested gaze her way. No wasted movements. Deliberate. Decisive.

"Headed for Zeon or Trag?"

"Zeon."

Odds were the Aktarian was a mercenary. On Zeon, a dozen legitimate armies recruited mercenaries and a hundred corporations hired security specialists. Either money or the need to escape drove a man to the outer regions. Perhaps both. The small scar on his cheek did little to dispel the soldier-for-hire image.

His gaze slid over her, hesitating on the white undershirt clinging to her breasts, then on the weapon riding her hip. Heavy boots, dark green trousers and a matching fitted jacket bearing the corporate logo completed her ensemble. Not the usual come-hither attire. Her gaze dropped to his callused hands. Her nipples tightened at the thought of those long fingers caressing her breasts, touching her between her legs.

The hunk's gaze settled briefly on her breasts. Hers dropped to his mouth. Would he suckle her breasts? Go down on her? Take time to please her? She ached to find out.

His gaze fastened on hers. "What brings you to Pyxis?"

She considered lying to him about her job, but few were permitted to carry weapons on skyports. "I'm running a Capha2 to Vidar."

"Commercial freight?"

Ria nodded. "The *Telum's* big and slow, but she's mine."

"Deep run, but the Caphas are built for it. You're a long way from home. How long since you've felt solid ground beneath your feet?"

Ria liked the long runs. She had no desire or reason to return to Sark, but the corporation demanded crews submit to full medical evaluations every five years on planet.

"A couple of years. How about you?"

"Spent six weeks at home. I'd forgotten how good grass feels beneath my feet. I'm contracted for the next year."

The drink trolley rolled silently toward their table. Aden picked up their selections and handed Ria one of the frosted blue glasses.

"Visiting the wife?"

A smile worked the corners of his mouth. "My parents, brothers and sisters. I'm not married."

She sipped the cold drink. "It's nice to know I'm not flirting with a married man."

"You're out of practice."

"Woefully. You speak like a native."

"I'm in communications. It's a necessary skill."

He lied well. Or told a half-truth. He might be in communications, but he wasn't an ordinary soldier. Except for the last three years, Ria had spent her life in the military. And those ridged calluses on his hands were common only to the Lord Chancellor's Elite.

Forget his profession. He's single, gorgeous and interested.

She finished her drink. "So let's communicate."

"Shall we rent a cube?"

When she reached for her currency card, he shook his head. "My employer can afford a cube."

His fingertips danced across the console. "Level four, number 801."

"Your employer is generous," she said, thankful they wouldn't have to manage in one of the less expensive sleeping cubes. She'd whacked her head once or twice in those while the *Telum* underwent a full pest eradication last year. Arc Transports refused to pay for the type of cubicles on level four. Standing up and having toilets weren't considered necessities.

Within minutes they were inside a vacant elevator sliding toward level four. He slid his arm about her waist, pulling her tight against his broad chest. His lips met hers, firm and warm, demanding her response. His tongue plunged into her mouth. She sucked on it gently at first, increasing the pressure, deepening the kiss. Every synapse fired, her skin burned in need and anticipation. She reached down and brushed her hand over the hard ridge of his cock.

He moved her against the curve of the elevator, pushed a thigh between her legs. She rubbed her breasts against the hard muscles of his chest, her belly against his erection, her center against his thigh, aching for more contact.

A recorded female voice announced level four. They wrenched apart before the doors slid open to an empty hallway. He picked up his valise and stepped out of the elevator. Hand-in-hand, the hunk escorted Ria past rows of doors. Finally, they arrived at 801. One quick scan of his currency card and they were inside the dark, windowless room, locked in a hungry embrace. The door closed, shutting out everything and everyone except the furious need to join and find mindless, momentary oblivion.

Ria pressed against the hard ridge of his cock. Impressive. She wanted to strip him, take him in her mouth to ensure she hadn't imagined his size. Seizing a handful of material, she yanked his shirttails out of his waistband and opened the seam of his pants. Her fingers closed about him, slid along his length.

"I want to suck you."

He pushed her jacket from her shoulders and shoved it down her arms. It fell to the floor. "Demanding. I like that."

She dropped to her knees. "It's been a long time."

He filled her mouth. Hot silk over steel; too long and thick for her to take all of him inside. Cupping his balls with one hand, she fondled his tight sac. Her lips and tongue teased his flesh.

His groan warned her a second before his salty climax hit her tongue.

"You may be lousy at flirting, but your mouth—"

He drew her to her feet, into his arms, against his heaving chest. His lips covered her, his tongue twining and dancing with hers. He cupped her breast, squeezing, teasing her nipple to a tight peak. His fingers slid beneath the hem of her shirt. His warm palm covered her breast while his thumb flicked her nipple.

His hands were magic, touching and caressing her aching breasts. Her clothes were too confining, her skin too hot. "Let's get naked."

He pulled her shirt over her head. "Lights on or off?"

"Off. I just want to feel."

Ria didn't want to think. She wanted, no needed, mindless coupling, utter release. Aden's big, thick cock was made for pleasure. She intended to use every hard inch of it.

She removed her weapon belt, boots and pants. He caught her about the waist. She gasped when her naked breasts touched his chest. Thick, hard muscles, devoid of hair, rubbed against her nipples. His cock pressed against her belly. Rivers of hot need sliced through her middle, heated her blood. Between her legs, she throbbed.

"I want to taste you," he said. "All of you."

He lifted her until his lips nuzzled a breast, encircled her nipple. He suckled, drawing on her flesh, creating a burning need in her center. A cry caught in her throat. Her heart, trying to keep pace with her body's long ignored demands, pounded furiously.

Ria wrapped her legs about his waist. His hands cupped her buttocks, his fingertips intimately caressing her pussy, heating her flesh, separating her swollen labia. His finger slid inside her, moving in-and-out, giving pleasure and priming her for penetration.

"Fuck me."

He kissed her, fucking her mouth with his tongue as he maneuvered her across the small space. They fell upon the sleeping platform. She reached for his cock, stroking his heavy length, positioning her body beneath his.

His tongue trailed down her neck, her chest, over a nipple, then down her belly. He spread her labia and licked her. Her hips lifted off the bed, her flesh demanding more. She creamed in pleasure. His tongue lapped her swollen, ready folds. With the tip of his tongue he flicked her clit, then suckled.

Her climax came in sharp, sudden waves. She grabbed him by the hair and ground her pussy into his face, bringing another wave of release.

Her hands drifted to his shoulders, kneading his thick muscles. Her chest heaved and her breath came in hot gusts. He climbed between her legs, probed at her still thrumming center. Wet and slick, she stretched around him, taking him inside her in three easy thrusts.

He licked her lips. "You're so tight, I could come."

"Don't. I need this."

He withdrew leaving only the tip inside. "Fast or slow?" he asked, burying himself to the hilt.

He withdrew again. She wrapped her legs around his waist. "Fast. Slow. Fuck me!"

With each withdrawal, his tempo and her need increased until his cock pounded her relentlessly. He slid a hand beneath her buttocks and lifted her closer. Nearing climax, Ria clamped around him, holding him so tight, he arched, stilled. She flooded, cried out.

He pushed deeper, pining her to the mattress while his breath exploded from his chest, fanning her skin in hot waves. The tension left his arms and legs. He rolled her on top of him.

"For the price, you'd think the sleeping platform could be larger."

"At least you can stand in here," she said. "We'd never have fit in the sleeping cubes on the lower levels. These weren't made for giants."

"I'm not that big, but my feet are dangling off the end."

She reached down and stroked his cock. "You're big. How long are you?"

He squeezed her breast. "Enough to keep you happy."

"Seriously, how long?" Odds were she'd never see him again. Tired of the twins' tales of conquest and their endless teasing about her lack of action, Ria wanted bragging rights. "Doc will ask the moment I return. The whole crew will be waiting for details."

"What kind of crew do you have?"

"Five females. Our runs are long and boring. Sex is their favorite topic."

"Minimal crew for a Capha." He stroked her back down to the curve of her buttocks and back again. Slow, sweet, gentle strokes of a lover. "Tell me about them. What kind of women sit around in the deep cold and talk about the size of a man's equipment?"

His request surprised Ria. By now she figured he would have dressed and made some excuse to leave. Instead he held her, caressed her, and took the time to have a conversation.

"Women who have a poster gallery of naked males."

He laughed. "You're kidding."

"When I was in the army, I recall plenty of photos of naked women."

"Army. Supply transport?"

"I served on a Capha2 running supplies to the Outer Regiment. How about you? Ever in the army?"

"I've served. Tell me about your crew?"

"My second officer and communications technician are Sarks. My cargo loaders are Aktarian. Six total. Other than Doc, we're all single. Her husband's in medical school."

"Why doesn't she work on-planet?"

"The Vidar runs pay well, especially if we maintain schedules. The medics qualify for bonuses if the crew remains healthy and productive. Medical school's expensive."

"She supports him?"

"Yes, and misses him. She's very faithful and very—"

"Horny?"

He laughed, a gentle rumble in his big chest. Ria snuggled closer. "We've been off-planet for months."

"What about you?"

"I'm horny, too."

"Thank the Gods. How long have you commanded the *Telum*?"

So the hunk had been listening. "I took command about two years ago, before that I served as second officer."

"What happened to the male crew?"

"The Sarks transferred immediately, but my Aktarian com-tech stayed on to finish his contract. Eventually, I replaced them all with females. Despite the laws, Sarkian corporations are reluctant to promote females."

"Except when the corporations need to meet quotas."

Ria rose from the warmth of his body. He caught her by the arm. His hold firm, but gentle. "Don't leave."

.J. McCall

"Time."

A computerized voice quoted the time in several languages. "I have to leave. My time is short."

He rose to a sitting position. Drawing her onto his lap, he said, "Give me what time you have. I want to do something different."

Ria prayed he wasn't into something weird. After all, she knew nothing about him, except he knew exactly how to touch her, how to please her with his hands, his mouth and his cock.

"We've fucked. Now I want to make love."

She straddled him. "We'll never see each other again."

"Perhaps, but I want you to remember me."

She wrapped her fingers around his cock, stroking him. He stiffened beneath her touch. "I'll remember you."

His fingers played in her curls. He licked her nipples. "I want you to miss me, ache for me, think of me while you lie in your lonely bed out there in the cold deep."

"You make me hot."

His finger slipped inside her, stroking her, making her wet. "Remember my heat."

"Remind me."

"Lights, red, level one."

Overhead a soft red glow spread throughout the room. Aden smiled. Her heart did a quick thump.

"I want to see you come. I want to look at you while we make love." He removed his finger from her pussy and sucked it. "I like your taste."

He cupped her breasts in his hand, thumbed her nipples to taut peaks. "I like your nipples."

He leaned down drawing one peak between his lips, his tongue working magic on her flesh. Rivers of heat shot from her breast to her pussy. She grabbed his cock, positioning the broad head to enter her.

Aden released her swollen nipple. "Ride me, find your pleasure, but don't just fuck my cock! Make love to *me*, Ria."

She lifted her hips, slowly lowering herself on his cock. He remained still, letting Ria set the tempo, wanting her to enjoy their mating. Lifting, lowering, in-and-out, she took him inside her heat, inch by inch, until she surrounded his full throbbing length. With each flex of her pussy, the urge to come intensified.

"You're so tight, so hot." Even his breath burned his throat. Gyrr cupped her firm buttocks, slid a finger down the sweet crease. She touched her nipples to his chest, her lips to his. Her tongue slid in his mouth, moving in rhythm with her pussy. From head to toe, he burned.

He slid his lips down her throat, suckling her soft flesh. Capturing a nipple, he nursed. She threw back her head, arched her back to give him easy access. He suckled hard. She pounded her pussy on his cock.

When her pussy flushed with hot cream, Gyrr released her breast. He wanted to see her come. Head flung back, Ria cried out. Her fingers dug into his shoulders. The strained muscles of her face softened in pleasure. She looked at him and smiled, her eyes and that exquisite mouth expressing her satisfaction. His heart thudding against his chest wall, he came.

Pulling her tight to his chest, he kissed her. He needed the feel of her in his arms, while the final spurts of semen spilled deep inside her womb.

When she pulled away, he understood she had to leave. This time he didn't want to kiss his temporary lover goodbye and return to life with nothing more than a fading memory.

"How long are you staying at Zeon?"

"If the cargo is ready, perhaps a day or two. If not, the corporation decides if the *Telum* remains or continues on to Vidar."

"Lights, normal, level four." The red glowed faded to a soft gold to low level light. He wanted to look into her eyes, read her reaction. "I want this again. I want to see you again."

A flicker of pleasure slid across her face, but her dark eyes were serious. "I don't want a relationship. My job, the long runs, it doesn't work."

"What about Doc?"

"She's married. She's in love."

"Has it been this good before? I want an answer from your heart."

She glanced away, shifted on his lap. His cock slid out of her. He waited, hoping she'd tell him the sex was as incredible for her as it was for him. Given his position, he never lacked for sexual partners. Until now, he hadn't wanted a permanent relationship. He didn't know how everything could change in one, too brief encounter, but it had.

"If we happen to meet in Zeon...it was good. You're good."

"I'll look for you." He'd look until he found her. "Time."

She pushed off his lap before the computerized voice finished and began to dress. "I'm late. I'll be fined if the *Telum* leaves late."

Pulling on his clothes, Gyrr asked, "I'll walk you to your ship."

"Fine, just don't slow me down."

CHAPTER TWO

Within minutes, they were on an elevator speeding toward the docking bays. The utilitarian hallways leading to the commercial freighters were akin to warehouses unlike the ornate entrances given to passenger vessels. Ria had remained silent during their ride. While they walked along the hallway, he took her hand in his.

She paused before a recessed air lock. "My ship."

He lifted her chin with the tip of his forefinger. "Don't say goodbye, kiss me."

"Aden, I don't know if we'll meet again."

Damn, she wanted to blow him off. "Kiss me."

He drew her close. From chest to thigh their bodies touched. Although thoroughly fucked and completely satisfied, he wanted her again. His cock stirred.

"Your appetite is healthy."

"My appetite is for you."

"Perhaps—"

Gyrr jerked. Pain, sharp and intense stung his thigh. He turned, faced the danger. Shoving Ria behind him and into the shelter of the doorway leading to her ship, he confronted three Veks.

Veks! The terrorist tools of the Sutumi! How could they know his identity? Who had betrayed him?

If he could hold them off, Ria would find safety in her ship. Dart tubes raised, they approached. The nails on their furry feet scraped the metal floors. Their yellow eyes narrowed. Gyrr pulled his ice blade.

Roaring in Glacidian, he ordered them away. One retreated until, the leader started to chatter. The three stepped forward. Behind them several more appeared, blocking them. He used the valise as a shield.

"We must get to your ship. It's our only escape."

Two darts struck the valise. How to avoid taking another in the body?

He'd taken one. Gyrr calculated he could handle five before he dropped. Extending his arm, he lunged, slashing the ice blade at the nearest Vek. Howling, the Vek grabbed his shoulder.

A dart stung Gyrr in the shoulder. Another caught him in the arm.

His left leg shook in spasms. Immobilized with pain, his right arm dropped to his side, useless. The blade fell out of his hand. A laser burst exploded, singeing his sleeve. The closest Vek crumpled, a smoking hole in his chest. Another burst exploded. The Vek fled and disappeared.

Gyrr's knee buckled. Ria caught him about the waist.

"If you hadn't gotten in the way, I could have protected your ass. What are Veks doing on Pyxis?"

Weak, he leaned against the wall. "My blade."

Ria scooped up the weapon. Upon contact, the lethal blade retracted. She shoved it in his jacket pocket.

"I've got to call for help. There's a hospital on level ten."

Gyrr's vision began to blur. "No. Never make it. Ambush. Get safe."

Holding onto the valise, Gyrr tried to walk. Willing himself, he put his good leg forward. He wobbled and reached for Ria. "Get inside. Go. I'll…"

Gripping him about the waist, Ria's legs nearly crumpled beneath his weight. She heard the scraping of nails. The Veks were returning. "Hold on, Aden."

Somehow Ria managed to hold Aden upright and press her hand against the air lock panel.

Docking Code.

Ria answered the automated security system.

Airlock secured. Proceed.

When the air lock began to open, Ria shouted orders. "Aden, forward! Move!"

Anchoring Aden to her side, Ria pushed the swaying giant inside the narrow tube. Behind her, the air lock sealed. They were safe. The valise slid from his grasp and thudded to the floor. Grunting beneath his weight, Ria hauled Aden toward the *Telum's* hatch. Her legs quivering, every muscle burning, Ria prodded Aden forward. Several feet from the hatch, his leg gave way. He fell to his knees, taking Ria with him.

Scrambling to her feet, Ria punched in the hatch code. Stepping inside, she grabbed the emergency lever. A siren sounded, alerting the crew. Within seconds, Doc and the twins, Loci and Falara, responded.

Ria pointed to Aden. "Get him to sick bay. Be careful he's been hit by darts."

The twins grabbed Aden beneath the arms and dragged him inside the ship. Despite their size and strength, they could only move him a few feet.

Loci called for the loading robots. Falara raced into the air lock tube to retrieve the valise. Doc kneeled at Aden's side. "What happened?"

"We were attacked by Veks."

"Veks? But that's impossible." Doc peered closely at the dart sticking out of Aden's shoulder. "Nasty things."

Finally, the robot loader skimmed toward them. Loci instructed the robot to lift Aden and take him aft to sick bay.

"Take care of him, Doc. I've got to get us out of here."

Her dark eyes widened. "He needs a doctor."

"He comes with us."

For the first time in their months together, Ria saw fear on Doc's face.

"I don't know how to treat him. He needs hospitalization."

"You have to help him. You're all he's got."

"Call the port security for an ambulance. They'll help us."

"The Veks are out there, waiting for him. I killed one, perhaps two. If we wait for the port security, we'll be questioned. Detained. You ready to give up your bonus for a couple of Veks?"

Doc shook her head.

"Good. Save his life, Doc."

Ria headed for the bridge. Why were the Veks after Aden? Looking back, she noticed Doc still standing at the hatch. "That's an order."

The medic nodded, turned and ran down the corridor toward sick bay.

When Ria rushed onto the bridge, her second officer stood at the helm. Ania was taller than the average Sarkian female and the fittest of the crew. Ria hadn't missed a daily workout since Ania came aboard. "Have you received clearance?"

"Yes, Captain."

Thankfully, security hadn't cancelled clearances in the docking bay, but give them a few more minutes and the whole sector could close. They had to leave. "Take her out, now."

Ania's long, slender fingers danced over the controls. "Hatch sealed. Airlock detached. We're clear. Steady as she goes."

Gracefully, the huge ship began moving away from the docking bay. With each breath, Ria's heartrate slowed. After they were underway, Ria intended to contact security and report the Veks. She wouldn't admit to shooting the scruffy creatures, nor did she plan to report her unauthorized passenger.

"Do you wish to take the helm, Captain?"

Unaware of the events leading to Ria's return, Ania's calm concentration remained on maneuvering the huge ship. "Negative. Take her out. Set course for Zeon."

Ania turned. Her dark eyes shining, she flashed a smile at Ria. "Aye, aye, Captain."

Sitting at the com-center, the technician, Ula, swiveled around. "The whole skyport is going on alert. Did something happen, Captain?"

"Once we've cleared Pyxis, I'll explain."

Like her, Ula and Ania were military brats. Their fathers had served in the Sutumi War. On duty, they were dedicated and followed orders. Off duty, they were hard-drinking and fun-loving.

Although short and stocky in build, Ula loved to dance. While in port, the tech spent every waking hour in the hottest club.

Ula returned to her duties, her long dark hair swinging as she swiveled to face her console. Ania steered the *Telum* clear of the docking station. Ria respected her crew, and never more than now. If they hadn't been prepared, the *Telum* wouldn't have undocked on time.

Missed schedules cost the crew points. High performance points meant bonuses. Female officers had to perform better, faster, than their male counterparts. Determined to hold onto her job, Ria pushed her crew when necessary, gave liberties when she could. This fiasco with the Veks could impact her career with Arc.

The urgency of undocking over, Ria's thoughts returned to her passenger. Doc had to save Aden's life. Once the *Telum* docked at Zeon, she had to get him onto the skyport without the authorities or the corporation finding out. The enormity of the task overwhelmed her.

"Set course. If you need me, I'll be in sick bay with Doc."

Ania and Ula stared at her, but said nothing. Ria knew they had questions, and she intended to give them answers, but later.

"Carry on." After she exited the bridge, Ria sprinted to sick bay.

* * * * *

Heads bent, Doc and the twins surrounded the patient. Upon joining them, Ria understood why. Aden lay on his back, naked and out cold. Falara and Loci held his bent leg tight to his body, exposing the dart embedded in back of his thigh. The twins' gazes were locked on his genitals. Even immobilized, he appeared every inch a warrior. Scars she hadn't noticed in those too short minutes in his arms marred his body.

"Hold his leg. Steady," Doc warned.

Doc had removed the dart he'd taken in the shoulder. It lay in an open container on a mobile table. Scanner in hand, she hovered over the dart embedded in his leg. Another dart remained in his arm.

"How can I help?"

"Place the dart in the analysis unit. Until I know the toxin injected, I can't give him an antidote. Thank you, Captain."

Ria picked up the container and placed it in the analysis unit. Grabbing several containers, she put them on the utility table next to Doc.

Using a pair of slender surgical pliers, Doc delicately removed the dart and dropped it into a container. "He was struck by three. His traveling bag wasn't so lucky. One struck his currency card instead of his chest."

Ria glanced at Aden's valise. Five darts were embedded in the lightweight nyplex bag. Against the dark material of his jacket, a dart gleamed. She picked up the jacket. She recalled Aden slipping his currency card back into the inside pocket of his jacket.

"Be careful of those darts," Doc warned.

Gently, Ria released the jacket and returned to the operating table where Aden lay unconscious. The twins were swabbing the entry wounds with a gooey blue substance then placing clear bandages over each affected area. Doc scanned the final wound. Within seconds she plucked out the final dart.

In a well-modulated masculine voice, the computer announced: *analysis completed.*

"On screen," Doc requested. She stared at the results for seconds. "Vektar pymal."

"Snake venom?"

"The Veks are immune. Their methods are barbaric, but effective. The victim never awakens."

"But Veks like to slash and tear," Loci said. Her twin nodded in agreement.

"Since the Sutumi were forced out to the far side of the galaxy, the Veks were stripped of their weapons," Ria said. "Perhaps a silent weapon suited their purposes."

"Darts are silent and effective." Doc picked up a dart displaying the long, thin needle protruding from a thin cylinder. "The cylinder holds a small amount of propellant. If fired in close range, the needle will penetrate skin and muscle easily."

Ria watched as Doc retrieved an injection pistol from a cabinet and loaded it. Pistol in hand, Doc stood over Aden. "If you had taken just one in the chest, we'd be fighting to save your life, Captain."

"I was armed. He shoved me behind him."

Loci stroked Aden's leg letting her fingertips graze his balls. "A real hero."

Ria resisted the urge to reprimand her. "Will he be all right?"

Doc nodded. She placed the nozzle of the pistol to the pulsing vein in Aden's neck, then to his thigh. "If he'd taken more darts, he'd never awaken."

"He'll live?" Ria asked. "You're sure?"

"Yes, I've injected a toxin-blocker. He'll revive slowly. Still, I think we should watch over him."

"We'll take shifts," Falara volunteered.

"Is he in danger?" Ria asked.

"Given the amount of pymal in the three darts and his body weight, I'd say no, but he'll wake up with a major headache. I want to be sure he doesn't convulse."

"But you gave him a blocker?"

"He's not a Vek, Captain. He's—"

"Hung."

Ria glanced at the cargo loader. Loci held Aden's flaccid cock in her hand. A fierce shot of pure jealousy shot through her middle. She wouldn't share her hero lover.

"You're dismissed." Ria's gaze moved from Loci to her twin. "Return to your duties."

Reluctance written all over her beautiful face, Loci caressed Aden's cock a final time before releasing it. The twins knew when to retreat.

"You can't blame them. He is hung." Doc smiled. "No sharing with the crew, Captain?"

"Not on your life. Just because he's Aktarian doesn't give them rights."

"That's just it. He's Aktarian, but he's also Sark and Glacidian. He's everything."

"Glacidian? Are you sure?"

"You don't run across Vek darts every day so I scanned his blood and his genes for defects and allergies."

"Do the twins know?"

"I doubt they have the training to read the scan output."

Ria released a breath. Given the population of the two planets, those with mixed blood were rare. The combination of the three reduced the numbers dramatically. She brushed Aden's hair off his forehead while Doc placed a transparent bandage over the small wound on his arm.

"He doesn't have any defects. He's absolutely perfect."

"No one is perfect, Doc. Aren't those with mixed blood prone to defects?"

Doc nodded. "The number with mixed blood isn't large, but a high percentage are prone to disease. Aden's genes are perfect."

"Perhaps he had embryonic surgery."

119

"Possible. He's wearing lenses, very high tech, very expensive."

Whose life had she saved? "Explain."

"I'm not an expert at this stuff, but his eyes aren't blue and the lenses he's wearing aren't available to the ordinary consumer."

"So, maybe he's vain." Even as Ria said it, she didn't believe it. Aden was confident, precise, gentle and brave. Vain didn't fit. Aden had mentioned his employer could well afford the cost of a sleeping cube. Perhaps the special lenses were also on the affordable list.

Doc opened Aden's left eyelid. "So vain he could fool an Ident scanner?"

Who was Aden's employer? Who was Aden? Why did the Veks attack him? What had she gotten herself into?

Brushing Aden's long blond hair away from his face, Doc pointed to the base of his left ear. "And there's this."

Ria rounded the table and leaned closed. Behind the lobe of his left ear was a small bump. She looked at Doc.

The medic grinned. "Glads have a pleasure node."

Extending her finger, Ria focused on the small bump. "I've heard about it, but—"

Doc grabbed her wrist. "Too much pressure and you can kill him."

Ria pulled her hand back.

"Just the right amount of pressure, and you can make him climax."

She locked gazes with Doc. "I thought that only worked for the women."

Smiling from ear-to-ear, Doc shook her head. "Men too."

Ria wasn't sure what to think. If Aden lived, the possibilities were interesting.

"Don't get any ideas. Manipulating the node for sexual pleasure takes training. If you get too excited, you'll accomplish what the Veks couldn't."

"Let's keep this information to ourselves," Ria said. "If the twins find out about this, he's doomed."

At the door, Ria turned. "And destroy that gene scan."

Deep Heat

* * * * *

After verifying the *Telum's* progress and a quick review of the ship's log, Ria returned to sick bay. Doc had covered Aden with a monitoring blanket. The thin material would detect any changes from temperature to heartrate and relay the information to the pager clipped on Doc's belt. "How's he doing?"

"The same. I expect he'll sleep for hours, perhaps through tomorrow. I suggest you get some rest, too, Captain."

Resisting the urge to touch Aden, Ria turned her attention to the pile of discarded clothing sitting atop his traveling bag. Perhaps Aden's identity docs could shed some light on the situation.

"You can handle them. I've removed the darts."

"Has anyone else touched them?"

"The twins helped me cut off his clothing, but other than that, no."

Ria scooped up the clothing, tucking the items in the crook of her arm. In one hand she held his boots, in the other, his bag. "Until further notice, sick bay is off limits."

Doc nodded. "I'll sleep here tonight. If his condition changes, I'll let you know. Get some rest, Captain. Doctor's orders."

Ria retreated to her quarters to inspect Aden's belongings.

His clothes were new, of excellent quality, but common in style. His boots were well worn. The Aktarian labels supported his story of a recent visit home.

Ria removed Aden's document cards from a wallet tucked inside an inner jacket pocket and settled into the chair before her desk. The docs included an Ident card, a ticket and travel permit to Zeon via Pyxis, an employment card and and a currency card issued from a major Aktarian Bank. The Vek dart had left a dent that may have rendered the currency card useless, but had also saved his life.

Pushing the other cards aside, Ria picked up the Ident card. The picture and the description matched the man lying in sick bay, but the eye scan on the card would correspond with the blue lenses. Few ordinary citizens could afford the lenses, or have the necessary contacts to obtain an Ident card accurate enough to pass through Aktarian and skyport security.

What color were Aden's eyes? What else about him was a deception? Had he truly been interested in seeing her again or had he simply used her as a short diversion for pleasure before fulfilling his contract?

Dropping the Ident card, Ria picked up his employment card and scanned it. The embedded employment contract information began to upload on her computer. Her crew carried similar employment cards. Every cargo container had a card the crew could scan for destination, weight and content. Most of the *Telum*'s cargo came from Sark. Aktarian and Glacidian products were loaded at Pyxis.

Aden had told her he was contracted for a year. Finding out who had employed him could shed some light on the situation.

The information appeared on her screen. The wording was that of an ordinary contract. When she read his profession Ria's emotions reeled. *Communications!*

Heart pounding, Ria read the work contract twice. The knowledge that she was a momentary diversion pierced her ego. If anyone should understand his profession, she should. She couldn't believe the money. Sex paid well.

Although she had wanted nothing more than quick sexual release, Aden had somehow kindled something inside of her. He'd warmed her heart and had her wanting more. His request to see her again on Zeon had planted a seed of hope. For a moment her thoughts had moved beyond lust.

Reality filled her computer screen.

Ria slipped out of her clothes and into her bunk. She needed to think and to rest. She hadn't closed her eyes in the last twenty-four hours.

Between the recent, amazing sexual activity and the adrenaline rush of the confrontation with the Veks, Ria gave into the sudden exhaustion overwhelming her. Ria ordered lights out.

She had several days, and nights, to work through the puzzle of Aden Conr before the *Telum* reached Zeon. Recalling Aden's lovemaking, Ria smiled. Aden had chosen the right profession. He'd made her whole body come alive.

* * * * *

After a quick sonic shower and several minutes in her sun tube, Ria called the bridge while she dressed. Ania verified the *Telum's* course and time. Satisfied with the ship's progress, Ria headed for sick bay.

Doc stood at the edge of Aden's bed. "I think he's coming to."

"Did he speak?"

Grinning, Doc lifted the blanket. Aden had an enormous hard-on. "Is it as good as it looks?"

"Better, but then that's his business."

Doc glanced at Ria briefly. "Business?"

"He's a sex consort."

Ria tried to keep her voice level. Thankfully, Doc's attention was centered on Aden's genitals.

"He certainly has the equipment for it. He didn't charge you, did he?"

"No. He didn't tell me. I found a contract in his docs. He has a long-term date waiting for him on Zeon."

Doc replaced the blanket. "Sounds like our boy was taking a night off. It's a legitimate living, especially for an Aktarian. They live to fuck. Just look at the twins."

Ria had a vision of Aden and the twins in an Aktarian three-way. No way was that going to happen. Not on her ship.

So he didn't tell her he had a mistress waiting for him on Zeon. And not just any mistress! Portmaster Sy was easily twice his age, but few challenged the Siluko on any level. The woman was a legend.

"You could wake him up."

Ria recognized the silky tone in Doc's voice. "Would it help?"

"It certainly won't hurt him." Doc removed the pager from her belt. "Think about it. I'm going to the galley. Shall I bring coffee for two in ohhh…about twenty minutes?"

"Please. What if he doesn't wake up?"

Already at the door, Doc turned. "He will."

Ria locked the door behind Doc and returned to Aden's side. She caressed his cheek. Stubble greeted her fingertips. She touched her finger to his mouth, running the tip along the seam of his lips. When his lips latched on her finger, she gasped. He suckled her finger.

"Aden, can you hear me?"

His eyelids fluttered, then closed. Ria figured he was trapped in the twilight between sleep and awake. She didn't want to jar him into consciousness.

Leaning down, she kissed him. He responded briefly then drifted. Reaching beneath the blanket, she grasped his cock. Slowly, she stroked him. He was thick, hard and wonderfully long. Her sex flexed.

She removed her jacket and pulled off her tank top. She shouldn't tease a semi-conscious man, but her nipples beaded in anticipation. Moving her torso side-to-side, she ran a nipple over the seam of his lips. His mouth latched onto her and suckled. Streams of heat raced through her.

He suckled, tugging and drawing on her eager flesh. Ria reached down and caressed the broad head of his cock. A bead of semen wetted her fingertips.

"Aden?"

When she pulled her nipple free of his mouth, he moaned. She stroked his cock, slid her fingers over his balls. His eyes remained closed.

Hard and hot to the touch, Ria stroked him again. She wanted him awake. She needed him to cool the heat flooding her body. Doc had suggested physical stimulation. Ria released him for the short moments required to remove her boots, pants and underwear.

Naked, she climbed atop him. Impaling herself upon the thick head of his swollen cock, she rode him, furious with her own need. Angry at his deception, she pounded her pussy against his heat until she climaxed.

A fine sheer of perspiration clinging to her skin, Ria realized she'd taken unfair advantage of Aden. Despite his profession, she had no right to abuse his condition.

"You fuck like a Goddess."

She looked into his eyes. Those beautiful eyes that weren't blue. "You're awake."

His fingers wrapped about her arm. He pulled her close until her face was mere inches from his. "And you're beautiful. I could come just looking at you."

Apparently he didn't mind that she had used his glorious cock for her own pleasure. "How do you feel?"

"Head aches. Thirsty." His stomach growled. "Hungry as a mank—where am I?"

Ice mank? The Glacidian fur-bearing creature was so rare hunting it was forbidden. Did he realize he had slipped?

"Aboard the *Telum*. You're in sick bay. Do you remember the attack?"

He massaged the back of his neck. "Veks. How long have I been out?"

"About thirty-six hours."

He swore. "I missed my flight."

"I had to leave Pyxis. I'd discharged a weapon, killed a Vek, perhaps two. Security would have detained us for hours. Either way, you would have missed your flight."

"You're headed for Zeon?"

"Yes. You'll get there. It's just going to take you a bit longer."

"Help me up?"

"Take it slow," Ria said, pushing up from his chest. She straddled his torso, letting her weight rest on her knees. His cock slid out of her. His gaze dropped to her pussy. A sexy smile shaped his lips.

He caressed her thighs. "Come here."

"Where?"

He dug his fingers into the backs of her thighs, urging her closer. When she positioned her pussy over his face, he whispered, "Here."

"I thought you were hungry?"

"I'll have my dessert first—"

His words were lost as his tongue burrowed between her labia. He plundered her pussy, licked her hot juices. She resisted the urge to cry, to scream her joy. When he latched onto her clit, Ria surrendered.

After regaining a near normal heart rhythm, Ria climbed off of him. Clutching his head, Aden rose up on one elbow.

"Doc warned you'd have a headache, but it will pass."

Eyes closed, hand spread, he rubbed his temples with a thumb and finger. "How many darts did I take?"

Ria plucked a water container from the cold unit recessed in the wall. "Three."

He opened his eyes, swept her body with a concerned gaze. "And you?"

She placed the container in his hand. "None, but I can't say the same for your luggage."

Parched, Gyrr drank, emptying the entire container. Ria made no move to cover her nakedness. Dressed in her honey-colored skin, she was glorious in her natural state. Looking at her made him ache with a need that transcended mere physical pleasure. She wore her dark hair pulled back in a braid. The style accentuated her delicate features. Her eyes were brown, her nose petite and her lips lush. Thanks to the Veks, he'd have more time to explore this amazing female.

How had the Veks discovered his presence on Pyxis?

"I remember now." Gyrr pushed himself up to a setting position, dangling his legs off the edge of the infirmary table. "You nailed one or two with your laser. I should have stood behind you."

"Thanks for protecting me."

"I need to use the—" He looked for a door. His breath froze in his lungs. "Great Gods."

On every wall were pictures of naked males with enormous hard-ons. Most were Aktarians with a few Sarks scattered in between. "This is sick bay?"

Ria laughed. "My crew claims these help them recuperate."

"I'm glad you were here when I awoke." He shuddered. "This could really be a nightmare to any sick or injured man."

Ria moved between his knees. "I thought Aktarian males spent their youth cavorting about naked."

He loved her wicked grin. He knew she was thinking about sex. "I spent mine with women, girls."

"No locker rooms? No army barracks?"

"Sure, but never sporting an erection." He slanted his head. "I save those for…" He licked her lips. "For you."

"Exclusive use?"

He wrapped an arm about her waist, splaying his hand wide across her fabulous ass. He touched the tip of his nose to hers. "For as long as you want me."

"I have a crew of horny women. Two of them, beautiful Aktarian twins."

"Twins! You do like to tempt a man."

Despite their teasing banter, her grin disappeared.

"You have the sweetest pussy in the all the planets. Your breasts are like the lush leche fruits of Sark. And your mouth...I want you, Ria. Only you."

"Until we arrive at Zeon, then what happens?"

No matter how much Ria fascinated him, the mission came first. "I have commitments."

"You expect me to wait a whole year while you fuck your way to wealth."

His chest tightened. He wished he could explain. "You've read my contract."

"You're talented. Your choice of profession suits you."

He prayed the edge to her voice was due to jealousy instead of disgust. Aktarians had long ago ceased viewing prostitution as an immoral occupation. Despite the changes to Sark's Code of Laws freeing the sex slaves, many still discriminated against the women forced by birth into the life-style. Their daughters continued the tradition and their sons served as soldiers until the slavery laws were repealed.

"Are you saying I'm a good lover?"

"You're very good."

He slid his forefinger between the crease of her buttocks. "Will the Captain allow me the pleasure of repaying her for my pitiful life?"

She wrapped her arms about his neck. "If I'm able to walk when we reach Zeon, you will have failed in your duties."

By the time they reached Zeon, Gyrr vowed she'd be his, forever. "I am yours to command."

CHAPTER THREE

"Where is my wallet? My clothes?"

Doc scanned his chest. The medic was petite, with short, dark hair, and a generous smile.

"Heartrate is normal. They're in the Captain's quarters."

Ria had dashed off when Doc returned. Although he felt fine, Doc insisted on checking him over. She replaced the bandages over the dart wounds.

"You'll have headaches for another day or so. Other than that, you're in excellent health."

His stomach growled. "Sorry. If you're finished?"

"I've ordered a meal."

To his utter disgust, Doc retrieved a large bowl of porridge from the nutrition unit. Sarks loved the sticky goo. Raised on the stuff, his father consumed a bowl every morning. Like his mother, Gyrr hated porridge.

"You Aktarians! You'd think I was serving fried Vek."

"I'd eat fried Vek."

The medic placed the porridge-laden tray next to him. "You'll eat this. And then you'll sleep."

Her gaze dared him to protest. Gyrr picked up a spoonful. Grimacing, he swallowed.

"Good. I'll check on you later."

The door locked behind her. Between the wall display of erections and Sark porridge, Gyrr wished he'd taken another Vek dart, maybe two. Great Gods!

His stomach grumbled. Focusing on the floor, Gyrr shoveled the porridge in to his mouth. Yekkk! He downed another container of water to rid himself of the taste. After a quick sonic shower and shave, he stretched out on the infirmary bed. Closing his eyes, he decided his first request to the Captain would be to move out of the cock gallery and into her quarters. His second would be her.

"Just one look, Doc. What's the harm?"

Two voices. Gyrr opened his eyes, turned his head. Doc stood in the doorway. Two blonde females towered over her. The twins Ria had mentioned.

"Captain's orders. Now back to your duties."

Door closed and locked, Doc approached his bed. "How's the headache?"

Gyrr sat up. His head no longer pounded. A dull ache remained. "Better. Why am I held prisoner?"

He enjoyed the shocked look on the medic's face. "Prisoner?"

"You've taken my clothes. You've locked me in. You force me to eat vile food."

"The Captain has your clothes. If we don't lock the door, the twins wouldn't let you rest, much less sleep. My porridge is healthy."

"I'm kept under lock and key for my own good?"

"Not exactly. Do you like Dansi tea?"

Gyrr nodded and the medic filled a pot from the hot water unit. After the tea was added to steep, she collected cups.

"How am I not exactly a prisoner?"

"The twins double-team their partners," she explained. "They're not gentle when it comes to sex. We've had complaints from other ships. R&R has a whole new meaning when the twins are on leave."

Gyrr grinned. As a youth he'd known a girl who'd tested his stamina. Perhaps that girl had twin sisters. "I can't stay locked up until we reach Zeon."

A secretive smile curled her lips. "The Captain wanted to ensure you'd recuperate as quickly as possible. She has declared you off limits."

"Off limits to whom?"

She handed him a steaming cup. "The crew, especially the twins."

He sipped the tea. "Excellent. What is your name?"

She slipped into a chair facing his bed. Apparently, she didn't find his size and nakedness the least bit intimidating. "Everyone calls me Doc."

"What does your mother call you?"

"Cirrii."

"Ria told me you plan to attend medical school."

Her eyes widened in surprise. "I do."

"Good. You're talented. Freighter medics don't handle Vek darts on a daily basis."

"Our medical computer is excellent. Thankfully, the corporation bought the best."

Gyrr drained the cup and set it aside. "Cirrii," he began, keeping his voice low. "I want my clothes. Then I want directions to Ria's quarters. I will not spend another hour in this cock gallery." He eased off the bed and stood in front of her. "And if you ever feed me porridge again, I'll hang you by your toes."

Ignoring his threat, her gaze focused on his crotch. "Are all Aktarians as large as you?"

"Yes, we all look like this," he said, sweeping his hand toward the row of pictures on the walls.

"May I touch it—you."

So much for size intimidation! "What?"

"Just once, please."

Before he could give permission, her hand shot out and touched him. Gently, she ran her fingers over his cock, stroking him in examination of his width and length rather than for sexual pleasure. She rubbed the tip with her thumb. Despite her clinical approach, his cock stiffened slightly. Her fingertips cupped his balls, testing their weight. Her inspection was over as quickly as it had begun.

"You're really magnificent."

"You could have done that while I was unconscious."

"I gave you a thorough examination, but it isn't the same. Rather like those pictures aren't real. You have a marvelous penis, Aden. I've never seen one so large. It's like a wonderful weapon you can brandish at will."

"I have yet to use it to inflict pain."

Cirrii sighed and rose to her full height. The top of her head didn't reach his shoulders. She looked up at him. "I'll get your clothes, but I think you should reconsider the porridge. It's really good for you."

Cirrii left. Within seconds, Ria arrived, locking the door behind her.

Standing before him, her gaze dropped to his partially erect cock. "Is that for me?"

"Cirrii examined me."

"Apparently, *Cirrii* has an excellent bedside manner."

"No need to get jealous. She fondled me like I was some specimen. Those little hands of hers were measuring me."

"I'm not jealous."

He ignored her protest and pulled her into his arms. "She promised to get my clothes. How long will it take her?"

"Doc's quick. She doesn't dawdle."

Cupping her face, Gyrr kissed her. Why this woman should be the one to take his breath away, he didn't know. What he did know was the effect she had on him. His heart pounded. His cock ached. Every nerve fired. He wanted to suck every inch of her delicious flesh from her tiny ear lobes to her toes: the journey in between sheer pleasure.

The heat of her mouth seared his. The way she sucked his tongue drove him mad with need. He wanted her naked, hot and wet, with her sweet pussy tight around his cock.

Taking her by the waist, Gyrr lifted her onto the infirmary bed. He peeled open the seam of her waistband, separated the side seam of her trousers. Sliding his hands beneath the material, he guided her legs about his hips. "When she brings my clothes, you could order her to leave."

"You want to fuck?"

He wanted to make love, too. By the time they reached Zeon, Ria would understand the difference. Once he'd completed his mission, perhaps she'd forgive his deception.

"Isn't that my job? This bed has great positional options." He cupped her ass, bringing her crotch to his. "Like this one."

Stepping back, Gyrr lifted her off the bed and turned her around. He pushed her chest down on the bed and her thighs apart. He placed his cock against her buttocks. "This one has great possibilities."

Ria activated her wrist unit. "Doc."

"Captain."

"I have something to discuss with our patient. Could you return in half-an-hour?"

"Aye, aye, Captain."

Pleased Ria had chosen him over her duties, Gyrr eased her trousers down. He stroked the insides of her thighs, up-and-down. Beneath his hands, her silky skin heated. Her enthralling sighs teased his senses. He needed to touch, to taste, to inhale her scent. Dropping to his knees, he licked the curve of one buttock, slipped a finger between her legs. Moisture pooled on the pad of his finger. He touched her clit. Again, she moaned.

She rocked her hips. "Please, Aden."

Gyrr ignored her pleas. Instead, he took a moment to appreciate her quivering, pink flesh. Slowly, he inhaled her hot scent. Every receptor in his system fired. His cock stretched, straining to touch, to join. He rubbed his face against her buttocks and thighs.

His sensitive Glacidian olfactory system gloried in Ria's perfume. He licked his fingers and touched her. His fingers burned at the moist contact. Her pussy flexed. His balls ached. Gyrr reached down and stroked his swollen sac. Great Gods, he wanted Ria.

Thrusting his face between her spread thighs, Gyrr licked her pussy, drawing her hot moisture while he stroked his balls and cock.

Ria squirmed. Beneath his tongue, her ready flesh plumped. Juices drenched her pussy. The taste of her nectar drove Gyrr mad with need. Heart pounding, he suckled her clit until she climaxed. When her tensed muscles relaxed, Gyrr held her thighs apart, rubbed his face over her pussy, wetting his skin with her juices.

His hands slid from her thighs. Gyrr closed his eyes and flung back his head. His face burned with a cold heat, like ice against his skin. His breath caught, the air trapped in his lungs hot and searing.

Although, Glacidian males accepted this reaction as their fate, Gyrr never expected to experience it.

Logic defied his physical reaction. He couldn't bond with a Sark. Yet, all his senses told him the process had begun.

"Aden, are you all right? Should I call Doc?"

His lungs released with a decided whoosh. He sucked in cool air. Only a Glacidian male could understand what he'd experienced.

He opened his eyes. Ria, her trousers about her ankles, stood before him displaying her glorious thatch of dark curls at eye level. "No. I'm fine. Just a bit dizzy."

Dizzy didn't begin to describe it!

"Maybe you're not strong enough to indulge yourself. Even sex consorts must pace themselves."

He reached out and grasped the edge of the bed. Hauling himself to his feet, Gyrr looked at his straining cock. Drugged with Ria's scent, he'd remain like this until he mated. "Turn around, Captain. I'm going in deep."

Smiling, Ria leaned over the bed and presented her exquisite backside. In a ritual as old as life on Glacid, Gyrr licked her back. Reaching between her legs, he caressed her already wet pussy.

He fingered her clit. "I'm going to love you, Ria. Hard and deep. Can you take it?"

"Ohhh. Yes."

"Do you want it?"

She shifted her hips. He slid a finger inside her tight wetness. She moaned.

He withdrew his finger and sucked it. His heart thumped hard in his chest. Although Ria did not understand, his need for direct contact, especially to her sensual juices was an integral part of the binding ritual.

Again, he dipped his finger inside of her. "Love me. Fuck my finger."

Hot and wet, she pumped her hips. Using his fingers, he played with her pussy until she climaxed.

After withdrawing his hand, Gyrr turned her around. Again, he licked her cream from his fingers, savored the flavor of her on his tongue.

Drawing her close, he slanted his head. Her lips parted. Her climax still on his tongue, Gyrr kissed her. His tongue slid over hers, mating, exchanging the nectar of sensual pleasure. He rubbed his chest and belly against hers, mingling the light sheen of perspiration dewing their skin.

He traced a wet trail down her neck to her breasts. Her nipples were hard eager points. Capturing one, he suckled, deep and needy.

The moan from deep in her throat telling him she wanted his eager nursing.

Needing more, he kneeled between her legs. Despite the intense pain of his erection, ritual drove him onward. He plunged his tongue inside the swollen folds of her labia. Easing his tongue in and out, he teased her hot flesh.

"Ohhh. Do they teach you this?"

Grinning, Gyrr withdrew his tongue. "Love me. Fuck my tongue, Ria."

With a delighted sigh, she shoved her pussy against his face. He needed her to climax, to spill her sweet juices on his tongue. He licked her pussy, suckled her clit until she shuddered. Plunging his tongue inside, he absorbed her pleasure as a thirsty man would drink.

She leaned on the bed for support. "My legs feel like jelly."

"How does your pussy feel?"

She smiled. "Pleased, but—hot. I need this." She reached out and stroked his cock.

"I'm not finished," he warned. His cock pulsed with the need to mate. "Turn around and spread your legs, Captain."

Without hesitation she turned and leaned over the table. Warmed by need, her golden skin glowed. Her pink pussy beckoned him to enter. When he touched the tip of his cock to her heat, his heart jumpstarted. Ria arched her back, positioned herself to receive him. He entered slowly, pumping his hips, easing his cock into her wetness. Again, he licked her back. Her scent filled his nostrils. Her taste melted on his tongue. Her flesh undulated around him, her moisture penetrated his skin with each stroke, drawing him deep, binding him, forever.

She clamped down on his cock, holding him tight and fast. Sweat beaded on his forehead. Every muscle shuddered. His heart swelled, banging against the wall of his chest.

Fully embedded, he spread his arms as if to embrace the sky. His head flung back in the traditional stance of worship to the distant, life-giving sun, Gyrr swore an oath of fidelity, spoken by lifemates for thousands of years, words as ancient as the ice of Glacid, in utter silence.

His climax wrenched free of his balls, thundered through his cock, spilling into Ria's wet heat.

Great Gods!

He sucked in a deep breath, then another. His legs trembled. Finally, the hammering of his heart subsided. Never had he experienced anything so exhilarating, not his first climax, nor his first battle could compare to this mating. Without Ria's knowledge, he'd chosen her as his. Now, Gyrr confronted the real battle, winning Ria's heart.

"I don't think I can move."

Understanding she'd feel exhausted, Gyrr lifted her and laid her on the bed. She'd curled into the fetal position. He joined her, curving his body about hers. He stroked her breasts, her belly.

"I feel strange."

"Sleep for awhile. You'll be fine."

Gyrr's heart swelled. Had his semen caused a chemical reaction? Ria displayed the symptoms of a female accepting her mate's semen, except Glacidian women were usually in their fertile cycle. When they awoke, they were hornier than ever. How would Ria react?

"You're amazing. No wonder you get paid to fuck. I want…more."

Her eyes fluttered once, then closed.

Although loving her compliment, Gyrr hated the necessity of deception. His mission demanded secrecy, but once accomplished, he'd tell Ria the truth.

He prayed she'd come to love him. Love him enough to understand the reason for his lies. Love him enough to accept him as her lifemate.

If she didn't, he'd live out his life alone and celibate.

Celibate! Great Gods!

Holding her prisoner in his bed held far more interesting possibilities.

* * * * *

Ria awoke naked, with Aden's arm draped over her and his big body curled along her back. She turned in the narrow bed to face him. His eyes opened.

"How do you feel?"

"Wonderful."

He smiled. Warmth flowed through her as if she were glowing from the inside. Nothing in her experience explained how Aden made her feel. Ria considered herself a normal, healthy woman with a reasonable, but easily controlled, sex drive. Although horny, she ignored her body's desires and had remained celibate for the last three years. Aden had changed everything.

How could she look into his eyes, knowing he wasn't truthful, and still want him with insatiable desire?

Every cell in her body wanted him. Her heart pounded at the very sight of him. Her blood ran hot at his touch.

Her brain told her to keep an emotional distance. Her senses told her to indulge, to wallow in his sensuality, and her heart told her to love.

Before her brain had a chance to control her heart, Aden kissed her.

Two days ago she would swear she'd been kissed well. Now, she knew better. Aden's lips moved over hers in a sensual dance, blinding her to everything except him. Like a powerful drug, he ruled her, yet she felt safe. When he touched her, she belonged to him, heart and soul.

The absurdity of her emotions shocked her. Soon enough they'd arrive on Zeon and they'd part ways. For now, she would wallow.

Aden drew her into his arms. When her breasts touched his chest, she rubbed her nipples against his smooth skin. Her body, every curve and hollow, molded to his. His cock nestled into the notch between her legs as if they were made for one another.

"How is it we fit so perfectly?" he asked.

"Do you read minds?"

"No, do you?"

"The same thought had struck me."

"That you fit me like a glove? That your breasts fill my hands just right?"

"When you touch me, I feel like I'm melting inside."

Why had she opened the door to her heart? She'd learned early that pain and emotion came hand-in-hand.

He smiled. Gently, he traced a finger along her thigh, over her hip, down into the valley of her waist, up over her breast, along her throat to touch the pulse pounding there.

"When I look at you, my heart races. It happened on Pyxis, it's happening now."

She wanted to bask in his words, let her foolish heart believe once again. Then she remembered his contract. Within a week he would say sweet words to another. He'd melt another's insides.

"I turn you on?"

His gaze narrowed. "Yeah, you could say that."

"Then teach me."

"Teach you?"

"Your tricks. Your specialties. I want a crash course in fucking."

"I'll give you the royal course. Shall we continue in sick bay or move to your quarters, Captain?"

She noticed his voice has changed. The coaxing, sensual tone had an edge. His cock had lost its rigidity. "You've serviced the rich, the famous, the royals?"

"Yes."

"Aktarian or Sark?"

"Both."

He slid off the bed. Ria sat up. He took her by the waist, lifted her onto her feet. "Get dressed."

She noted the command in his voice. At one time Aden had to have served in the military. She'd seen him in a crisis. He hadn't cowered. He'd faced the enemy and attacked. He'd protected.

Ria dressed quickly. "What about your clothes?"

"I fuck for a living. Clothes aren't an essential part of my profession. You can order your crew clear, or you can give them a show."

A challenge to test her? She didn't want the crew to see Aden naked, but since Doc and twins had already had the pleasure and Ula and Ania were manning the bridge, Ria picked up the gauntlet he'd thrown.

Despite her quickened pace, Aden remained at her side. "My quarters are sparse. Not what you're used to."

"You have no idea what I'm used to."

"True, but I'm sure a man of your talents is treated well."

Instead of responding, Aden smiled. They ducked through a narrow hatch. In an emergency, Ria could seal off sections of the ship. Turning into another corridor heading forward, they met Doc.

"What are you doing out of bed?" Doc dragged her gaze from Aden and looked right at Ria. "He should be in sick bay."

"Don't worry, Cirrii. Your Captain will tuck me in the moment we reach her quarters. Are those mine?"

Doc handed over his clothes and boots. "Report to sick bay in twenty-four hours for an examination."

Aden turned to one side, allowing Doc to move past him in the narrow corridor. Again, Doc's gaze slid over Aden's nakedness. Sinfully gorgeous, Aden carried his beauty with confidence, but without conceit.

"Thank you, Cirrii."

Ria noted Doc's reaction to Aden's silken voice and sweeter smile. He had a way about him. Surely, he'd left a trail of heart-broken females in his past. Would she too be a short memory in his sexual journey?

"Shall we continue?"

They'd walked the length of the corridor before he spoke.

"You hide your jealousy well."

Ria ignored him, or tried to. How do you dismiss a naked hunk able to turn your insides to molten goo? She stopped before a door. *Captain Ria Torr*. Silently, the door slid open.

He followed her inside and dropped his clothes and boots onto the floor. "You have no reason to be."

She removed her jacket. "Be what?"

He advanced toward her. "Jealous. Tell me you love me, Ria."

"I thought we came here to fuck?"

"That's all you want from me? My cock inside you?"

Although he spoke softly, his voice held a serious tone. "Do all your mistresses fall in love with you?"

He ran his fingertip along her bare arm. "Are you my mistress?"

"As long as you're aboard the *Telum*, you are under my command."

He placed a fingertip against the pulse at her throat. "Do I require your permission, or am I allowed to take the initiative?"

"When we're naked, you can do anything you like."

He wrapped his long fingers around her neck and drew her close. "Do you want to fuck or make love?"

She couldn't bear it if they made love. She had to hold onto her heart. "I want to fuck."

"Will you let me show you the difference?"

She shook her head.

"Then I shall fuck you until you're ready."

Ria expected him to kiss her. Instead, he released her. His gaze searched her cabin, settling briefly on her bunk.

"May I use the cleansing unit?"

"Of course." Upon her command a section of the wall slid open, revealing a narrow sonic cleansing unit. If Aden were lucky, he might be able to turn around. "*Sun tube.*" Another section of the wall opened. Ria exposed a control panel next to the shower for his use. "Feel free to use any facility."

Ria ordered cold tea from the nutrition unit. She called the bridge to verify the *Telum*'s progress and status while Aden used the facilities. In less than four hours, she would relieve Ania. She should sleep. Hoping to catch an hour's rest, Ria set the alarm on her wrist unit.

When Aden stepped out of the cleansing unit, Ria noted he ignored the sun tube. Sarks required daily exposure. Aktarians required less, while Glacidian tolerance levels were minimal. Watching him stroll the short distance to her bunk, Ria was struck anew by his amazing display of honed muscle and quiet grace.

Retrieving the cold drinks, she joined him. His gaze remained on her as he drank. Complimenting the tea, he handed her the empty glass.

"I'm going to touch you, Ria, and kiss you, until you beg me to end your suffering."

His quietly spoken words held authority. He would do as he promised. The glasses threatened to slip from her fingers. Setting them aside, she glanced at his cock. Already, he grew hard. Licking her lips in anticipation, Ria stripped off her clothes and entered the cleansing unit.

Raising her arms, Ria gave the command. Within seconds, her skin was smooth and hairless. Next, she removed the hair on her legs. What would Aden think if she…he'd love it. Legs slightly apart, she gave the command.

She caressed the smooth skin surrounding her sex, gasping when her fingers slid over her clit. Never, even in her youth, had her body craved a man's touch with such intensity. No, she craved Aden's touch. Only Aden's.

Ria unbraided her hair, letting it fall free, and gave the cleansing command.

When she stepped out of the shower, Aden rewarded her with a slight gasp of his own. His gaze swept over her, hesitating on her sex.

"You take my breath."

Ria's heart fluttered. She wanted to believe him, but compliments delivered by a silken voice were expected from a professional consort. Even silent, Aden's tongue worked wonders.

When he reached out, she moved eagerly into his arms, burrowing against his wide chest. He kissed her, his lips softly demanding. His tongue slipped into her mouth, thrusting sweetly. His slid his hands into her hair.

She curled her tongue around his. Flush with heat and need, her breasts felt tight and full. To relieve the ache, she rubbed her breasts against his chest, spearing him with her taut nipples.

He tugged gently on her hair, forcing her head back, exposing her throat. Suckling a gentle path, his lips moved down her neck.

Cupping her breast in one palm, he licked her nipple.

"Tell me how you feel."

"Hot. Heavy." She reached for his cock.

He brushed her hand aside. "Hot? Tell me."

Would he torture her with questions? "I burn for you."

He caressed her breast, fondling her with expert fingers. "Where?"

"Everywhere."

He brushed her lips with his. "Here?"

"Yes."

He squeezed her breast. "Here?"

"Yes."

His fingers trailed down her belly. He cupped her sex. "Here?"

"Yes. Yes." She rolled her hips, creating a delicious friction. She wanted his fingers inside her. Her sex flexed in need.

"You're wet."

"You make me wet."

"You're hot."

"Aden."

He lifted his hand and licked his palm. "I love you, Ria."

"No more games."

He pressed her onto her back and settled his hips between her thighs. "No games. I'll give you what you want, but I want you to look at me, Ria. While we fuck, look into my eyes. When you climax, see *me*."

Adjusting his hips, he pressed the tip of his cock to her sex. Ria arched her hips, gasped when the thick broad head slid inside.

Aden pulled back, withdrawing from her.

"You closed your eyes."

She had. Ria stared into his eyes. Again, she wondered why or what he was hiding behind those beautiful blue orbs.

He placed the tip of his cock against her sex. "That's better."

Looking into her eyes, he began to move his hips, entering her gradually. Quivering with need, Ria grasped his hips. He smiled at her efforts. Taking her hands, he imprisoned them in his and forced her arms over her head. His thighs pressed hers, his legs holding her fast beneath him. Leisurely, he stroked her ready folds, dipping deeply and withdrawing. Although her body trembled in near rapture, this taking wasn't for mere mutual pleasure. Aden wanted her to know for this moment, she belonged solely to him.

Time stilled, nothing existed but Aden, his gaze intense, his measured penetration making her mindless. She tried to pull her hands free.

"Don't resist. Tell me how you feel."

"I want to touch you."

"Touch me with your pussy. Let your eyes tell me what your heart feels."

When he began to withdraw again, she clamped down on his cock. She wanted him deep inside, pumping, thrusting. He wanted to ensnare her heart as he had her senses. She couldn't fall for him. Tuned by his fingers and mouth, her body had become an instrument only he could play. She wanted Aden. The near obsession frightened her. She couldn't give him control of her heart.

It's only sex.

"I want to climax."

An easy smile curling his lips, Aden pushed deep. She grabbed him.

"You're tight as a fist. You test me, Ria. All I want to do is fill you with semen."

He withdrew to the tip, teasing her, then slid deep. She tried to hold back, to play this game he invented. Her breasts ached for his touch.

"Look at me, Ria."

Again, he withdrew, only to penetrate her once again. Heat radiated from her center. She couldn't hold back.

"I love how your pussy gets hot, then wet." He withdrew gradually. "I love how you—"

She grabbed his cock. "Now! Please."

Aden plunged deep into her core. He pumped his hips, giving her the release she needed. Perspiration beaded his forehead. His thighs, slick with sweat, slid against hers. Heart pounding, Ria cried out. He stilled his hips. His gaze held hers while the fire he'd built between her legs exploded.

He sucked in an audible breath. "You're like a terraquake inside. A million tremors surrounding my cock."

Once her breathing returned to something akin to normal, she realized his words created as much heat as his cock. His sensual tone, his sex talk could make her climax. One day, she'd have to the test the theory.

"You're still hard."

He released her hands and grasped her by the waist. Sliding his thighs beneath hers, he shifted to a kneeling position, raising her pelvis. Despite his maneuvering, his cock remained inside her.

Ria wrapped her legs about his waist. "You've had practice."

"Sex is an art. Art requires practice."

Palming her buttocks, he began to move. She clenched, holding him tight, loving the way he filled her, needing his special heat. Ria understood why women would pay for his services.

"You are an exquisite artist."

He glanced down at her sex. "I'm inspired by the sweetest, barest pussy in the universe."

Each slow stroke of his thick cock sent tiny shudders along her center.

He pumped his hips, increasing the tempo of his thrusts. "I love fucking you."

"I like fucking you."

Placing the pad of his thumb against her clit, he began rolling the sensitive bud while he drove into her. Thick and hard he filled her again and again. Tremors followed in his wake. Fire raced in her veins. Her breasts ached for the feel of his mouth.

"Look at me, Ria."

His thumb flicked her clit. She tore her gaze from his cock.

"Do you merely like it, or do you love it when I fuck you?"

The tremors radiated, overtook her. "I love it," she gasped.

His quick smile faded as his thrusts pounded her sex. Ria heard her name, a whispered groan, as he emptied himself deep inside her. He stilled. Pulses rippled along his length, she answered with tiny quakes.

Needing to hold him, Ria raised her arms. Smiling, he drew her close and wrapped his strong arms about her waist and back and lifted her to him. She laid her cheek against his and held him tight about the neck. A lone tear slid down her cheek.

Ria brushed it away. When they reached Zeon, Aden would leave with more than a memory of a romp with a ship's captain. He'd take her heart, but she could never let him know. Like a good little soldier, she'd say her goodbyes and lick her wounds in private. She'd done it before. She'd do it again.

* * * * *

Gyrr stroked the smooth skin between Ria's legs. Soon duty would call her to the bridge and he wanted to make love again. It wasn't lack of satisfaction driving him, but the need to join with this female. He'd heard of the bliss Glacidian grooms experienced while mating during the bride's fertile cycle. Warriors told of hours, days filled with lovemaking. He'd believed the tales were exaggerations. Now, he understood.

Awakening, Ria stretched. The graceful uncoiling of her exquisite body sent a flood of need right to his balls.

She opened her eyes. "You like the shaved look?"

"I love looking at you." He touched a fingertip to her clit. She flexed. Gyrr loved how readily she responded. He leaned down and kissed her briefly on the lips. "All of you."

She rose to a sitting position, raised her arms above her head, stretching her muscles. "I have to relieve Ania. She's had the bridge for hours."

Gyrr rolled onto his back. "Before you go, one favor?"

Lowering her arms, she turned toward him. "Time is short."

"But my need is great."

Laughing, she crawled on top of him. Her silky dark hair brushed against his skin, tickling him. Gyrr grabbed a hank. "Come here."

She scooted up, rubbing her pussy against his chest.

He pulled gently on her hair. "Closer."

Finally, she straddled his face. Her tight, pink pussy hovered above him. His cock stretched. "Make love to me, Ria."

She lowered herself to him. When her pussy touched his face, she began to undulate her hips. Clutching her thighs, Gyrr plunged his tongue between her moist folds, licking her sweet moisture, reveling in her soft wetness. Using his tongue, Gyrr explored her slick channel.

When Ria placed a fingertip on her clit, he pushed her hand aside. He kissed her heated pussy, covering her labia with his lips, suckling her clit. She rewarded him with a gush of sweet nectar.

His cock ached with need. He wanted to sheathe himself in her wetness and ease the pain, but this intimate oral mating was as necessary as it was pleasurable. He craved the taste of her sexual juices, needed her liquid heat penetrating the soft tissues of his mouth and tongue. Gyrr understood his Glacidian blood demanded this exchange as part of the binding process. Ria's sweet secretions were as essential to his soul as air to his lungs.

Her hips pumping wildly, she moaned. Gyrr plunged his tongue deep inside her hot pussy. She stilled. The muscles in her thighs clenched, then relaxed. Another hot climax drenched his mouth and tongue.

Gyrr rubbed his face in her wet pussy, saturating his skin.

Ria brushed her hair from her face and smiled at him. "Why do you do that?"

Not ready to explain the binding process, Gyrr told her a partial truth. "I love your pussy."

Crawling backwards, Ria straddled his waist. She reached behind her and stroked his straining cock. Her hands were warm on his flesh.

"Is this for me?"

"Forever."

She laughed, thinking his response was mere jest. One day she'd know how serious his words were. Then she'd understand their mating had transcended the usual physical sex act, he had accepted her as his lifemate. His cock would never penetrate another. His heart belonged solely to her.

He reached up and cupped her breast. "Kiss me."

Her lips touched his. Gyrr kissed her deeply, plunging his tongue into her mouth, letting her taste the sweetness of herself.

Wriggling her backside, she positioned her pussy on the tip of his cock. Gyrr lifted his hips and drove into her. He gasped. Wet and tight, she grabbed his cock. She placed her hands on his chest.

"Look at me, Aden. Look into my eyes."

Joy touching his heart, Gyrr smiled at her demand. "Make love to me, Ria."

She rode him hard, pounding her pussy on his cock as if to deny the act of love. Her brown eyes remained open, her gaze never wavering. Finally, she slowed her furious pace. Her hips undulating, Gyrr caressed her inner thighs with his thumbs. His balls ached.

"Next time, I want to fuck in the dark."

Her demand suppressed the climax building in his balls. The first time they'd made love, she'd wanted darkness. Ria had wanted release, nothing more.

"It's too late, Ria. You'll know it's me kissing you, my lips on your breasts. You'll know it's my tongue deep in your pussy, my cock buried inside you. My heart pounding against yours. Darkness cannot change how we feel."

She stilled and closed her eyes. "I don't want to care about you."

Reaching out, Gyrr slid his hand around her slender neck and drew her close. Her breasts pressed soft and full against his chest.

"Can you feel my heartbeat?"

Ria nodded. Her silky hair slid through his fingers. "Don't fight me."

She shuddered. How to make her believe? Right now all he could do was ask her to follow her heart. "Trust me, Ria."

He kissed her gently. Rolling her onto her back, Gyrr moved with slow deliberation, sliding in and out of her in a tender cadence. She wrapped her legs around his hips. The fire between them burned slow and hot. The air in Gyrr's lungs heated. His veins turned to liquid fire. His heart threatened to explode.

Gyrr reveled in her softness, her wetness, in the magic of her body. A thousand tiny tremors surrounded his cock. Her climax drove him over the edge. He burst, filling her with evidence of his love.

CHAPTER FOUR

Late for her shift, Ria rushed to the bridge. Ula tried to stifle a yawn, but Ania looked unaffected by the long hours. Given their distance from the busy skyport, Ria could handle both the com-center and the helm. Although she officially relieved Ania and Ula, neither left the bridge.

Ula spoke up. "What happened on Pyxis, Captain?"

How to explain? Best to stick to the truth. In the long run, lies always caught you. "My escort and I were attacked by Veks."

Ania folded her arms beneath her breasts. "The Aktarian?"

The underlying contempt in her second officer's tone sparked a swell of protectiveness in Ria. Although she had signed the required oath of loyalty to the Federation before accepting her position, Ania cared little for Aktarians and hated Glacidians.

"Aden saved my life and was hit by several darts loaded with pymal in the process. I couldn't leave him to the Veks. Entering the air lock saved both our lives."

"You could have called port security, Captain." Ula said. "They would have come to your aid."

Ania shook her head. "We nearly missed our schedule as it was."

Ria didn't miss Ania's admonishment. Her tardiness hadn't left her any options. "I killed one of them."

"Way to go, Captain," Ula said, clapping her hands together. "Nasty things, Veks."

"Captain, you realize security could have demanded we return to dock or sent a patrol ship after us?" Ania said. "The *Telum* could have been detained for hours."

"Thank you for reminding me of my responsibilities and failures, Officer Onacc. I doubt the portmaster wanted to broadcast the appearance of Veks on Pyxis. Since I made no official report, no incident exists."

Ula nodded in agreement. "That would raise a question or two about Pyxis security." A slight grin formed at the corners of her mouth. "When do we get to meet Aden, Captain?"

"He's resting. Doc's orders. He'll meet everyone before we dock at Zeon."

"He's unauthorized, Captain." Ania said. "How do we explain his presence?"

"I'm working on that." Ria directed her next statement to Ania. "I take full responsibility. I have no intention of reporting him to corporate security. If I do, we all suffer. If headquarters finds out, you have no knowledge of the situation. The man was wounded and you were acting under emergency orders by me. Is that clear?"

"Yes, Captain."

Ria turned to Ula and received her affirmation.

"Relieve me in eight hours, Ania." Although her usual shift was twelve hours, Ria wanted, no needed, to return to Aden. She didn't understand how or why she craved him. She just knew she did. As for the hours, she'd make them up to Ania on the long run to Chedd.

Ula left, but Ania lingered. "Permission to speak freely."

Ania had never appreciated Ria's informal style of leadership. Ria understood she should maintain some distance from her subordinates, but preferred the softer approach. Despite all the corporate rules, Ria enjoyed her crew. The weeks and months of isolation either tore a crew apart or pulled them together. "Permission granted."

"Once the unloading begins, you could take him out through the cargo bay."

"That might work," Ria said, a little surprised by Ania's willingness to become involved. Ania's by-the-book approach to her job assured superior ratings, few errors and good bonuses. Until now, Ria had no reason to bend the rules concerning unauthorized visitors.

"Is the Aktarian confined to sick bay?"

"Aden is staying in my quarters."

Ria waited for a reaction to her news. She'd never taken a lover while in port and she expected keeping one in her bed would cause comment, perhaps criticism, from her second in command, but Ania simply asked, "He has recovered?"

"Doc's keeping an eye on him. By the time we reach Zeon, Aden will be fine."

"That's good. I think you should restrict him to the living quarters."

"I doubt Aden has any interest in our cargo."

"That may be true, but if headquarters did find out about him, at least we could guarantee he wasn't poking around in cargo holds or had accessed the power supply."

Ania had a point. Corporate security would slap a violation against Ria for giving an unauthorized person free reign about the ship.

"I'll confine Aden to the living quarters."

"I'll give some thought to slipping him out one of the cargo bays." Ania turned at the bridge door. "Once he's on Zeon, he'll have to figure out how to get through security."

"I don't think he'll have problems with Zeon Security."

"Zeon has the tightest security of all the skyports."

"Aden works for Portmaster Sy."

"He—" Ania braced her weight against the door with one hand. "Does she know he's aboard?"

"Negative. Don't be alarmed, when Aden reports the Vek attack—"

"He can't report it!" Ania pushed away from the door and stepped toward her. "If he does, he'll expose us. Corporate will find out everything."

"I saved a man's life. Corporate has to take that into account. Besides, Portmaster Sy has influence."

Ania's hands clenched. "The war's been over for a long time. Many think General Sy was banished to Zeon."

"Lord Commander Thrane had many mistresses. The General served bravely." Ria touched Ania's arm. She understood her fear. Security problems could affect careers and like Ria, her second officer wanted her own command. "I'll talk to Aden. I'll explain the consequences. We'll work something out."

"Your actions could affect the whole crew. I like the *Telum*. I don't want to give corporate a reason to reassign us."

"Neither do I."

"What does the Aktarian do for Portmaster Sy?"

"He's her sex consort."

"This is not the time for levity, Captain."

"When he arrives on Zeon, he's contracted for a year as a consort."

"This isn't good."

"We saved his life."

"Let's hope the Portmaster appreciates that fact and isn't the jealous type. With the strike of her seal, she could impound the *Telum* for weeks."

"Perhaps pulling out my nails will appease her?"

Ania's eyes narrowed. Her mouth contorted. "This is serious business, Captain. I pray you know what you're about."

"I'm fully aware of the situation and the possible consequences."

Ania nodded, muttered a good night, and left Ria to ponder the possible repercussions of her actions.

* * * * *

A few hours later, Doc requested permission to enter the bridge. Ria welcomed the intrusion. The more she thought about Aden's presence, the more she realized how impossible the situation. Odds were headquarters would find out about Aden and the Vek attack. If she were lucky, she'd be demoted.

"How's our patient?" Ria asked when Doc settled into Ula's com-seat.

"Good. He slept, once you gave him a chance."

Ria grinned. "He wasn't complaining."

"Neither are you. I think Aden is good for you. I think you should keep him."

Ria would love to do just that, but she'd learned attachments lead to promises. Promises end in heartbreak. "He has a contract. I don't think his employer will appreciate my visits whenever the *Telum* is in port."

"I suppose not, but he strikes me as a man in love."

"He has a year to forget me."

Doc rose. Ria should have expected the gentle hug, but Doc's uncanny ability to know when one was sorely needed always dumbfounded her. Right now, Ria needed support. Two days ago, the *Telum* and its crew were all that mattered.

Over the last two years, Doc had become her confidant. By choice, Ria had few friends. Her medical officer forced her to take a few hours leave while in port. She made her laugh. They passed many hours talking, but even Doc didn't know about Ria's parents and why she would never take a lifemate.

After squeezing her shoulder, Doc settled back into the com-seat. "Why do you think the Veks attacked the two of you? It's common knowledge ship's captains carry weapons."

Used to Doc's abrupt changes of topic, Ria began to unbraid her hair. "I don't think I was the target."

"Aden?"

"He's hiding something behind those blue lenses."

Doc nodded in agreement. "Why don't you ask him?"

She'd thought about doing just that, but ask wasn't the word that had come to mind. "I should confront him."

"I was thinking you could ask him about the Veks? See what he has to say. Probe him a little before you question him about his identity and his Glacidian ancestry?"

Ria scanned the ship's instruments, verifying course and speed. Despite the automation of the system, Ria liked the security of reading the critical data instead of relying on the computer. Perhaps the action made Ria feel more like a pilot.

"If I'm going to lose my job, I'd at least like to know his real name."

Doc shot out of the console chair. "Lose your job?"

"How am I going to explain his presence on board? Or the Vek attack?"

"We had an emergency. If you hadn't entered that air lock you'd be dead. One of those darts could have killed you."

"By the book, I should have called security. I should have notified headquarters."

"Which do you think corporate cares about, an unauthorized passenger or the morass of security paperwork and security checks? We'd have been confined to port for hours, perhaps days."

A glimmer of hope presented itself. If Aden cared, he'd help. If not, Ria would take the heat and do anything she could to save her crew. Ania could handle the run to Vidar. By the time the *Telum* returned to Sark, she'd have earned her veteran status. The Vidar run tested the best.

"As soon as Ania relieves me, I'll return to my quarters and have a heart-to-heart with Aden."

Doc leaned forward. "He's not in your quarters. The twins took him for a tour. They begged. I hope they don't tire him."

"What?"

"Don't worry the twins know Aden is off limits. They asked him about news from home. He's well informed. It seems he's actually met one or two of the royal princes. I couldn't follow all they said, but the twins were hanging on his every word."

"I'm not worried about the twins."

She was a little, but breaking her word to Ania albeit inadvertently done, worried her more. Ria needed her second officer's loyalty and support. "I think I should confine him to quarters. If headquarters does find out, I can tell them he remained restricted while on board."

"So Aden sees a few cargo containers. Every dockworker sees them. They're sealed while in the holds. The twins don't have access to the power supply and only you or Ania can grant access to the bridge."

"That's true. I think he's familiar with a Capha. He didn't ask the usual questions about the ship when we met. It was as if he had knowledge of the freighters. Just a feeling more than his words."

"Ex-military?"

"Definitely. When you examined him did you notice the ridges on his hands?"

"I did. I meant to ask him, but I became sidetracked."

"You touched his cock."

"I'm sorry, Ria. I was curious. Those posters hanging in sick bay...I wondered if they, if the men's, if real men had cocks that large. Pol isn't...well he's Sark. He's normal."

After all their conversations about men and sex, Doc's verbal fumbling surprised Ria. "Perhaps you should have married an Aktarian."

"In my next life, for sure." Doc smiled sweetly. "When Pol and I are together, I don't think about his size. I think only of how my heart pounds at the sight of him. How I love to hear his voice. How he touches me, holds me. How I feel when he's around. He can be in the next room and I'm so happy. He's always pleased me."

Ria heard a catch in her friend's voice. When Doc was alone, she'd cry. "That's good. Aden knows how to please me, more than anyone ever."

Rising to her feet, Doc grinned. "And you know how to keep him occupied and confined until we reach Zeon."

At the bridge door, Doc turned and asked, "What about those ridges on Aden's hands?"

Ria hesitated before she spoke. The person she trusted more than anyone was Doc. Could she trust Aden? "He's adept with a sword, but not just any sword. A Sarkian falx. Those ridges are a result of years of practice."

"But those are only worn by the Lord Chancellor's Elite troops!"

"Yes, those sworn to Lord Aaxis." Ria stood. "They are subject to no laws, but his. Their allegiance is to no nation, only to him."

Doc's eyes widened. "You can't leave the Elite except by death!"

"Either Aden's on the run, or he's covert. What's your best guess?"

"But he's a sex consort!"

"A cover, and an excellent way to gain access to Zeon and parts beyond. Portmaster Sy is no stranger to the Lord Chancellor."

"Great Gods! What have we gotten ourselves into?"

"I don't know. Despite Aden's skill, I don't buy the sex consort story. The Veks wanted to kill him or at least capture him. Why would they kill a consort?"

"You thwarted their plan. Do you think they'll try again?"

"If they can penetrate Zeon security, they'll try, but after what happened on Pyxis, Aden will be on his guard."

"Now we know why he's wearing those Ident lenses."

And why he carries an ice blade!

"Don't discuss this with anyone. When you're with Aden, play dumb. Don't ask him about the ridges, the Ident lenses or his heritage. Any knowledge of his mission could be dangerous to you, to the crew, to anyone you tell. If he's Elite and he's undercover, his business is serious."

"What are you going to do?"

"I don't know. I'm not afraid of Aden, I fear for him."

"If he's covert, I doubt his name is Aden."

"We may never know his true identity. Perhaps that's best for us all."

"You mean it's best for you. The rest of us are incidental. When he leaves, will you see him again?"

Ria shook her head. Her heart ached at the thought of losing Aden. No matter the outcome, she'd never forget him.

"What about when his mission is finished?"

"Few of the Elite take wives. Their dedication is to their Lord, before their family, even their children."

"You're in love with him, aren't you?"

"Crazy for him is the better description. What woman wouldn't be?"

"How did you know about the ridges?"

"When I was little, I used to know an Elite."

"Who?"

Doc had questions. Ria could see it in the medic's eyes. She couldn't speak of her father. Nothing good would come of it.

"It was a long time ago. Promise me, you'll say nothing. You'll forget what you have learned about Aden."

"I promise."

"Go, now, before Ania comes to relieve me."

"You can't carry this burden alone."

"What choice do I have? If an inquiry arises, why should everyone have to pay? I'm the one who met Aden. I'm the one who was late. I pulled him into the air lock. Horny female captain meets sex god. My story to corporate will be the truth. Maybe nothing will come of it all. Maybe once we arrive on Zeon, Aden will report to his mistress as he's supposed to do and we'll fly on to Vidar as if nothing had happened."

"Why do I feel it isn't going to be so simple?"

"Just make sure when our patient arrives in Zeon, he's healthy."

Doc touched the lock panel. The bridge door slid open. "Aye, aye, Captain."

* * * * *

Ria entered her quarters. Aden lay sprawled on his stomach across her bunk fast asleep. Struck by the beauty of his perfect male form, the doubts and worries plaguing her for the last several hours melted in a surge of sexual heat so profound, Ria's breath hitched. She pulled off her uniform jacket. Her boots and socks came next, followed by her trousers.

Aden rolled over onto his side. Wearing nothing but her underwear tank and panties, Ria dove for the bed and for him.

Laughing, he caught her to him. "Does this mean you missed me?"

"Uhmmmm." She stroked his cock.

His blue eyes glowed and his mouth softened in a sensual curve. His nostrils flared. Ria's mouth went dry while her sex moistened in anticipation.

Her response amazed her. Did the mystery surrounding her lover add to the excitement? Or had Aden cast some ancient spell over her? An ancient spell called love?

His mouth covered hers. His tongue slid across her lower lip. His hand cupped her breast. Gently, his thumb stroked her nipple through the soft material of her tank into a tight, needy bud.

No, she wouldn't love him.

His tongue slid inside her mouth. His lips covered hers in a feverish pressure as if he were as starved as she for the taste of passion.

A hot, wet path followed his tongue down the column of her neck. He paused where her pulse pounded, suckling gently. Finally, his mouth covered the nipple he'd teased to a deliciously taut point with his thumb.

He suckled drawing on her nipple through the thin material of her tank, creating an incredible sensation of wetness, heat and friction. Moaning, her nails dug into his shoulders. He released her breast only to capture the other and work his magic. He suckled. She burned.

Lifting his head, he blew gently, grazing her nipple with his heated breath. She gasped. "Again."

He complied. She shuddered.

Lust glowed in his eyes. Ria knew what he was thinking as he shifted his weight and slid his shoulders between her thighs. Her sex quivered, expectant and wanting. When his tongue, his lips touched her sex through her panties, Ria cried out. Capturing her clit, he suckled until she was wet with need. Drenched with her response, the soaked material clung to her swollen labia. Using his tongue, he caressed and fondled, tormenting her. Writhing and close to climax, she arched her hips.

When his hot breath skated across her clit in measured gusts, Ria surrendered.

Aden lifted his head and looked at her. "So you did miss me."

Her sex continued to quiver in the delicious aftermath of her climax.

"I want to suck you."

"Is that an order or a request, Captain?"

"A necessity."

Aden climbed off the bunk and stood. Legs slightly apart, his thick erection jutted proudly from its nest of golden curls. "Your needs are my pleasure."

Eager, Ria scrambled off the bunk and dropped to her knees. The size, the length of him, the memory of the feel of him made her tremble. Touching her lips to the broad, silky head of his cock, Ria suckled him gently. Slowly, she drew on his flesh, sliding her lips over the smooth crown, inching her way down his hard length, back-and-forth, conforming her lips, tongue and mouth to his size and shape. Aden's groan of pleasure urged her to take him deeper.

Cupping his sac, she tugged lightly on his balls. He gasped, shuddered, then his hips moved in a slow sensual grind. Beneath her hand his thigh grew damp with a light sheen of sweat.

He wrapped a hand in her hair. "I'd rather come inside of you."

Releasing him, she grinned. She loved licking, sucking, caressing him. She couldn't get enough of him. "You will, but right now I'd rather see you ejaculate and lick the semen from your cock."

To demonstrate, Ria licked a bead of semen from the tip of his cock.

"You torment me by withholding your pussy?"

The sensual curve of his lips told Ria he loved her foreplay.

"Torment you?" Ria rose. Stepping toward him she urged him backwards toward the bunk. "Why didn't I think of that?"

He cocked his head to one side and stepped back. "What do you have in mind, Captain?"

"Unauthorized persons may be confined, Merchant Code 864."

"Confined?"

Placing one hand on his chest, Ria pushed lightly. He sat on the edge of her bunk. "In an emergency, at the Captain's discretion, unauthorized persons may be restrained, Merchant Code 864.9."

"Do we have such an emergency, Captain Torr?"

"We do. We have an unauthorized person interfering with the Captain's duties." Ria touched his chest with the tip of her forefinger, pressing until he lay on his back.

He ran his forefinger along her thigh. "Duties?"

"The Captain is responsible for the crew's morale."

Grinning, he traced a crescent pattern on her belly. "You're forcing me to pleasure your crew?"

Ria crossed the room and opened a built-in storage space. She retrieved four lengths of flex cuffs. "Specifically, one crew member's morale is in need of improvement."

His gaze shifted from her sex to the cuffs she held. "I'm to remain confined and restrained until the Captain deems the task accomplished?"

Taking his arm, Ria cuffed his wrist to one of the bunk's support. When Ria desired more floor space, she could raise the bunk to the cabin ceiling. When she cuffed his ankles, Aden tested the restraints.

"These aren't toys."

Ria hadn't encountered a situation requiring the use of cuffs. If corporate found out about Aden, she'd tell them she had confined him to quarters, even restrained him for a short time.

When he tried to move, the muscles in his legs flexed. Having total control over Aden's powerful body made her nipples tingle and her sex wet.

"Do you often use cuffs to improve your morale?"

She placed the last cuff on his wrist. "Never, but having a warrior at my mercy makes me hot and wet."

"Warrior?"

"Women fantasize about warriors." Ria ran her hand along his arm. "All that hard muscle and male strength."

"I thought that fantasy would be about submitting."

She traced a pattern on his ridged palm. "This is about submitting."

His gaze caught hers. He tested the restraints and laughed. "No wonder I love you. How do I earn my release?"

Ria stroked his handsome face. "By pleasing me."

"Will you kiss me? Begin my imprisonment with gentle passion?"

Leaning down, Ria touched her lips to his. His lips clung to hers. Sweetly, gently, she kissed him. His tongue slid inside her mouth.

She loved kissing him. Aden had the ability to make her believe he truly cared, tempted her to indulge in the hope of love everlasting. Foolish hope.

Aden sighed when she pulled away. "When you kiss me like that, I want to hold you in my arms."

"When I'm thoroughly pleasured, warrior." One blond eyebrow shot up. "When your cock is too limp to revive, I'll release you."

Smiling, Ria opened a drawer built into the bunk's frame. She withdrew a fur mitten from her collection of sensual toys and slipped it on. Caressing his chest, she teased his nipples. "I find fur stimulating."

"Show me."

Using the mitten, Ria stroked his belly and thighs. Finally, she ran the fur along his cock, teased his balls. He jerked.

"That tickles. When you're alone, do you caress your nipples?" he asked, his voice suddenly deeper, huskier. "Do you rub your pussy?"

Straddling his groin, Ria touched the mitten to her breast. Her nipple peaked.

"Does the feel of fur on your nipples make you hot?"

Ria rubbed her nipples. The combination of the fur and Aden's husky voice caused a familiar ache.

"Open your legs. I want to see your pussy."

Rising to her knees, Ria followed his directions. His gaze dropped to her exposed sex.

"Touch your pussy with the fur."

The feel of the fur against her shaved sex sent shivers of need coursing through her.

"One day you'll lie in my furs. When we make love, my furs will tease your nipples to lush points, excite your clit until you cry with need, while I take you from behind."

"You like to fuck the ancient way."

"I like to fuck you in every way, every position."

Ria ran the mitten over her breasts, her belly and her sex.

"How does it feel when I fill your pussy? When I thrust deep? When I fuck you hard and fast? When I love you slow and easy?"

Aden could talk her into a climax. If she recorded his voice she could imagine he shared her lonely bunk during the long journey to Chedd. But right now, she had him in the flesh.

"Make love to me, Ria. Take your pleasure, now. Suck me. Ride me. Use me."

Shifting her position to kneel between his thighs, Ria took him in her mouth, swallowing his length with each down stroke, tugging lightly on the upstroke, loving him with her tongue and lips. Placing the mitten beneath his balls, she fondled his sac as she suckled him.

He arched, thrusting his pelvis toward her. "Great Gods! I'm going to explode."

Ria released him and withdrew the mitten. Grasping his balls, she tugged gently. "Not yet, my eager warrior."

His chest heaved as he drew several deep breaths. "You torment me, Ria."

Straddling him, Ria stroked her drenched panties against the length of his cock. Shivers ran the length of her spine. She leaned toward him and teased his lips with an erect nipple. On her third pass he latched onto her breast.

Moaning in delight, she stroked him with feather-light contact while he drew eagerly on her breast. A river of heat coursed from her breast and pooled in her center. Her clit vibrated. He suckled with fervor, tugging relentlessly until Ria swore she could take no more. But she could, she did. Ria welcomed the heavy waves of pleasure radiating from her center.

When he released her breast, her nipple remained red and plumped and ever so sensitive.

"If I wasn't restrained, I'd rip your panties off and lick your pussy until cream dripped onto my tongue."

His voice affected her like a sex drug. Ria climbed off his chest and wriggled out of the wet panties.

"Come closer, let me lick your pussy."

Ria straddled his shoulders. "Please me, warrior. Make me scream."

He obeyed, lapping her slit with long, lush strokes of his experienced tongue. She undulated her hips, sliding her wet sex against his lips, silently begging for sensual invasion of his tongue. He slid his tongue inside of her, teasing her flesh with rapier quick stabs.

Ria tugged on her nipples, rolling the sensitive points between her thumb and finger, until she hovered near the brink of joy. When Aden captured her clit and began a slow, intense suckling, Ria succumbed.

After the shattering climax subsided, Ria watched Aden lick her nectar, savoring the moment as one would a favorite dessert.

"Why do you swallow my come?"

"For the same reason you swallow my semen. You hunger for it. You need it. I love your passion honey. It's sweet and unique to you."

How did he know how she craved his semen? Never had she wanted to feel a partner's cream on her skin, in her mouth and womb. She wanted Aden. And she wanted his child.

The thought shocked her. Long ago, Ria decided not to pass onto a child the cloud of her heritage. Aden had tossed her well-organized, detached life into a vortex of new feelings, new emotions and reevaluation of her rules.

Aden. Was that his name? Ria knew in her heart this man she wanted beyond all reason wasn't born with the name of Aden Conr.

His amazing blue eyes narrowed. "What's going on in that brain of yours? Does the idea of loving me frighten you, Ria?"

Automatically, her defenses rose. "Loving sex and loving you are two very different things."

"Sex and love *were* different for you, but no longer. You'll crave no other, Ria, ever again."

"That's not true."

"You can fuck me, and forget me?"

"I won't forget you. I doubt any of your lovers have forgotten you."

"I want you. I want you at my side, for the rest of my life. I want my sons and daughters to suckle their mother's milk from your exquisite breasts."

The image of a golden-haired babe at her breast flashed in a brief, agonizing moment. Ria pushed the image away. If he truly knew her, he wouldn't make such foolish promises. "Your profession doesn't lend itself to taking a lifemate."

"I'll leave my profession."

She placed her fingers over his mouth. "Don't."

"I love you."

His words whispered against her fingers. She touched the ridges on his palms. "Don't make promises you cannot keep."

"Don't dismiss what we have. When I come home to rest in my bed, I want you there."

"Lovers, never lifemates. That's all I can give."

"I won't accept that."

Ria shook her head. "Soon, we'll dock in Zeon. After that, I'm delivering my cargo to Chedd. If you're on Zeon when I return, perhaps we will be lovers again."

"You're traveling to Chedd?"

She wondered at his interest in the small, gaseous planet. "We deliver to Vidar's main skyport, then to outer skyport serving Chedd. Why?"

"It's rare to meet anyone who visits Chedd."

Few ships docked on Chedd's skyport. The Cheddians working in the Aktarian sector of the port wore canisters providing the necessary gas mixture for them to breathe. They wheezed as they spoke and made disgusting sucking sounds as they inhaled. Ria preferred to remain in the Aktarian sector whenever possible rather than donning the required portable oxygen mask to enter the main section of the port. No ship remained in port longer than necessary.

"We never go on planet. Just deliver to the skyport. The place stinks from five miles up. I can't imagine what it must be like to live there."

"The Chedds live in gas. The Sarks in heat. The Glacidians surrounded by ice."

"Have you visited Chedd?"

He hesitated a bit too long in his answer. Was he deciding whether to lie or tell her the truth? "I have. During my time in the military."

"Did you like it?"

"The military time or Chedd?"

"Chedd."

"No. I prefer Aktares."

Although, she believed his words were truthful, he'd left much unspoken. At least he hadn't lied.

"When you return from Chedd, I'll be waiting."

With each kiss, each climax she lost more of her heart to Aden. Why promise? If she saw him again, fine. She didn't want to expect him to be waiting for her when she returned to Zeon. If he wasn't, she couldn't handle it. Ria started to climb off the bunk.

"Don't leave. You've said we could be lovers." When she hesitated, he pulled on the restraints.

She stroked his flaccid cock. Beneath her fingers, his flesh began to stretch. Their time together lessened as the *Telum* journeyed silently toward Zeon. Ria wanted every precious minute.

"Please. This captured warrior begs for your mercy."

His easy banter pushed aside their serious discussion. Taking him in her mouth, she suckled him until his cock grew thick and hard.

"Suck my balls."

Tracing a slow wet trail with her tongue, Ria moved down the underside of his cock to his balls. Delicately she drew one orb, suckling tenderly. Moving to the other, she caressed his sac with her tongue while pleasuring his cock with her hand.

"Great Gods. Please, I want to come inside you."

Ria wanted to taste his climax as he had hers. She drew firmly on his swollen flesh until he tugged on his restraints and every muscle in his body clenched. Releasing him, she watched, fascinated, excited as semen burst from his cock. Scooping up the hot cream, Ria rubbed it on her lips, her breasts, her belly and her sex.

She'd never performed such an act, but the eroticism of Aden's semen on her skin was suddenly necessary. When she finished, her gaze caught his. Aden smiled like a man who had won a great prize. "Does it please you when—"

"When you rub my semen on your body, it pleases me beyond measure."

She leaned down and licked the remaining cream from the tip of his cock. Exhausted from lack of sleep and her intense orgasms, Ria lay beside Aden snuggling close to his chest.

"Rest, warrior," she said, throwing a thigh over his. "When we awake I'll have further need of your glorious cock."

He kissed her hair. "Will you ride me, Mistress?"

"Uhmmmmmmm. With fury."

Aden chuckled. "Then sleep, my love, and dream of me."

* * * * *

Hours later, Gyrr awoke. Every muscle protested against the restraints keeping him flat on his back. Ria had turned in her sleep. Her soft bottom touched his hip and his biceps pillowed her head. Her long, dark hair lay draped across his chest. Moving slowly, he flexed his knees. Thankfully, she'd left about four inches of slack when she'd decided to make him her sex slave.

Having sex slaves were common for upper class Sarkian males until his father had finally convinced the council to eliminate the practice in favor of legal consorts. Females who chose to remain in the life could, but their daughters could not be forced into sexual bondage. Since male consorts were illegal on Sark, an independent, intelligent female like Ria must enjoy breaking the rules.

Gyrr flexed his arms and Ria stirred. When she rolled over, her hair slid across his chest. She opened her eyes and lifted her head.

"Morning. Or is it? I've lost track of time."

"Does it matter?"

She rose, tossing her dark mane over her shoulders. Stretching, she lifted her arms above her head and arched her back, thrusting her magnificent breasts toward him. Her dark rose nipples puckered. A sudden need surged in Gyrr's groin. His balls felt heavy and his cock stretched.

She reached for him, caressing his cock with her soft fingers and warm palm. She cupped his balls. "Are you rested, warrior?"

Gyrr enjoyed their playful bantering. Far too serious, Ria needed to indulge in play, to relax and have fun. "Yes, Mistress. My weapons are at your disposal."

"Do you think if I talked about fucking you, without ever touching you, I could make you come?"

"Yes."

She had no idea he could touch a dozen naked women and never climax, but her voice had the power to activate his receptors. Glacidian lifemates could climax by looking into one another eyes. Thank the Gods for his Glacidian blood.

Of course, nothing could equate the sex act itself. His cock ached for her slick female sheath. How could he say goodbye to her on Zeon?

The importance of his mission weighed ever heavy on his mind. Duty would override his need of Ria, but he would suffer as every Glacidian soldier had when called to leave the homefire.

Ria had options. She could forget his existence on the long journey to Chedd. If she chose, she could take a lover.

While he...he couldn't control her feelings. If she took a lover, what then?

Gyrr shook his head. He couldn't fight these demons until they presented themselves. Perhaps, he never would.

"You promised to ride me, Mistress."

She straddled his hips. With her thighs open, Gyrr could see the soft folds of her pussy. Fully erect, his cock strained as Ria slid her hands along his flesh.

"Shall I kiss you, Mistress?"

She leaned toward him. Her breasts dangled before his face. "Your breasts are like the sweet melons of Ardith. I have sucked on their juices since I was a babe. Would you like to be suckled, Mistress?"

Smiling, she cupped one breast, offering him the taut, dark rosy nipple. Gyrr latched on, suckling greedily as a hungry babe. He prayed one day, he'd share the nursing ritual with Ria. After the child delivered, Glacidian fathers drew the first drops of mother's milk then placed their son or daughter at their lifemate's breast.

His father had performed the ritual for all his children signifying the babe was the responsibility of both mother and father.

Aktarians accepted the ritual, their understanding natures applauding the principle, but Sarks rejected it. Would Ria?

When Ria positioned the tip of his cock at the entrance of paradise, the question vanished from his brain. She rocked backwards, pulling her engorged nipple from his mouth and pushing his cock deeper inside her moist slit.

His blood heated with each stroke, each clutch of Ria's pussy. He watched his cock disappear as she took him deeper, hotter until he was fully embedded in her tight heat.

"Does it excite you, warrior? Do you like watching my pussy devour your weapon?"

"Do you like the feel of my weapon inside you?"

She rode him, pounding him hard. Her dark eyes sizzled with a heat as intense as the delicious friction created by the wild thrusts of her pelvis. When she grasped her breasts and began to massage them, Gyrr's hands clenched. Agonized by his restraints he nearly lost it when she touched her forefinger to her clit. Head flung back, she closed her eyes and climaxed. Her walls grabbed his cock with such force, Gyrr fought to control his own release. Unwilling to ruin Ria's entertainment, he asked permission to climax.

"Can I fill your pussy with proof of my pleasure, Mistress?"

"Fill me."

Muscles tensed, his climax wrenched free of his balls. When he exploded inside of her, Gyrr cried out.

Slick with sweat, Gyrr sucked in several deep breaths. When Ria fucked him, she sucked him dry. His balls still hummed from the intensity of his climax.

"Why is it so powerful with you? Why do I crave your cock?"

"We belong to each other, Ria. Each time we make love, the bond between us grows stronger."

She climbed off of him. Although his cock was limp with satisfaction, Gyrr loathed the separation. He needed to hold her.

"Release me, Ria. I need to stretch."

After she had removed the flex cuffs from his arms and legs, Gyrr waited for her to use the cleansing unit before using the facility. When he emerged, Ria stood before a built-in closet. She stepped into a pair of white panties and slipped a tank top over her head. With practice ease, she flipped her long hair over one shoulder and began to braid the shining mass. She turned and smiled.

Gyrr's breath caught. Her dark nipples were visible through the thin material. He remembered the first time he saw her on Pyxis. Her full breasts and taut nipples had enticed him, but her eyes had held mystery. Despite his mission, Gyrr couldn't resist the unexplainable, but instantaneous link between them. He'd wanted her as he never wanted another woman.

Even the Vek attack couldn't diminish the pleasure of Ria.

He strolled toward her. "I like you naked."

"After we eat dinner. I'm famished."

He brushed his lips to hers. "As long as you don't serve that gruel Doc passes off as food."

"How about stew? It's the best the *Telum* has to offer."

He wrapped his hand around her braid. Silky soft, the dark mass slid through his fingers. "You're the best the *Telum* has to offer."

"Trying to talk me back into bed?"

He retrieved a pair of underwear from his satchel. "Always."

Ria laughed. Gyrr loved the joy he heard in her voice. In a few short days, her happiness had taken on an importance no other female in his life, other than his mother and his sisters, had evoked.

Ria ordered stew from the nutrition unit. Although she had ordered a double portion for him, within minutes they both had consumed the stew.

She rose from the bunk and disposed of their utensils and bowls. Meals on the *Telum* were intended for efficiency, not leisure.

"Will Doc let you have wine?"

"I'm fine. After the exercise you've given me today, I can handle a little wine."

She slid open a panel, several bottles of wine lay on their sides. She selected one. "I've been saving a bottle for a special occasion."

He joined her. "I'm flattered you think I'm special," he said, purposely keeping his voice low and serious. He wanted her to know their conversations were more than easy banter between mutual sex partners.

She looked at him, her gaze penetrating. Sadness flickered briefly. He thought she would speak, instead she handed him the wine, saying, "I'll get the glasses."

"Again, I'm flattered," he said, opening the seal. "The Captain's quarters, wine service, real glass. I'm traveling premium class."

She placed the glasses on a small service table with one chair. Gyrr poured. He figured she took her meals here when she preferred her own company. Although she'd expressed an enjoyment of her crew, Ria maintained a solitary air about her. Anyone who piloted a Capha2 and juggled crews, schedules, and the loading and delivery of cargo to distant ports such as Vidar required an agile mind and a tough skin. Yet, Gyrr sensed a deep vulnerability within Ria.

Either life had delivered a few hard knocks or a prior lover had hurt her deeply. Gyrr couldn't change the past, but he could offer Ria a home, children and a life of love. All he needed to do was touch her heart.

He feared Ria took care to shield her heart. After handing her a glass, he lifted his. "To us."

She hesitated before touching her glass to his, but she didn't repeat his toast. He complimented her on the wine.

"There are some rewards to this job. We handled a shipment of wine on our last run to Trag. Upon arrival, the distributor gave me a case of their best. This is the last bottle."

"When did you drink the others?"

"If you're asking me if I shared them with lovers, the answer is no."

She read him well. Women as beautiful as Ria attracted men. A woman with as healthy a sex drive as Ria would take lovers. "I'll be jealous of any man who looks at you with desire in his eyes. I'll learn to handle it."

"I'm not the enchantress you think I am. When I'm with the twins, males don't know I exist."

The wine slid down his throat, smooth and nicely matured. "The twins are charming, but easy. They present no challenge, while you are selective. A man feels he has to work for you."

"If I recall, you bought me a drink and I asked you for sex."

"You dismissed me at first. I waited until you looked again. I don't know why you chose me, but I believe had I been any other man in that relaxation lounge, you wouldn't have looked a second time."

When she made no comment, he asked, "Why didn't you tell me to get lost like the others?"

"Others?"

"You told a Sarkian lieutenant and a navigation officer from the inter-skyport fleet you weren't interested. Do you have any idea how much courage it took for those two to approach you? The young lieutenant was sweating buckets."

"You were watching me?"

"When you walked into that lounge, there wasn't a male in the room unaware of your presence. Your captain's stripes would grab any man's attention. And, you fill out a uniform well."

She sipped her wine and smiled.

He took her hand and led her back to her bunk. "So why, Ria? Why me?"

She leaned against the wall and faced him. After sipping her wine, she licked her lips. "I was curious."

He waited for her to explain.

"You're handsome, Aden, but you know that. I've only fucked Sarks, I wanted to find out if you measured up to those pictures in sick bay."

Gyrr could feel the heat staining his cheeks. Surrounded by his brothers, he hadn't realized how well endowed he was until he spent two years training with his father's Elite unit on Sark.

"You chose me for my cock?"

Smiling, she set her wine glass on the small stand next to her bunk. "Don't tell me my ability to fill out my uniform had nothing to do with you approaching my table. You stared at my breasts."

"You do have magnificent breasts, but your eyes—"

"Are brown. Ordinary. Most Sarks have brown eyes."

He set aside his empty wine glass and cupped her face in his hands. "That's like saying water is blue. How can one compare the oceans of Aktares or the ice forms of Glacid to mere water? Look at me the way you did that night."

She did. Her eyes glowed, warm with a hint of golden heat. "What are you thinking?"

"The same thing I was that night. I'm thinking about how your hands would feel on my breasts, between my legs. I wanted you to touch me."

"So it wasn't my cock."

"At first, yes. But when we shook hands, I wanted you to touch me."

"Some are frightened I'll hurt them or my touch will be harsh."

"Because of the ridges?"

"Yes." He slid his hands beneath her tank and cupped her breasts. He caressed her, letting her feel the ridges on his palm. Her eyes fluttered closed as she arched toward him, thrusting the firm, full mounds into his spread hands. Beneath the rasp of his thumbs, her nipples tightened to hard points.

Without opening her eyes, she pulled off her tank top.

Gyrr leaned down and licked her nipples while caressing her. Choosing a ripe nipple, Gyrr suckled her. His blood heated, filling his cock until he ached to be inside her. When she moaned and clasped his head, he drew deeply. Responding to his eager, but gentle massage, her breasts firmed and tightened.

She fisted his hair and guided him to her other breast. When his underwear became too uncomfortable to bear, he released her breasts. Her nipples were distended and beckoning. His mouth watered, wanting again to suckle.

He shucked his underwear and hers. Positioning her beneath him, he settled the tip of his cock at the moist portal of her pussy. Sucking in a breath, he eased his length inside her and pumped his hips. Finding her pussy already slick and moist, he thrust. Eyes closed, she gasped as he plunged deep.

"Wrap you legs around me."

She lifted her legs, clutching his hips with her thighs. Gyrr buried himself to the hilt. Her hot sheath held him tight, bathing his cock in wet heat. He shuddered and willed his body to hold back. Balancing his weight on one arm, he cupped her left breast with his free hand. With slow purpose, he moved within her while caressing her breast.

His heart thumped hard. Love swelled his chest, thrummed in his balls, burning hot in his blood. Never had a woman captivated him as Ria. Never would any other woman make him shudder with pride and lust and passion.

"I love being inside you," he whispered. Although they were alone, his words were intimate, meant for sharing when passion entwined hearts as well as bodies.

Her eyes opened. In their depths, Gyrr saw need, heat and doubt. Had no one told this woman she was loved?

Gyrr wanted her to know, he loved her body and soul.

"I'll never get enough of you," he said. "I could make love to you every night for the rest of my life and never have enough of you."

She reached up and pushed a lock of hair from his face. "Make love to me now."

Moving with deliberate ease, he slid back-and-forth within her slick passage. When her muscles flexed about him, squeezing and releasing as he moved, an intense shudder ran the length of his spine. The deeper the penetration, the tighter Ria grabbed him.

He slid his hand from her breast down her side to cup her bottom in his palm.

She grabbed his hand and guided it back to her breast. "I like the way you touch me."

Wanting only to please her, Gyrr caressed the yielding mound of firm flesh he held in his palm. His thumb rasped across her nipple. He pushed deep into her softness, withdrew and penetrated, again and again, until hearts pounded and bodies slapped making a special, erotic music only they could share.

When Ria cried out her pleasure, Gyrr released, joining his chosen lifemate as she sang her sensual song.

* * * * *

A message alert sounded in her cabin. Instantly awake, Ria's head snapped up from the pillow of Aden's chest. "Open communication."

"Captain." Ula's voice came loud and clear over the intercom.

"Speak."

"Captain, you're needed on the bridge."

Springing to her feet, Ria ignored her underwear and grabbed the pair of trousers she'd left lying on the floor. "Explain."

"A vessel, identifying itself as ZSC1 will rendezvous within the hour. The Portmaster's office contacted us about our passenger."

"Why didn't you inform me immediately?"

"Doc said to let you rest."

Ria fastened her trousers and picked up her crumpled tank top. "I'm on my way." She yanked the top over her head. "Where's Doc?"

"Sick bay."

Dropping to the floor, she yanked on her socks and shoved her feet into her boots. "Close communication."

Aden rolled out of bed and began to dress. Shoes fastened, Ria stood. Their gazes caught for a brief moment. Like her, he understood their too brief interlude had come to an end.

"Take your baggage and report to sick bay. It will be better for both of us if Portmaster Sy thinks you've been recuperating."

Snatching her jacket off the floor, Ria rushed for the door. Aden grabbed her arm and swung her around. Her chest slammed into his. He kissed her, hard and fast. "No matter what happens, remember I love you."

"Right now, let's just try to keep my ass out of trouble." Grabbing his neck, she kissed him again, briefly touching her lips to his.

With Aden close on her heels, Ria sprinted toward the bridge. She should have anticipated the Portmaster would search for her expensive lover. Headquarters hated inspections. Infractions, even minor ones, resulted in fines. Hopefully, the Portmaster would retrieve her lover and head back to Zeon without a formal boarding.

Ria and Aden parted at one of the twelve hatches strategically placed throughout the *Telum*. Should the air supply or the ship's hull ever be comprised, the hatches could be sealed off.

As she sprinted toward the bridge, Aden called to her. "We will meet again, my love."

Without turning to look at him, she waved and entered the bridge. Ania sat at the helm looking calm and collected while Ria's hair hung loose and tangled, and her breath came in ragged puffs. Using the bridge's facilities, she washed her face, braided her hair and straightened her uniform. By the time the Portmaster arrived, Ria was composed and ready to present herself as the Telum's captain.

"The rover is coming along starboard. Portmaster Sy is requesting permission to board," Ania said.

"Permission granted."

Ula transmitted Ria's message.

"Do you wish to take the con, Captain?"

Ria shook her head. "Remain at helm. Synchronize speed. Open access portal when the rover's docked."

Gathering her hair, Ria twisted its length into long rope and formed a loose knot at the base of her skull. It was the best she could do under the circumstances.

"How many in the boarding-party?"

Ania glanced at Ria. "Three."

Ria expelled a breath. Portmaster Sy had a reputation for surprise inspections. An inspection required a larger party. Ria doubted Veks would manage to sneak onto Zeon as they had done on Pyxis. The skyport offered safety for any legitimate trader. Smart smugglers avoided Zeon.

"Have the twins meet me at the starboard access portal. I'll escort the Portmaster to sick bay. I doubt we'll be inspected. The Portmaster has come to retrieve Aden."

Relief washed over Ania's face. "Aye, aye, Captain."

Along the passageway to the starboard portal, Ria took several long, slow breaths. The twins were waiting at the portal.

"Secure air lock."

While waiting for the rover's airbridge to dock with the starboard portal, Ria smoothed her uniform and fastened her jacket. When the hatch opened, two good-looking Aktarian guards dressed in Zeon security uniforms boarded the *Telum*. The guards stood on either side of the portal ready to protect the Portmaster. Ria glanced at the twins. Already, each had picked their man. When the *Telum* docked, the twins would have new lovers.

Ria contacted Doc and requested she bring Aden to the starboard portal.

The guards snapped to attention when Portmaster Sy approached. Almost as tall as Aden and imposing in her black uniform, Portmaster Sy ducked her head to enter the *Telum*.

Ria welcomed her aboard. The Portmaster responded in Sark. Her voice reminded Ria of the purr of a large cat. When she smiled, Sy exposed a pair of healthy incisors. Would Aden enjoy the scrape of those teeth on his cock?

The Portmaster's question concerning Aden ended Ria's speculation.

"Aden Conr is aboard," Ria said, trying to keep her voice neutral. "He's in sick bay."

"Sick bay? He is ill?"

Ria noted the fear and concern in Sy's voice. Her piercing eyes bored into Ria's. Wide and slanted, the Siluko's eyes allowed for extensive peripheral vision. No matter where one stood, her eyes could follow causing rumors the Portmaster could look inside one's brain. As an interrogator, the Portmaster could extract the truth easier than any drug or torture.

"We were attacked by Veks on Pyxis."

"Veks?"

Ria swore the Portmaster growled. An involuntary shudder slid down Ria's spine.

"Mr. Conr took three darts. He is recovered and will join us shortly."

"He's well enough to travel?"

"Yes, Medical Officer Minn has taken excellent care of Mr. Conr."

"Thank you, Captain Torr. I must speak with him."

Again, Ria heard something akin to a growl combined with the word Vek emit from the Portmaster as they waited for Aden's arrival. The twins teased the guards with tempting glances. Neither responded. Given Sy's military record, the former General would demand total attention to duty.

When Aden entered the small portal space followed by Doc, Ria noted the Portmaster's response. A purr of relief tinged her words.

"You are well."

Sy's deep blue eyes scanned Aden from head-to-foot.

"General, forgive me, Portmaster Sy, it is an honor and a blessing."

Ria pondered Aden's words. Although the Portmaster had received the Sarkian medal-of-honor during the Sutumi campaign, Aden's greeting of respect spoke more of a military man meeting a honored superior than a sex consort's first encounter with his mistress. The thought of Aden and the Siluko having sex, making love, sharing the wild and the tender moments she had shared with Aden tore at Ria's heart.

When the Portmaster touched Aden's face, tracing a slow pattern from his forehead to his cheek with a curved nail, she purred. "We were concerned."

We? Was the Portmaster's use of the plural a mere grammatical mistake when speaking in Sark? In her gut, Ria knew Aden's relationship with the Portmaster had more significance than a contracted male companion.

Did the Portmaster know Aden's true identity?

The Portmaster cuffed Aden with her large hand; the gesture intended to tenderly berate rather than inflict pain. "You are late. The time will be reduced from your contract. That is, unless your abilities can compensate for keeping me waiting."

"My apologies. While escorting the Captain back to her ship, we were attacked by Veks. Thanks to Captain Torr's quick action, my life was saved. I owe her the highest degree of gratitude I can grant."

The Portmaster turned to face Ria and placed her fisted right hand over her heart and bowed: her gesture a salute given only to those of royal Sarkian rank. Ria had had the privilege of giving this salute only once in her life when the Lord Chancellor Aaxis had inspected the Sarkian skybase where she'd been stationed.

"We must leave. I have a meeting on Zeon I must attend. Are you prepared, Aden Conr?"

"I am. But before I say goodbye to my friends, I wish to introduce Medical Officer Minn. She tended my wounds." Aden smiled at Doc. "And forced me to eat porridge. Even my father never convinced me to eat porridge."

Sy's gruff laugh held the deep resonance of a male's, but given the shape of her breasts and curve of her hips, no one could doubt the

Portmaster was female. She would certainly offer Aden a challenge in the bedroom. Despite her years, Sy appeared fit and agile.

The Portmaster thanked Ria, and with her guards in tow, stepped into the air lock bridge. Aden hugged the twins, speaking briefly to them in Aktarian. He kissed Doc on the cheek. Finally, his gaze met Ria's.

"Remember what I told you, Captain Torr?"

Her throat suddenly too clogged to speak, she nodded.

Although she wouldn't hang her heart on the idea of being in his arms again, she'd always remember him. Always, love him.

She fought the tears forming in the corners of her eyes. She lost. Aden leaned down and kissed them from her cheeks.

"The taste of your tears shreds my heart. I am leaving, but my heart remains with you. Take care of it."

How many times had she heard soldiers say that ancient phrase to their lifemates, lovers and mothers before off-planet deployment? It was said to those left behind and to whom the soldier thought most precious. No one had offered the star-soldier's goodbye to her before, and Ria had said it to no one. It was on the tip of her tongue to repeat the phrase. "Go Aden, please, before I act like a fool."

He kissed her briefly on the lips. "Believe in *us*, Ria."

With those words, he ducked through the hatch and disappeared from view. When the hatch closed, Ria felt an isolation she hadn't acknowledged in many years. The emptiness of her life weighed on her heart. Like a fool, she'd given it away to a man she knew nothing about. Not even his true name.

Nothing except the way his heart beat against hers, the way his voice touched her soul and how his ridged palms caressed her body.

Could she, dare she, believe?

CHAPTER FIVE

Although Gyrr had spoken the words of a departing soldier, he knew, given Ria's military experience, she would understand the significance. Her tears had revealed feelings she hadn't expressed; she would miss him. And he would miss her. Aware of a deep longing he'd never experienced before when leaving a lover, Gyrr finally understood the anguish his father experienced when leaving his mother behind.

Settling into a comfortable seat, Gyrr turned his attention to his mission. Sy secured the cabin door and sat opposite him.

"You must contact your father when we arrive on Zeon." She spoke in Aktarian. "In my private quarters I can provide encrypted transmissions. The rover hasn't the range for a high-level, secure transmission."

Sy spoke with an underlying purring sound. Although odd, Gyrr found it soothing. "How is my father?"

"Worried. When you didn't arrive on Zeon as scheduled, I contacted Pyxis and discovered you had cleared security on arrival, but hadn't departed. Given the importance of your mission, your father assumed the worst. I scanned your spent credits: drinks for two in the relaxation lounge and a large sleeping cube didn't add up to the worst to me. Was I wrong?"

Gyrr thought of Ria. "You weren't wrong. I met Captain Torr in the lounge. I was escorting her back to the *Telum*. I intended to say goodbye, but the Vek attack took us by surprise. She dragged me into the *Telum* air lock and sealed the hatch. She saved by life. Blew a Vek to the next universe."

A feral sound, something between a purr and a growl, curled about Sy's words. "I like her already. The attack took place in the docking bay?"

"Yes. They had lain in wait. Not a hint until we were standing before the *Telum*'s air lock door."

"They could have disembarked a ported ship, conducted their attack and scurried back on board."

"Logically, yes. What I am unsure of is whether the Vek attack was random or if my mission has been compromised. Experience has taught me to not believe in coincidence."

"I'll investigate. I'll review the list of skyships in port at the time the *Telum* was docked. Pyxis security reported an incident, but nothing was mentioned of Veks. When I discovered you had missed your transportation, I began making inquiries. I contacted every ship that had left Pyxis and was bound for Zeon. I didn't expect to find you on a freighter."

"Father must be informed of the problems on Pyxis."

"Veks on a skyport. It's unacceptable. I told your father years ago, we should destroy their planet."

Gyrr couldn't imagine his father considering the idea of wantonly destroying a whole planet.

Sy purred. Briefly, her dark blue eyes softened. "Aaxis finds value in everyone, even Veks."

Gyrr wondered if his mother knew how Sy felt about his father. Perhaps, one day, he'd ask.

"Is Uyin still on Zeon?"

"Yes, he's agitated with the extended wait, but I told him your transportation was delayed and assured him you intended to meet with him."

"Has he told you anything?"

"I've questioned him, but he refuses to speak with anyone but a royal Thrane. He's afraid his information will not find your father's ear."

"Then he doesn't understand your relationship with my father?"

Again, Sy emitted a purr. "No one does. If they did, my usefulness would be greatly diminished. My communications with him are encrypted and routed through a blind source. If my communications were traced, they would not be tied to your father. An amazing amount of information passes through a skyport."

"Thank you for helping me on this mission."

Sy raised her large hand, curled nails tipped each finger. She touched her fist to her heart. "My allegiance is to the royal Thranes. My loyalty to your father passes to you."

"Have you met my mother?"

Large incisors appeared as Sy smiled. "I've had the privilege on several occasions."

"Does she know you're in love with him?"

Sy's extraordinary eyes fastened on his. Gyrr couldn't have looked away even if he had wanted to. His father's sexual adventures hadn't interested him before, but now that he had committed himself to Ria for life, the complexities of his parents' relationships intrigued him.

"Yes. When he went to war against the Sutumi, I stood at his side. Your mother understood I would protect him at all costs, and granted the privilege. From that moment my loyalty to Aaxis included Queen Tayra, and all of you."

"Thank you for being our friend."

"Forgive me, your Highness, but I must ask a question."

"As your friend, I wish to be called Gyrr."

"As you wish. You formed a relationship with Captain Torr?"

Now it was Gyrr's turn to smile. "Yes. She does not know my mission or my true identity. May I tell you something of importance, something I have yet to share with my parents?"

Sy nodded. "What we say as friends is between us along as I perceive no threat to your father. I ask you never bring that conflict to our friendship."

"Nothing so serious, Sy. I have fallen in love with Captain Torr. After this situation is resolved, I intend to ask her to become my lifemate. So, I ask that you keep a watch on the *Telum*. She's headed for Vidar and after speaking with Uyin, I must return to Aktares. I will inform my parents of my decision then."

"Then you know her history?"

Something cold coiled in Gyrr's gut. "I know she served in the military, then used her training to become second officer on the *Telum*."

"She told you nothing of her personal life before the *Telum*?"

"No. You've investigated her?"

"Given your mission, I felt it my duty. Since you have chosen her as your lifemate, then she should tell you. It is not my place."

"Is she a murderer? A thief?"

"You are a royal. Everything in your life is public, whether you like it or not. The woman you take as lifemate is subject to the same scrutiny. My advice, as a friend, is to learn everything about her life.

Every detail. Your family will surround her and protect her. But you should learn it from her."

"Her life has been painful?"

"Events have shaped Captain Torr. You must decide if you are willing to accept what she cannot change."

"For Ria, I would challenge the universe. If necessary, I will insist Father relieve me of all royal responsibilities."

"You would do that for her?"

"Yes."

"Our Captain is a very fortunate woman." Sy purred. "My advice as a woman?"

Gyrr nodded. His father respected Sy's judgment as well as her skill as a warrior. He'd given the Siluko the immense responsibility of protecting his back.

"Let her tell you."

Sy rose. She poured two generous vessels of kvass and handed one to Gyrr.

The cold brew slid deliciously down Gyrr's throat. Often, he and his brothers had emptied a keg of kvass. Memories of those close, family experiences brought forth a need to go home. He wanted Ria at his side. He envisioned her joining his mother and sisters planning birthday celebrations and family outings, and taking her place beside him at the large dining table in his parents' home.

Drink in hand, Sy settled in her chair. "Now, while we have a brief time before arriving on Zeon, tell me of your family. I understand Xxan is considering a political marriage with the house of Zadar."

* * * * *

After assuring his father of his health and well-being in an encrypted message, Gyrr removed the blue lenses in preparation of his meeting with Uyin. Two years earlier, Gyrr had met the rebel leader during an official visit to Vidar. Then Uyin had held the position of Viceroy. When the Vidar Tetrarch refused to acknowledge the

Cheddian request for independent rule, Uyin resigned and joined the rebel movement.

Upon entering the secure room within the Portmaster's offices, Gyrr's olfactory senses were assaulted by the Cheddian's unpleasant odor. Uyin was small of stature and slight of build. His eyes were small, bright green orbs. His dark skin had a greenish tinge and a thick mop of frizzy black hair stood atop his head. He was dressed in a long, black robe. The noxious gas surrounding Chedd clung to Uyin's person. Thankfully, several high-powered air-cleansing units circulated fresh air. Otherwise, Gyrr would require a breathing canister with tubes threaded through his nostrils as well.

Gyrr introduced himself and Uyin held out his small hand. After a proper clasp of hands and the required social inquiries as to the leader's comfort and accommodations, Gyrr and Uyin sat opposite each other. A table supplied with liquid refreshments stood between them. For Gyrr, Sy had selected Glacidian spring water, for Uyin something akin to dark-green slime with a sucking tube provided. As agreed, no notes or recording devices were allowed.

A disgusting sucking sound accompanied each inhalation of gas mixture necessary for Uyin's survival in this oxygen rich environment. "The Lord Chancellor is aware of Chedd's fight for independence?"

Gyrr nodded. "He is."

"We do not wish to secede from Vidar, only to have the right to govern ourselves, and our resources."

Chedd's resources were the issue. The raw crystals mined on Chedd provided the essential energy source for Vidar. Chedd's bid for independence would guarantee their right to sell the crystals to other worlds desperate for energy. Vidar controlled the Cheddian crystal market, providing Chedd with only a fraction of the profits.

"We are asking for the Lord Chancellor's support of our efforts."

"The Federation does not interfere in Vidarian domestic issues."

Uyin took a deep breath. The resulting noises sent a shudder down Gyrr's spine. Trained to remain passive and polite, lest he offend, Gyrr waited for the Cheddian to speak.

"I understand. Would the Lord Chancellor offer mediation if a meeting could be arranged between representatives of Chedd and the Tetrarch?"

Gyrr understood his father had already offered his personal services to the Tetrarch. "The Lord Chancellor will consider such an offer if the rebels cease the violent attacks on Vidarian officials and militia stationed on Chedd."

"I have always chosen the path of non-violence. Vidar is our mother planet, but there are others who are impatient with diplomacy. They seek to remove Vidarians from our world through lethal means and they are gaining support of our young people daily. This must stop before Vidar takes action that will cost many lives and will begin a civil war that Chedd will lose.

"Before the crystals were discovered, Cheddians depended upon Vidar as children depend upon a parent, but now we have means to support ourselves. As any group of peoples, we want independent rule."

"Why have you requested this face-to-face meeting?"

"If you, as the representative of the Lord Chancellor, will give Chedd your support to achieve a fair and reasonable solution, I will accept your word as that of Lord Aaxis, and give the Federation information concerning a plot that concerns the peace of both our worlds."

"The Lord Chancellor will support a fair and reasonable solution. The Federation will officially ask the Tetrarch to openly debate your requests. We will act as mediator. We will not favor Vidar over Chedd, but treat both equally."

"Thank you. The Lord Chancellor has stood for peace. I pray he can bring harmony to the Vidarian system."

"Your information?"

"The Nejd have formed a plot to bring war to Vidar by supporting the rebel movement."

White-hot anger speared Gyrr's middle. The Nejd, Sarkian purists and sworn enemies of his father and the Federation, were responsible for many acts of terror. One such act had cost the life of his infant brother, Seti.

"Explain."

"They are providing weapons to our rebels. After Chedd wins independence, they'll take control of our resources. Our young hot-heads don't realize that the Nejd care nothing for our people and will only use Chedd as a means to challenge the Lord Chancellor and the Federation's rule on Sark."

"What kind of weapons?"

"Sonic blasters to shatter the sealed units where the Vidarian militia are housed. High intensity, portable light thrusters designed to take out Vidarian rovers and transport ships."

"But who will use these weapons? Chedd has never trained an army. The Nejd couldn't bring enough soldiers to challenge Vidar."

"Veks will serve as the Nejd's soldiers."

"Veks?"

"The Nejd have promised the Veks an unending supply of energy if they will serve as an army against the Vidarian forces. Veks are not affected by Chedd's atmosphere. Vektar has a similar mixture, but with a higher concentration of oxygen. They are fiercely adaptable creatures. If the Nejd doesn't control them, they will control Chedd and eventually Vidar."

The puzzle of the Vek attack became suddenly clear. The Nejd had planned the attack on Pyxis. "Did you tell anyone of your meeting with me?"

"No one. My ship left the Chedd skyport undetected. My crew does not know my true mission."

"I was attacked by Veks on Pyxis. They intended to kill me. I thought perhaps the attack was random, but given your information, I know it was planned. One of us has a traitor."

"The death of another prince of Thrane would inspire the supporters of the Nejd. According to my sources, many lurk in business and government. Your father must review those serving in the Chamber of Lords."

Gyrr knew once he told his father of the plot, the news would open the wound young Seti's death had left upon his family. Even his grandmother, who openly opposed the Federation because of her hate for Glacid, had wept for Seti's senseless death.

"Do you know how the weapons are being delivered to Chedd?"

"They are disguised as mining equipment and shipped through regular channels."

"Mining equipment?"

"The pressure drills we use are specialized. The drills are made of the same materials and match the size and weight of sonic blasters and light thrusters. Like the drills, the weapons are not fully assembled when shipped. When scanned the weapons will appear to be drilling parts. The scans will match the bills of lading."

"And the source?"

"A Sarkian corporation called Excavation Technologies. They listed on the exchanges as EXTech."

EXTech. He'd seen that name recently. "I thought their specialty was antiquities? I recall their equipment was used to uncover the ancient city of Sadr."

"It is. But in recent years they expanded to precise drills use for precious minerals mining."

"Like Cheddian crystals."

Uyin agreed. "EXTech ships equipment throughout various systems. Any merchant ship could be carrying the weapons. We should concentrate on the ships traveling between Sark and Chedd. The number cannot be many."

Gyrr thought of the *Telum*. Then it struck him. He'd seen EXTech's logo stamped on several large commercial cargo containers during the tour the twins had given him. Impossible! Ria couldn't be part of this plot to destroy the Federation.

"I wish I had more information concerning the ships, but—"

"You have my word, Viceroy Uyin, no more weapons will be delivered to Chedd."

Uyin rose and bowed. "I will assure my fellow patriots of the Lord Chancellor's support. Together, we shall find a peaceful solution."

Gyrr remained in the small conference room thinking about the Viceroy's information and recalling the details of the tour the twins had given him while aboard the *Telum*. Finally, Sy entered and took the chair Uyin had vacated.

"I need a list of all ships traveling between Sark and Chedd in the last year. Can you provide it?"

"We track all ships traveling through this sector. It was necessary in the years after the war. Your father and I choose to remain informed as to who moves between the Vidar and Aktarian system."

"I also need to know any ship carrying mining equipment destined for Chedd by a corporation called EXTech."

"What am I looking for?"

Gyrr related his conversation with Uyin.

Sy leaned forward. "The Vek attack was not random?"

"The source had to be in Viceroy Uyin's camp. Only my parents, Husi and the two of us knew of my mission."

"You continue to call him by his former title."

"He deserves the respect. What I want to know is why our intelligence failed on Sark. The Nejd is active, and Father knows nothing. It's unacceptable."

Sy rose. "When I have the information concerning the cargo shipments, I'll bring it to your quarters. It's best we meet in the consort's unit."

Reminded of his cover, Gyrr felt a slight burning of his cheeks.

Incisors appeared as Sy smiled. "Don't worry, son of Aaxis, no actual consort duties will be demanded of you in private."

Despite his mission, Gyrr still had a role to play publicly while on Zeon. His covert mission to assist in what he thought was a Vidarian domestic issue had taken on serious proportions. The Vek attack had served to confirm the Viceroy's information.

When Gyrr entered the relaxation lounge on Zeon, heads of various shapes, sizes and origins turned to look over the Portmaster's new consort. Gyrr would have preferred to remain in Sy's offices focusing on the Nejd problem, but consorts were social creatures and known to enjoy the amenities offered in the lounges. While drinking Zeon blasters and losing several games of Staracer, Gyrr thought of Ria and those containers he'd seen on the *Telum*. His gut churned. Ria couldn't be involved with the Nejd.

If he was so confident, why hadn't he told Sy of the cargo the *Telum* carried? He'd told himself a hundred times that the containers were packed with mining parts, not weapons. Why did his gut tell him otherwise?

The *Telum* made regular runs from Sark and actually docked at the Cheddian skyport. According to Sy, most ships docked at the larger Vidar skyport and left the unpleasant duty of transporting goods to Chedd for the Vidarians.

An all female crew aboard an unremarkable Capha2 may serve the purposes of the corporations involved with the Nejd. Both were expendable. His computer search for the holding companies involved with EXTech and Arc Transports should be finished. Pleading duty first, Gyrr left the lounge amid quiet snickers and knowing smiles.

Perhaps if the situation wasn't so dire and Ria hadn't come into his life, he could enjoy the carefree life of blue-eyed Aden Conr for a few days. But Ria had a firm hold on his heart. If his mother dared to give him such a cover again, he would refuse the mission. When the *Telum* docked, Gyrr wanted to be standing at the air lock bridge, but given his cover his presence wasn't warranted. What would Ria think when Sy boarded the *Telum* and removed her and her crew from the ship for an official inquiry?

Searching those containers was vital to federation security.

* * * * *

Ria's heart plummeted when a dozen of the Portmaster's guards marched aboard the *Telum* the moment she opened the main portal hatch. A full inspection wasn't half the disappointment of Aden's absence. Ria expected to see him. She'd believed his parting words.

She addressed the sergeant. "Our clearances and ship's manifest are at your disposal."

"Assemble your crew, Captain."

Ria scowled. Security's request was unusual, even for Zeon. Why hadn't the Portmaster made an official request? "My second officer will assist you with the bills of lading. I will provide the clearances and the ship's manifest. My cargo loaders will assist your inspectors."

"Now, Captain."

"What is this about Sergeant?"

"Portmaster Sy will address your questions. Your crew, Captain."

Puzzled, Ria spoke into her wrist unit. "All personnel, report to main portal. I repeat. All personnel, report to main portal."

The sergeant refused to say anything more. Ria waited, wondering why Security demanded her crew. Doc arrived first.

"What's going on?"

"I don't know," Ria admitted. "I assume we will be informed as soon as everyone had arrived."

The twins protested the interruption to their busiest time, but hushed quickly when surrounded by four Aktarian guards. When Ula arrived, two guards stood at her side. Ria ordered her silent before the com-tech demanded an explanation.

"Your second officer?"

Ria had no idea why Ania was delayed, but she supported her crew. "Officer Onacc is securing the bridge."

The sergeant glanced at two guards. Weapons drawn, they sprinted for the bridge. Ria complained.

"Do not speak, Captain. I am not the person you should address."

Suddenly, it struck Ria. Aden. This action wasn't about her clearances or her cargo, but Aden. Had the Portmaster discovered how Aden has spent his time aboard the *Telum*? Ria hated to think what could happen if she had angered the Suliko. Better her ass, than her crew's.

"I demand to see Portmaster Sy."

"Your weapon, Captain."

The sergeant relieved Ria of her laser unit. She'd done it now. The Portmaster could order a full inspection and write up every minor infraction, forcing the *Telum* to miss its scheduled departure, and its docking schedule on Chedd and Vidar. Arc Transports could dismiss her or if she were lucky, reduce her to a com-tech. If Aden tried to help her, most likely they'd both be out of jobs.

A short while later, Ania and the two guards joined the group crowded into the main portal area. Ania wore flex cuffs.

"Why is my second officer cuffed?"

"Order your personnel to extend their hands."

Expressions from shock to blatant fear flashed across the crew's faces. Ria nodded and all held out their hands. One-by-one, they were cuffed. When the sergeant locked gazes with Ria, she understood and allowed him to apply the flex cuffs without protest.

Separated from her crew, Ria paced the room. Six strides in any direction, blank walls greeted her. Two uncomfortable chairs and one table filled the secured space. She had little doubt Zeon's Security had blanketed the *Telum* the moment she and her crew were removed. Rubbing her unbound wrists, Ria sat down to wait. She worried for her crew.

When Sy finally entered the room, Ria stood.

"Sit down, Captain Torr. I have a few questions for you."

Ria noticed the Portmaster had removed her weapon. "My crew?" Ria took the offensive. "I demand to know why you have arrested them!"

"No one is under arrest. Your crew is well. They will remain in isolation."

Relief washed over Ria. But why keep Doc and the crew in isolation? "For how long? Have you contacted Arc? Our corporate counsel should be informed?"

Despite her size, the Portmaster slid gracefully into a chair. "I'm conducting an inquiry, Captain. You will answer my questions."

Inquiry! Inquires meant time, paperwork, delays. My ass is in trouble!

The Postmaster pointed to the chair. "Captain."

She sat. Trying to appear at ease, Ria leaned back and crossed her legs. Her heart hammered in her chest.

"Screen. View ZS, *Telum*, item 1."

An official security number? Not good. Not good.

A section of the wall slid silently into the ceiling, revealing a large screen. The *Telum*'s manifest appeared. At Sy's instruction the cargo listed on the ship's manifest scrolled past until a listing for a company called EXTech appeared.

"According to your records, these four containers were loaded on Pyxis."

"Yes," Ria said, deciding to answer only what was asked and to offer nothing.

"EXTech is a Sarkian corporation?"

"It is not within the scope of my position to scrutinize, or select the corporations transporting goods. I pick up and deliver as instructed."

"Who makes those decisions?"

The Portmaster's questions surprised Ria. If she had a question about a container, why didn't she open it and contact EXTech?

"Headquarters. I am given a schedule. I load cargo as instructed."

"ZS *Telum*, item 2."

Inquiry? The Portmaster had gathered and logged evidence.

The *Telum*'s schedule, complete with ports and cargo appeared on the screen.

"We requested this schedule from Arc headquarters. Is this the schedule you received?"

Sy scrolled through the document. To Ria, it appeared original. Unsure of the direction of Sy's inquiry, Ria agreed.

"Do you know what EXTech stands for?"

"No."

"Do you have any affiliation with anyone at EXTech?"

Why EXTech? The name didn't jump out at Ria as one of the larger or regular companies shipping to Vidar. The number of corporations with cargo aboard the *Telum* required an efficient database program. Some corporations shared containers to save on the shipping costs. One of Ania's talents and duties as second officer was tracking cargo and reporting all containers loaded and delivered. "I know nothing of the company."

"The EXTech containers were destined for Chedd?"

"If that's what is on the manifest, that's where I'll deliver them."

"Four containers. Did you verify the contents?"

The Portmaster must know how many containers were aboard the *Telum*. The bulk of the shipment was destined for Vidar with a quarter of the load going to Chedd. "Given the number of containers on the *Telum*, I have no recollection of specific containers. If the manifest and the custom stamp matches, it's loaded."

"What happens if it doesn't match?"

"Headquarters is notified. Unless we receive clearance, the container is left on port."

Sy's questions were puzzling. As Portmaster, she knew the drill. Ria guessed Sy wanted her answers on record, but for what purpose?

If infractions were documented, the corporation incurred fines and the captain and the crew lost points. Lower points meant lower bonuses. Was the Portmaster trying to make her sweat?

Had Aden seen something aboard the *Telum* and casually mentioned it to the Portmaster? Was EXTech suspected of something illegal? Or had Aden spilled his guts and told his new master he'd fucked his brains out from Pyxis to Zeon. Was this inquiry Sy's payback?

The Portmaster knew the cost to captains and crews missing those precious docking times. Penalties assessed to the corporation were deducted from the crew's salaries. Ria would accept the responsibility for her involvement with Aden, but the crew shouldn't have to pay.

"Whatever offense, misrepresentation, or transgression, I accept full responsibility. I request you arrest me and release my crew to fulfill the *Telum*'s schedule."

"Confessing, Captain Torr?"

Pain, sharp, intense pain speared her heart. Obviously, Aden had done the confessing. Ria couldn't let her crew pay. She should have listened to Ania, reported his presence to Zeon Security, and kept him under lock and key.

"Yes. My crew is not involved. I've said all I'm going to say."

"This is an inquiry, Captain. Your refusal to be forthcoming is a detainable offense."

"I confess. I'll resign my position. Release the *Telum* to Second Officer Onacc."

Sy emitted a low growl. Displeasing the Portmaster may not be the wisest thing, but Ria decided to call her bluff. If this was about Aden, Sy had no reason to hold the *Telum*.

Ready to return to her isolation cell, Ria stood and held her hands before her.

"Perhaps you require some time to rethink your decision."

* * * * *

Gyrr stopped pacing the moment Sy entered the consort's quarters. Furnished in a mixture of Sarkian and Aktarian styles, with many desirable amenities, such as a stocked intoxication unit, with every type of liquor and legal drug available in two star systems, an expensive entertainment system, and a large, comfortable bed he'd loved to share with Ria, Gyrr realized why the life of a sex consort could tempt a healthy, young male. Sy's consorts lived in luxury.

"She won't cooperate."

Convinced in his heart of Ria's innocence, Gyrr swore beneath his breath. "What did she say?"

Sy settled onto one of two plush leisure chairs. The chair molded to fit her form. Taking a seat on the edge of the sofa, he waited for Sy's report.

"She acknowledged the manifest, but claims to have no information or affiliation with EXTech. She took full responsibility."

"For what?"

"For any transgressions or offenses. I did not tell her what was in the containers. I asked her if she was confessing."

Heart thumping hard in his chest, Gyrr waited for Sy to tell him Ria's answer.

"She refused to say more. The Captain is strong-willed."

Zeon Security had removed eight containers with the EXTech logo from the *Telum*. Four containers held drilling parts and mining equipment, four were filled with weapons.

Leaning forward, Gyrr asked, "What if Ria and the crew knew nothing of the contents?"

"Captain Torr stated the cargo had to match the manifest, otherwise the cargo was left on port. Standard procedure. If the manifest doesn't match, an officer has to file an official request with headquarters to change it. Eight containers were loaded on Pyxis, instead of the four listed on the manifest I received from Arc Headquarters."

"Was there a request for the additional containers?"

"No record of the request with Arc or in the ship's log. The manifest retrieved from the *Telum* listed eight."

Falsifying records and transporting weapons were serious offenses. "How many crewmembers had access?"

"The cargo loaders, the second officer and com-tech all had access. Medical Officer Minn did not. According to Arc Transports, amendments to the manifest must be entered and approved by the captain."

The moment's ease Gyrr felt in learning Cirrii couldn't have altered the records was short-lived. The finger of guilt pointed at Ria.

"Did Ria approve the change?"

"Yes. Her coded signature appears on the altered manifest."

Gyrr clenched his hands. How could Ria explain her signature?

"Meaning, unless customs had reason to be suspicious a pick up of extra containers signed off by the captain would appear reasonable?"

"Yes. Cargo is added or left behind depending on the situation. A ship arriving late will leave cargo for the next ship headed for Vidar, Sark or Aktares, depending on the destination. Meteor showers have affected shipments to and from Trag for weeks. By law, corporate headquarters and customs are to be notified and a new manifest filed. Even if the filing is done, my team can't inspect every ship."

"It appears the Nejd is using legitimate ships for weapons delivery."

Sy nodded. "Someone had to set up the delivery. Is Arc Transports covering up or are they being used? Either way, someone aboard the *Telum* has be involved, otherwise the crew would have requested an official change to the manifest."

"Why wouldn't the crew just load the cargo and save themselves the paperwork?"

"Crews gets paid a low base salary, the real money is in the bonuses. The credit bonuses are paid if the ship remains on schedule and for the number of shipments delivered on time."

"But it's only four containers, one shipment."

"Unless the whole crew is in on it, someone is going to notice and complain. Especially, the loaders, who are the lowest paid crewmembers. They aren't paid if the ship docks on time. Their bonuses are tied to the number of actual unloaded containers. If they pickup extra containers along the route, they earn more credits. From the records I retrieved, the *Telum*'s loaders are hard workers."

His conversation with the twins supported the records. When the twins lost their father, they signed on with Arc Transports. Their credit bonuses provided income for their mother and younger siblings. While waiting for Sy he'd read the background reports on all the *Telum*'s crewmembers, except Ria. Sy had withheld hers.

"Are the four containers the only discrepancy between the manifests?"

"Our inspection isn't finished, but so far, yes."

"When was the *Telum*'s manifest altered?"

"I compared the manifest registered on Sark with the Interstellar Customs Department prior to the departure of the *Telum*. It matches the one I received from Arc Headquarters."

Gyrr's heart constricted. Even if Ria wasn't the one manipulating the records, by law her position as captain made her liable.

"I think you should speak with Captain Torr."

"Tell her what we found? See if she will talk?" Gyrr shook his head. "I don't think Ria will give up a crewmember unless we have hard evidence."

"Why are you so sure your Ria isn't responsible? The captain has the final say. Her coded signature is on the manifest."

Because he couldn't bear it if she were a traitor to everything he loved and held dear.

"I love her. Here," he tapped his chest, "I know she is innocent. Tell me, General, tell me everything about her."

"Talk to her."

"The situation is changed. A matter of treason is far more important than my royal position. Ria's life—traitors are still put to death on Sark."

He couldn't allow that. Nor could he let her languish in prison for the rest of her life. Where could he take her? Where could they go? How could he betray his family? His name? Renounce his oath to the Federation? He rubbed the barren finger of his right hand. He needed his father's council and the guidance of his mother's gentle heart and sharp intelligence. But his parents had yet to know Ria and come to love her. Gyrr had to trust his heart, his instincts.

He had to talk to Ria to hear the truth. If she were guilty, they would disappear into another star system. If innocent, he'd take on the Sarkian council and the entire federation to prove it.

"I'll speak with her, alone, without surveillance. I must know what is in her heart. Our conversation is off the official record. When I return, you must tell me everything you know about her."

Sy nodded. "I will arrange it."

"Put her in one of the interrogation units."

Although her dark blue eyes focused upon him for a long moment, Sy didn't question his request.

CHAPTER SIX

When Aden entered the interrogation room, Ria's emotions vacillated between anger, hurt and fear. She'd expected Portmaster Sy, but Aden had come. He wasn't a bystander in all this. She'd trusted him and look where it had gotten her.

Behind him, the security door slid silently closed. He wore a loose black shirt revealing several delicious inches of his broad chest, black trousers and boots. The trousers clung to his muscled legs. She caught herself staring at his crotch.

Despite her anger, Aden still had the ability to make her hot. Why did her foolish heart pound in her chest at the sight of him? When near him, why did her thoughts turn erotic? Why did she ache to fall upon her knees and…

He cocked his head to one side, a smile hovering at the corner of his lips.

"Did you miss me, Ria?"

If she answered that question, she'd have to lie. She chose to ignore it. "I expect you to reimburse my crew. Because of you, the *Telum* is behind schedule."

"I owe you and your crew my life. Agreed."

She had no idea how many credits a man like Aden might have in the banking system, but his easy agreement surprised her.

"You'll reimburse them?"

"On one condition."

Given his position as sex consort, what condition could he ask of her? Did Sy indulge her consorts? Stories were told and retold on Sark about the wild sex the Lord Chancellor had shared with the Siluko. Ria had never participated in a sex ménage, or experienced sex with another female. Could she do it for her crew? Her heart constricted at the thought of sharing Aden. The idea that he'd want her to…

Get tough. You can handle it. "I'll do anything to protect my crew."

He stepped toward her. "I'm going to ask you questions, Ria. I want honest answers."

So Sy had sent him to ask her questions. Had he promised the Portmaster, she would do anything he wanted?

"Agreed. Anything to get the *Telum* on its way."

He stood before her. Ria could feel the heat of his body and inhale his wonderful male scent.

"Another ship can take your cargo to Chedd."

"No, the *Telum* has to deliver her cargo—"

"Is the stop in Chedd important?"

She moved away from him. "The bonuses paid for Chedd are the most profitable. Doc has to pay for Pol's schooling. The twins have obligations. But what would you know about that kind of need? Fucking women must pay well or you wouldn't ask why bonuses are essential to females working on a Sarkian commercial freighter.

"I should have locked you up in sick bay and called the Portmaster to pickup up her toy."

His low chuckle brought forth memories of the wondrous hours they'd spent making love.

"I've missed you, Ria. I miss *us*."

Did he read minds? "Sure you did. That's why I'm locked in an interrogation room. And to answer your question, no, I haven't missed you."

"You agreed to answer honestly!"

She ached for him, but she wasn't about to tell him.

"I've ached for you every moment."

The man did read minds. "Then why couldn't you have lied? Why did you have to bring this down on my crew?" She turned her back to him.

He took her arm and spun her around. "I saw the containers aboard the *Telum*."

She tried to pull her arm free. He held onto her. "What containers?"

"The EXTech containers. The ones you picked up on Pyxis!"

"I picked up a lot of things on Pyxis, including you!"

He glared down at her. "Tell me, Ria. Do not lie."

Why accuse her of lying? Wasn't he the one wearing the phony Ident lenses?

"Who are you Aden? Did the Portmaster require blue eyes or are you the one hiding the truth?"

He looked stunned. "You knew?"

"Doc discovered the lenses. She's good."

"Why didn't you ask me before?"

"I would have, once you were safely off the *Telum*. No one knew, except Doc and I."

She wanted to ask him about his Glacidian bloodlines, but now wasn't the time.

"Did you fear for me, or yourself?"

"I was trying to keep my job. You were unauthorized. I didn't want to explain you to headquarters or Zeon Security."

"For fear of an inspection?"

"Headquarters deducts points. They look for a reason to reduce our bonuses. Inspectors impose fines for infractions."

"Would picking up cargo without requesting an official change to the ship's manifest be such an infraction?"

His grip had tightened on her arm, not enough to hurt, but to emphasize his question. "I always make an official request, otherwise Loci and Falara lose credits. I wouldn't do that to them."

"Do you ever delegate the task? Let someone use your coded signature?"

Why would he need to know that? Had she picked up cargo on Pyxis? So much had happened since she'd laid eyes on Aden.

"*Who* are you?"

His broad chest expanded as he drew in a deep breath. Why did her question cause him difficulty? He wanted the truth. Didn't she deserve the same?

"Answer my questions, Ria. The time will come for you to learn what I cannot tell you now."

"Are you a sex consort? Do you fuck women for a living?"

He cupped her face in his large hands. She felt the ridges of his palm against her skin.

"Is it important to you?"

B.J. McCall

"Yes." Why did she have to sound so breathless? His fingers slipped into her hair. She wanted to lean into him, and feel his strong body against hers.

"Because you care for me?"

"Yes."

"I give you my solemn oath. I do not fuck women for my living."

Despite his measured words, she feared he wasn't telling her the whole truth. How much of what he had said was truth or fiction? What was he to Portmaster Sy? The meeting she'd witnessed aboard the *Telum* wasn't two strangers introduced for the first time. She'd sensed something between them.

"You fuck them for pleasure?"

"You are my pleasure, Ria. Only you. If you believe nothing else I say, believe that."

Her heart twisted. Believe? She didn't know his name, his occupation, or why Sy allowed him alone with her in an interrogation room. Why didn't anything make sense?

Holding her by the hair, he lifted her to him, fastened his lips to hers. Her questions and suspicions melted in a vortex of warmth and need. He'd expected her capitulation. She couldn't let him distract her while her crew idled in detention. She bit his lip.

He pulled away and stared into her eyes. "Why resist? You want me as much I want you. You need me as much I need you."

"Are you calling the shots, or is Sy?"

"You're supposed to answer my questions."

"Release my crew and my ship."

"It's not that simple."

"What do you want, Aden?"

He released her so quickly she stumbled back. "The truth."

What had she done while docked in Pyxis? Ula had experienced problems with the comlink to Sark. They'd worked for hours together. Ania and the twins had handled the cargo. "I may have picked up cargo in Pyxis."

"The containers marked EXTech?"

"I don't remember any containers marked EXTech. The Portmaster showed me the manifest. The containers were listed. Tell Sy to write up the infractions. I'll resign. Ania can handle the Vidar run."

"The *Telum* isn't going anywhere."

"The whole crew will suffer. Isn't my job enough?"

"You can't trade your job for treason."

Treason! Had she heard him correctly?

"Portmaster Sy may be powerful, but fucking you isn't a treasonable offense."

"This isn't about us, Ria. The EXTech containers, did you authorize them to be loaded on Pyxis?"

"I don't remember them. I don't know anything about EXTech."

"Ria." He wrapped his fingers about her upper arms and stared directly into her eyes. "Those containers were filled with weapons."

Her blood roared in her ears. She shook her head.

"Weapons intended for Cheddian rebels."

Her knees gave beneath her. If Aden hadn't been holding her, she would have fallen. She closed her eyes tight, tried to shut out his words.

"Ria."

"No. No, no, no. No weapons. Not on my ship."

"Sonic blasters and light thrusters."

The implication of his words slammed into her. *Treason.* He thought she was smuggling weapons to Chedd. He wasn't a consort. He was a spy.

"You work for security!"

"In a manner of speaking."

She backed away from him. "That's why you approached me on Pyxis. You wanted to find out if I was a traitor."

"No, I knew nothing about the weapons until I reached Zeon. I wanted you—"

"Don't."

The wall brought her retreat to a halt. She couldn't escape. Fear rose so fast and quick, she could taste it. Convicted traitors were put to death. Someone was moving weapons on her ship. Either her crew was smuggling beneath her nose, which Ria refused to believe, or someone at headquarters had set up the cargo and changed the manifest. Whoever had masterminded the plan, intended to cast the blame on her when caught.

B.J. McCall

"You believe I'm guilty. That's why you've kept me in isolation. That's why you been questioning me. That's why you—"

Her heart ached. She'd fallen in love with a man who'd set her up for the ultimate downfall. Would he be there when they condemned her? Would he watch her die?

Hot tears filled her eyes. She swiped them away with the back of her hand.

He reached out and touched her damp cheek. She swatted his hand aside. "Don't touch me."

"Ria, tell me everything. I must know the truth."

"Truth. When did you ever tell me the truth?"

"I'm not at liberty to tell you everything, but one day, I will. I love you. Believe in me. Trust me."

Trust? How could he ask her to trust him? She stared into the blue lenses obscuring the real man. The man she'd just began to know.

"I don't want to hear your lies."

"Sy suspects you're involved. I wanted to hear the truth from your own lips."

"I have nothing to say to you, or Portmaster Sy."

"Don't do this, Ria. These charges are serious. Work with me."

Ria glared at him.

He grabbed her by the shoulders and slammed her back against the wall. His actions shocked her more than harmed her.

"Talk to me!"

She bit her bottom lip to keep it from trembling and locked her knees to keep them steady, but she didn't back down. After several minutes of silence so thick you could slice it with an ice blade, he released her and strode out of the room.

Wrapping her arms about her body, Ria sank to the floor. Who was calling the shots, Aden or Sy? How did one sort-of-work for security? If he worked for the Federation that would explain... What would it explain?

Had meeting Aden on Pyxis been coincidental as he claimed? Had the Vek attack been planned so he could get aboard the *Telum* and check out its cargo? How else did Veks get onto a skyport undetected?

If weapons were found on the *Telum*, she couldn't escape responsibility. Her job lost and her reputation tarnished beyond repair, Ria had to focus on fighting for her life.

Did Ania know about the EXTech containers? Had she or the twins been promised an unauthorized bonus for looking the other way? But the twins couldn't have altered the manifest. The twins and Doc weren't authorized. Only Ania and Ula had access. Did one of them know how to code her signature?

Ania would be the most likely choice. How many times had Ria entered her code in Ania's presence? During the last two years, had she ever given the code to Ania? But why would Ania smuggle weapons? Her father ranked among Sark's greatest military heroes.

While her own father… If charged, no one would believe she hadn't committed treason. Like father, like daughter.

Within minutes, Gyrr strode back into the interrogation room. Remaining seated on the floor, Ria looked up at him.

"Cirrii is cleared of any charges, but until we have a handle on the situation, your crew will remain sequestered."

"What about the twins? Their access to the manifest is restricted to viewing the list. They can't alter or input data."

"They control the loading of the containers."

"If they were part of this, do you think they would have taken you on a tour that included the area where those EXTech containers were stored? The *Telum* is a huge ship. They could have avoided that section and you'd never known the difference."

"What about your communications technical, Ula?"

"She has access to the bridge's computer. She handles the communications to and from headquarters, to the skyports, transmits reports, and maintains the comlinks to Sark and Aktares. She comes from a military family. Her brothers are both decorated officers. Her uncle is Colonel Waal."

Aden's eyes widened. "The Colonel Waal?"

Ria nodded. "I'm sure the Colonel has calluses matching yours."

His gaze narrowed, but instead of responding to her comment, he asked, "What about Officer Onacc?"

"Better still. Her grandfather is General Onacc. He is now called Councilmember Onacc."

He dropped down beside her and leaned against the wall. Propping an elbow on a bent knee, he asked, "And what about you, Ria?"

She didn't look at him. If he wanted her to tell him she had powerful friends or a respected family, she couldn't. She had no one to help her.

"I'm no one. My parents are dead. I have no siblings, no known family."

"How did you get into the military? Who sponsored you?"

Her father had collected one final favor from a friend before he'd faced the gallows. She'd been lucky. She hadn't felt lucky at the time, but without Master Quaa she could have spent her childhood in a government school.

"My learning master. Because of my lack of respectability, he recommended the military. He didn't think I could find a lifemate."

"Did you serve with honors?"

He would ask! No point in lying. Surely, Portmaster Sy was retrieving her records since birth. "No. I was released."

He didn't ask why. The silence between them stretched while her heart warred with her brain. How much should she reveal? The official version, he'd learn from Sy. If she told him the real story, would he believe her? Once he found out about her parents, he'd think the worst.

"Unauthorized activity. Unsuitable moral character."

"You had sex with a male officer?"

She hadn't spoken of Natrh in years. Ria didn't want to remember. "I was young and thought he was dashing, and brave. I was wrong."

"When you were discovered, he blamed you for enticing him?"

She wished it was as simple as that, but she'd heard of several females released for the same reason.

"Something, like that."

"I'm sorry, Ria. Whoever he was, he lost something precious."

His voice softened, curling around her sore heart. She didn't want his pity. "Don't be. I learned a valuable lesson."

"I think you learned not to trust."

Didn't he realize you have to feel safe to trust? Ria had stood alone for so long, then she'd been promoted to captain, and the *Telum* and her crew became home and family. Had she let down her guard only to be betrayed?

"After you were released, did you hire on with Arc Transports?"

"Arc needed pilots willing to take deep runs. I wanted to run as far as I could. Chedd looked good."

A skilled pilot, she'd left the bad memories and Sark behind. Aboard the *Telum* she'd found a home, a purpose, a life. Despite its age and its size, she loved her ship. She wrapped her arms more tightly around her body. Now she'd lost it. She'd lost her home.

"You think I'm guilty, don't you?"

He reached out and cupped her chin. Slanting his head, he kissed her. For a scant second her lips clung to his. She pulled back.

"You kiss me. I confess. Is that the way it works?"

Shaking his head slowly, he said, "I'm aching to kiss you, make love to you, but I need you to tell me the truth."

Ria wanted to believe in him, but given the seriousness of her situation she'd be a fool to pin her hopes on a man whose true identity and purpose still remained a mystery.

"I doubt you'll be there when Sark executes me."

He leaned toward her until his face was mere inches from hers. His piercing gaze held her rooted to the spot. "You're not going to die, Ria. You're going to talk and keeping talking until I know everything that happened aboard the *Telum* from the moment you left Sark. You're going to help me find the traitors."

Ria ached for the chance to prove her innocence. Eventually, Aden and Sy would learn about her mother. If they dug deep, her father's identity could come to light. If she were lucky, Aden would simply walk away. Natrh had punished her for her secrets.

"On one condition."

"Until I discover who is behind the weapons smuggling, your crew cannot leave Zeon."

"I want to see the real you. I want to see the man behind the blue lenses."

"You drive a hard bargain, my love."

"You speak of trust. If I am to trust you, you should trust me."

He stood and held out his hand.

"Where are you taking me?"

"Trust me."

Instead of returning to the holding cells, Aden guided Ria through a series of hallways. They stopped before a tube elevator. An Ident scanner flashed on Aden's right eye and the tube opened. Once inside, Aden commanded the lift to the Master Deck. The narrowness of the tube forced their bodies to touch as they zoomed upwards.

A hint of a leer touched his lips and eyes. "This has possibilities, but I'm not sure the Portmaster would approve of such a use of her private lift."

Before Ria could comment the elevator stopped, opening onto a foyer dominated by flowering plants. At a set of thick double doors, another Ident flashed. Once inside, Ria stopped in her tracks. After spending the last two years in the cramped crew areas of the *Telum*, the sheer size of the room amazed her. Six containers could easily fit inside the living space. Plants and flowers adorned gleaming tables. Comfortable looking chairs and seating units filled the room. At the far end, a wall of permashield exposed the vast dark blue vista of space dotted by the twinkling planets of the Vidarian system. The smallest, Chedd, glowed green beside its larger, bright yellow neighbors. A myriad of ships slid silently across the horizon in their docking patterns.

"Portmasters live well."

"If you lived on Zeon, how would you spend your credits?"

"If I earned enough of them, I'd spend them like this."

At Aden's command another reinforced door slide open to her left. "Wait till you see the consort's quarters."

"If you're not her consort why are you living here?"

"It's my cover." He placed an arm about her waist and guided her through the door. "I thought you'd figured that out."

"Isn't she going to object? After all, I'm under suspicion." Again, Ria stopped dead in her tracks. "Great Gods, she knows how to keep a man in style."

"Sy was a member of the Lord Chancellor's harem before his marriage. She learned to appreciate his comfortable style of living."

Without thinking, Ria fisted her right hand and touched her heart at the mention of the Lord Chancellor. Although she was no longer obligated to offer the salute, she did it out of respect. "I'd say she developed royal tastes."

His gaze dropped to her fist. "You're no longer in the military, Ria."

Ria dropped her hand. "The Lord Chancellor is our leader as well as your supreme ruler. He emancipated the women of Sark."

Aden had no idea what Ria's occupation would have been if not for Lord Aaxis. She owed him her life.

"I understand Queen Tayra has much to do with his modern thinking."

"He is influenced by his wife?"

"That is my understanding."

"Then the women of Sark owe her their allegiance."

"She doesn't have it?"

Ria walked through the room, touching the fine fabrics covering the seating units, admiring the paintings on the walls. "Many lost sons and husbands during the Glacidian conflict."

"Our Queen was instrumental in bringing the conflict to an end. Her marriage to Lord Aaxis brought peace."

Interesting that he'd used the term *our queen*. Although Lord Aaxis was the supreme ruler of Aktares, his wife had refused all official titles, other than her birthright as Queen of Glacid. His tone held respect. Aden must hold dear his Glacidian heritage.

"And the birth of Antar has joined us as one. Strength in unity."

"The royal motto. Do you find him handsome?"

What an odd question? "He's as handsome as his father. Almost. The twins nearly wet themselves whenever Antar is on the news."

"Lord Aaxis is over twice your age."

"Our leader is still an attractive and vital warrior. Surely, *you* aren't jealous of the royals?"

"I'm jealous of any man who catches your eye."

"You have no reason to envy any man. The royals are like a vision, beautiful, but distant. While you—"

Ria stopped before the permashield wishing she didn't feel the wave of heat coursing deep inside her. *Ignore it. Focus.*

Her gaze scanned the heavens. The view from the consort quarters was almost as staggering as the Portmaster's. "I can understand how Portmaster Sy can remain on Zeon."

Aden moved behind her and wrapped his arms about her middle. "Wouldn't you rather live on-planet?"

"I have no desire to return to Sark, ever. If it wasn't required, I'd never go back."

"What happened to make you turn against your homeland?"

Ria stiffened. She'd walked right into his trap. "I do not stand against Sark. I support my homeland and the Federation. I would defend it tomorrow, but Sark doesn't want me."

"I don't understand."

Ria moved out of his grasp. "No, you don't. My disappointment with Sark has nothing to do with containers or weapons."

"Tell me."

"After I was released from military service, I was lucky to get a job. No one wanted to hire me. It's not easy when you have no family. Heritage and ties are everything to us. That coupled with a release for moral character—I might as well of been a murderer. I grew tired of people viewing me as a women of questionable everything."

"Who hired you?"

"You mean why did they hire me? Look up my records. I don't remember much about the recruiter, except his last name was Issin and he had piloted a Capha during the Glacidian conflict. After a lengthy interview, he knew I could handle the ship and the job. I agreed to accept half the wages a man with the same training would receive and take the longest route. We met twice."

"Come here."

"Why?"

"You're not alone, Ria. You have me and I can protect you."

She shook her head. "Don't protect me, Aden. Stand clear. Nothing good will come of your support."

He took a step toward her and held out his hand. She shook her head.

"Take it."

He had no idea his faith in her would shatter the moment he learned the truth. She couldn't bear to see the look of disdain in his eyes. In her dreams, she'd relived the hatred burning in Natrh's eyes and his insults were forever seared into her memories. "I can't."

"I won't let you go. I'll take you captive and make you my sex slave."

He had no idea the pain his words inflicted. "That's illegal."

"Who will know? Who will stop me?"

The serious tone of his words frightened her. "You can't hold me against my will!"

"Try to leave."

Ria glanced at the door. Only an Ident scan would open it. "You'd force me against my will."

"I won't have to force you. I'll lick your pussy until you cream."

Relieved his words were only teasing, Ria rebuffed him. "What makes you think I'll cream?"

"We've been without release for hours. Tell me your sex isn't flexing with need. Convince me you aren't aching for my cock."

She did ache for him. Already, the need of him tingled between her legs, heated her blood. He moved closer. Her gaze slid to the obvious erection stretching his trousers, but this wasn't the time for recreational sex.

He grasped the lapels of her uniform jacket and yanked it over her shoulders and down, trapping her arms. "Your nipples defy your silence."

She couldn't deny his words. Her nipples poked at the white fabric of her tank. Her breasts swelled, eager for his mouth, his lips and tongue.

"I have more important things than fucking to worry about."

"Making love to you is the most important thing. You're not alone Ria, get used to it."

Holding her in a firm grip, he bent his head and captured one taut point. He suckled, drawing deeply on her breast, wetting the thin material of her tank. Closing her eyes, Ria lost her will to deny what burned in her heart.

Encircling her ass with his hands, Gyrr lifted Ria and shoved her up against the permashield. Great Gods, she made him burn. Needing her wet heat, his cock strained beneath the tight confines of his trousers.

"Lights off!"

The room went dark, leaving only the twinkling lights of Vidar and the sound of his blood roaring his ears. Here, at the edge of the skyport, he and Ria faced one another, seemingly alone in the vastness of space. In that dark, endless void, Ria had become the center of his world. Whether she liked it or not, they were one.

Gyrr shoved her jacket down her arms and thrust his hands beneath her tank. Cupping her full breasts, he groaned.

"Your breasts are exquisite."

Instead of resisting him, Ria tugged at his shirt. Within seconds he'd removed his shirt and freed her of the tank. Skin met skin. Heartbeats soared as her breasts pressed, soft and inviting, against his solid chest. He kissed her, reveling in the taste of her, as he released the seams of her pants.

His hand slid between her legs. She arched her back at the contact. Sliding two fingers inside her heat, Gyrr licked the swollen mound of her breast, flicking his tongue over her plump nipple.

Her slick flesh surrounded his fingers, clamping, grabbing, flexing with need.

He suckled, drawing eagerly until she moaned. He pumped his finger deep and fast into her wet passage until she shuddered.

Instead of removing his hand, Gyrr caressed her pussy. Silky wet, he took pleasure in the small gasps and subtle roll of her hips. His thumb grazed her clit.

"Did you miss me, Ria?"

"Fuck me."

His cock ached to be where his fingers remained, deep inside and stroking her sweet flesh. She'd admitted her feelings before, now she denied the depth of their passion. "Wrong answer."

Removing his hand, he touched his fingers to her lips. He nearly came when she suckled gently on his fingers, her tongue licking her pleasure from his skin.

Gyrr had no doubt, they'd spend hours making love and fucking for the sheer joy of it, but he wanted more than a physical union. He wanted Ria to love and to trust him.

Blood pounding in his veins, he removed her boots and trousers. Slowly he slid her underwear down her hips and thighs until they lay pooled at her ankles. Kneeling before her, he gently pushed her thighs apart.

Teasing her, Gyrr licked her belly, nuzzling her soft flesh. Rubbing her thighs, he skimmed the edge of her center, never touching her pussy. She shifted, communicating her desires. He ignored her provoking hints and continued to lick and kiss and suckle her thighs, her belly, and the sweet hollow between.

She shifted, thrusting her pussy toward his face. Gyrr inhaled her scent. Thanks to his Glacidian ancestors, his receptors flared, sending a delicious heat from his brain to his cock.

She grabbed him by the hair. "Aden, please."

Despite his agonizing need, Gyrr slowly licked the crease between her thigh and her pussy. "Please what?"

"Make love to me."

Smiling, Gyrr rested his mouth against her pulsing center. Ria kicked her underwear off her ankles and thrust a leg over his shoulder. He plunged his tongue deep inside her. Honeyed and hot, he tasted her desire.

His receptors flamed. She quivered, her pussy flexing wildly against his darting tongue. He intended to bring her to climax again and again until she was so exhausted she'd admit her need for him.

Closing his lips over her budded clit, he suckled, drawing deep. Her fingers dug into his scalp. Her leg clutched his back. She shuddered and gushed.

Gyrr lapped her nectar, feeding a need to taste, to absorb her climax. Her hands relaxed and she leaned against the shield.

"How do you do that? What is it about you?"

In the darkness he couldn't see her eyes. "Do what?"

Her leg slid off his shoulder. "When I climax, it's like you're sucking out my soul."

To thwart her sudden desire to distance herself mentally, Gyrr slid his hands up her thighs, squeezing her firm flesh. "Doesn't it feel good?"

She turned away from him and faced the shield. "It's too good. When I'm with you, it's different."

"It's different for me. What we have is special. It pleases me that you acknowledge our bond."

She leaned her forehead to the shield. "We can't bond."

Ria could deny it all she wanted, but Gyrr understood the binding process. She did not.

He stood and released the seam of his trousers. His pain eased as his erection sprang free. "Do you still want to fuck?"

Gyrr didn't wait for her answer. Reaching around her torso, he cupped her magnificent breasts and began a gentle, erotic massage.

He nudged her buttocks with his cock, wanting her aware of his need.

Grasping her nipples between thumbs and forefingers, Gyrr teased them to sensitive points. Sliding one hand down her belly, his fingertips grazed her pussy. She moaned deep in her throat.

Placing her hands on the shield, she leaned back against him and spread her legs. Her wanton answer to his question shot pure lust to the tip of his cock. Sliding his cock between her legs, Gyrr probed her moist center from behind. Slick, hot and ready, her pussy stretched to receive him. She held him tight, so tight, he gasped. Rocking his hips, he pushed deeper, boldly into her wetness.

Taking her hands, he pulled them away from the shield and pushed her gently against the shield. Pressing her breasts and pussy flush to the cool surface, Gyrr rolled his hips slowly. He wanted her to experience the sensation of her body between his and the shield.

When Ria moaned, he nipped her earlobe and licked her neck.

He pressed his thighs to hers and undulated his hips. "Do you like it?"

"It's cold. I'm hot. I'm coming. Ohhhh."

When her sex flooded, Gyrr rammed his cock into her, pounding her sweet flesh, reveling in the fierceness of their mutual need. "I love fucking you."

The words mingled with his release. Intense, hot, searing, he exploded.

Holding her against the smooth surface of the shield, Gyrr buried his face into the hollow of her neck.

This beautiful female he'd met by pure chance, now held his heart and his balls firmly, forever, in her power. A moan, a tiny gasp, a smile, a sultry look could squeeze either part of his anatomy. Her laughter brought him immense joy. Her fears tore him apart. He couldn't live without her.

I love you.

* * * * *

Rolling onto her back, Ria's eyes fluttered open. She yawned and stretched, considered snuggling into the luxurious softness of the slumber unit and hiding from the problems she faced.

She needed to confront Aden about her crew.

Sitting up, she surveyed the tasteful room the Portmaster provided for her consort's comfort. Sy, a large woman, had chosen the sleeping platform for its size and comfort. She and Aden had taken advantage of both, several times, before Ria had collapsed exhausted against his chest.

Soft light filtered from the ceiling. Before her the permashield provided the still stunning view of the Vidarian system and the slow dance of the ships coming into port.

After taking advantage of the oversized cleansing unit and sun tube, Ria searched the cabinets for fresh clothing, anything other than the uniform she'd worn for last two days. She chose a neatly folded, but familiar looking garment from a shelf. The items neatly stacked and folded were hers. Aden must have boarded the *Telum* and retrieved them. She noted he'd left her clean, spare uniforms behind.

He'd chosen the three loose caftans she'd brought with her from Sark. Although, she'd loved the traditional garments, she hadn't worn them. They reminded her of the past.

Was he telling her that she no longer held her position as Captain of the *Telum*? Accepting the reality of the loss of her beloved ship, Ria dragged the cream-colored garment over her nakedness. Ria noted Aden hadn't bothered bringing her clean underwear.

On a lower shelf she spotted her favorite shoes. She'd worn boots for so long, the intricate straps of the sandals felt odd and unfamiliar. She wriggled her toes and walked about the room.

She exited the sleeping chamber as Aden entered the front door. Dressed in black trousers and an unadorned black jacket cut in the short military style, he paused, letting his gaze sweep over her. A smile hinted at the corners of his lips. "I thought you'd like a change in attire."

Before he said something about her lack of underwear and distracted her, Ria asked, "Have I been dismissed by Arc Transport?"

"A crew is on its way to Zeon to take command of the *Telum*."

Drawing in a slow breath, Ria asked, "How soon before I'm remanded to the Sarkian authorities?"

"Ria, sit down."

Instead of choosing the comfortable seating in the living area, Ria moved to a small settee before the permashield. Gazing at the Vidarian system, she realized her days were numbered.

When Aden sat beside her, Ria leaned into the comfort of his broad shoulder, needing the support of his arm about her. "Did you handle the docking on Pyxis?"

"Yes."

"Did you handle the manifest changes?"

Ria shook her head. "Ula was having some problems with the com-unit. I left the cargo to Ania."

"Were you aware of the loading of the EXTech containers?"

Knowing she had nothing to do with the weapons didn't stop the trembling racking her body. Who would believe her? "No."

"Does Ania know your signature code?"

"No. I don't know. We've worked as a team for so long, I never worried about—" Ria tried to pull away from Aden. He held her tight. "I can't prove my innocence."

"When the security of the Federation is threatened, Sy is mandated to perform mind probes."

Ria stiffened. "I've heard of them, but I thought they were nothing more than rumors."

"The Siluko scientists perfected the probe some time ago. Specialized Siluko military units were trained to retrieve data. Sy shared her knowledge and now a few specialists on Aktares can perform the probe."

"Has she performed them on Sarks?"

"Yes. Also, on Aktarian and Glacidians but there were instances of brain damage. I know Vidarians, even Sutumi have been subjected to the probes. Veks are poor subjects. The probe has little to no affect on them."

"Why didn't you tell me this before?"

"When you accepted your position with Arc, you signed a waiver allowing any probe or brain scan in the event of an inquiry affecting

Federation security. Interplanetary transportation of contraband affects Federation security. I can't legally prevent the probe."

"Legally?"

"I've made plans to get you out of here."

He couldn't be serious. "You mean you want me to run? Where? How?"

"I have the means and the transportation!"

Condemned forever. No! Never. "I'm not a traitor and I'd rather be dead than branded."

"I'll not let you die."

"It's not your choice. Nor is it your life."

Aden touched his lips to her temple. "You're very much mistaken."

Ria felt a sharp pain at the base of her skull, then nothing.

* * * * *

"Are my quarters prepared?"

"Yes, all items bearing the royal markings have been removed. Are you certain you are making the proper choices, your Highness?"

Husi followed as Gyrr carried Ria into his sleeping quarters and settled her gently upon his fur-lined sleeping platform. She'd be out for several more hours.

When Sy realized he'd taken Ria, Gyrr knew she'd contact his father. Would his father understand the reason he'd violated the law? Had he made the right choice?

Logic told him Sy would do everything in her power to safely administer the probe. Gyrr had refused to take the chance Ria would become part of the one percent damaged by the probe. He'd rather die than see her harmed.

After closing the door, Gyrr headed toward the bridge with Husi hot on his heels.

"What is to prevent Portmaster Sy from disabling this ship and arresting us?"

"This ship can outrun anything Sy deploys. We'll be out of Sy's range within hours. Are all crewmen on port?"

"Yes, all except the pilot."

"This is insanity, the Queen— Do you realize? Forgive me, your Highness, but I must protest. Do you realize—"

"I do. I understand the ramifications of my actions."

He wasn't about to tell Husi all of his plans. The element of surprise would aid his escape from Zeon.

Upon entering the bridge, the pilot stood and saluted. "She's ready, Lord Commander."

"Follow me," Gyrr said, before turning on his heel. Arriving at the portal for one of three rovers used for short journeys to planets surfaces, he released a hatch and ordered both men to enter.

"I do not understand, Lord Commander."

"Are you refusing a direct order?"

The pilot saluted and entered the rover.

"Your Highness, in good conscience I cannot abandon you."

"I'll need you to work with Sy and my parents to clear Ria's name. She's innocent."

"I don't understand."

"She's my lifemate. The binding is complete."

"That's impossible!"

"I thought it so, but it's done."

"But she's a Sark. You can't bind with a Sark."

"I know the science. I don't know why or how, but it's happened."

"I'll contact our Queen. Perhaps something can be done."

Gyrr placed his hand upon Husi's shoulder. "I would not have it otherwise. I want her safe and alive and I'll travel to the ends of the universe to save her."

"Do not force your parents to make a decision. If you are not condemned to die, you will be banished."

"I'm begging for your help, Husi. Only a Glacidian can understand my need. I'm committed. I choose to live, only if Ria lives at my side."

Staring into Husi's eyes, Gyrr relived his own conflict. "If you choose not to help me, I'll understand. But you must go, now. I'll need time to leave the Zeon sector."

"Let me remain, your Highness. I'm far more help to you here than on Zeon."

Gyrr shook his head and guided Husi through the hatch. "Thank you, my friend," he said, before sealing the hatch and his fate.

The rover carrying Husi and his pilot launched, Gyrr returned to the bridge. Set on a path that would change his life no matter the outcome, he set course and speed. By the time Sy realized he wasn't aboard the rover, his ship would have cleared enough space to make it impossible for her forces to chase him. The hyperlink engaged, and the *Praesum* raced toward the rings of Aktares.

CHAPTER SEVEN

Leaving the control of the ship to the DK3 computer, Gyrr checked on Ria.

He could barely make out her features in the soft lighting he'd ordered when leaving her. He didn't want her to awaken in the dark, alone and disoriented from the drug he administered on Zeon. One prick to the neck and she had slid gently into oblivion. Would she forgive him for the steps he had taken?

Smoothing a strand of hair from her cheek, Gyrr whispered her name. Her eyes fluttered opened. "Where am I?"

"Aboard my ship, the *Praesum*."

"Your ship. Why are we here?"

He ignored her question. "How do you feel?"

"I remember looking at Vidar. We were sitting in—" She forced herself to a sitting position and clutched her head. "Did Sy administer the probe?"

"No. The ill effects will soon dissipate. You're safe, Ria. That's all that matters."

"I was cleared of the charges?"

"No." She needed a distraction. "Illumination." When she looked at him, Gyrr waited.

"Your blue lenses?"

"Discarded."

She continued staring into his eyes. "They're yours? No lenses?"

"They're real."

Soon he could tell her everything, his name, his mission. He ached to reveal his identity, to end the deception, but Gyrr held back. Before, his royal status caused him no discomfort, but now he needed to feel secure in Ria's love. Did she love him?

Gyrr wanted to be loved for himself, not as a member of the royal family and not as the son of Aaxis Thrane. He couldn't bear it if Ria's heart belonged to the title, rather than the man.

"Who is Glacidian, your father or mother?"

"You knew."

She reached up and touched his cheek. "Doc scanned your genes before she administered the toxic blocker. And Aktarians don't have this."

He grabbed her hand before she touched the nodule at the base of his ear. One day, he'd train her to give him the ultimate climax.

"My mother. My father is Aktarian and Sark. He served in the Elite."

"Your father was a soldier?"

Her slower speech, her need to concentrate as they spoke told Gyrr the drug still remained strong in her system. "Yes. Now he works for the Aktarian government."

"That explains the calluses."

"My father trained me and my brothers. We practiced for hours. I grew up with a Sarkian Falx in my hand. Are you hungry?"

She shook her head. "Thirsty."

Gyrr fetched her a container of Glacidian water. "Still tired?"

She drank deeply. "What did you give me?"

Instead of answering her question, Gyrr sat on the edge of the sleeping platform and removed his boots. "Mind if I join you? I've missed my furs."

After stripping off his clothes, Gyrr reached for her caftan. He slipped the garment over her head. His cock stirred at the sight of her. Her dark hair fell down her back and over her shoulders. Her skin glowed soft, deeply golden, and accented by her lush nipples. Her sensual mouth, ripe for kissing, held his attention.

"Why are we on your ship?"

He stretched out beside her on the furs. Great Gods, he'd missed his own sleeping unit. "This is my home."

She dropped her head on her bent knees and spoke through a curtain of hair. "I thought you lived on planet."

"I have a home on Aktares, but I spend most of my time on this ship." He stroked her back, caressed the gentle curve of her hip.

"Tell me what you've done."

Wrapping her hair about his hand, he pulled her close. Her breasts crushed softly against his chest. Her legs stretched out along his. "Sleep. We'll talk later."

"Answer me."

"Later. I'm exhausted."

Closing his eyes, Gyrr kept his hand about her hair. Ria would be furious when she realized what he'd done. She asked him a question, but sleep took him before he could formulate an answer.

* * * * *

The second time Ria awoke, hungry and thirsty, but with a clear head. Aden had already arisen and busied himself at the nutrition unit tucked into a small alcove in the massive room.

"I don't have porridge," he volunteered. Dressed in a white shirt, worn open, and drawstring pants favored by Aktarians, he appeared relaxed and at ease. His feet were bare.

"It's morning?"

"Yes. I'm preparing my favorite meal." He arranged eating utensils and cups upon a table set for two as he spoke. "Strong tea, feather-light cakes smothered in lansi sauce and sweet melon."

"Where are we?"

He pointed to an open door. "You have time to use the cleansing unit."

Ria did feel much better after a through washing. When she walked back into Aden's chamber, he held a caftan in his hands. Ria froze on the spot. His eyes were like silver crystals, with shots of gold. Amazing eyes. Nothing like she'd ever seen before.

"You are beautiful, Ria. No matter how often I see you, I am more enthralled than that night on Pyxis. Put this on before I forget you require nourishment."

"No more flattery. It's time to start talking and the first order of business is, what is your real name?"

"Gyrr."

"Gyrr?" She waited for his family name.

"Let's leave it at that for now."

What wasn't he telling her? Plenty. Why the continued mystery?

"You are of mixed blood, live on Aktares, and the only name you offer is a Sarkian name?"

"Many Aktarian parents honored the Supreme Ruler by giving their sons the same names as the royal princes. The name Antar is now quite common."

"Antar is an Aktarian name. Gyrr is a most honorable Sarkian name."

"That's what my father says. I understand it was the name of some ancestor of Lord Aaxis. From his Sarkian mother, I believe."

"Some ancestor!" Ria slipped into the black caftan trimmed in an intricate pattern of shimmering gold thread. "Gyrr is the warrior responsible for uniting Sark."

"Ohhh. Do you like it?"

Taking notice of the caftan, Ria realized the cloth and design were of the finest quality. The material caressed her skin.

"This isn't my garment."

"I purchased it on Zeon. When I saw it, I thought of you."

She couldn't recall the last time someone bought her a present. "Thank you, Gyrr."

"Come, sit, a delicious meal awaits."

After consuming the last of the melon, Ria sipped her tea. "I compliment your nutrition unit. I can't recall the last time I had so sumptuous a meal."

Relaxed and tired, Ria wanted to crawl back into the furs and sleep. The furs? Gyrr must have connections in high places. Mank furs were rare, so rare Ria wondered if his possession of them was legal.

"Ask."

Since she had awakened, questions, doubts and uncertainties had filled her thoughts. Whenever she'd tried to speak, he'd directed her to eat. Now, Gyrr settled those amazing eyes upon her and waited. She had far more important questions for him than how he gained possession of mank furs.

"Where are we?"

"The Odurh."

Ria placed her cup on the table. Passage through the outer rings of Aktares took skill and timing. No one willingly entered the Odurh. "We're headed for Aktares?"

"No. We're running between the particle streams."

"Great Gods! Are you insane?"

"Tracking is difficult in the Odurh, if not impossible."

"So is navigating. A minor error could obliterate this ship."

"We had to escape Zeon security."

She leaned forward as he spoke. "*We*? When did you begin making my decisions?"

"You weren't in a position to act. Sy was determined."

Ria jumped to her feet. "So you defy Portmaster Sy and brand me a traitor! Does your crew know they're fugitives?"

While her heart pounded furiously in her chest, Gyrr appeared calm. He rose slowly. "I ordered my crew to remain on Zeon. With two experienced pilots aboard and one of the fastest DK3 models operating the ship, we'll be fine."

A DK3! The more she learned about Gyrr, the less she knew about him. Either he made an immense amount of credits for his services or his father was a high-level government official. Or had he stolen a ship? The docking bays at Zeon offered a wealth of choices for a pirate. The whole Outer Regiment could be searching for this vessel. "Take me back."

"Not until your name is cleared."

"The probe would have cleared me."

"It could have killed you."

The horror of her youth and the fear of being exposed ripped through her. She'd spent her adult life trying to redeem the past. "Better to die a loyalist than to live as a traitor."

When he placed his hands on her shoulders, Ria wanted to lean into his strength, take comfort in his warrior's body, let his powerful arms hold her until she was safe.

"You don't understand. I must go back."

He shook his head. Ria tried to step away. Gyrr scooped her up, holding her firmly against his chest.

"You can't hold me against my will. You have no right to force me into being a fugitive."

"I've captured you my beautiful Sarkian maiden, and I'm making you my sex slave."

"This is not the time for levity. By now the whole Outer Regiment will be looking for us."

"They won't find us. You can't leave, or escape. You can't redirect our course. The DK3 acts upon my voice command."

He dropped her onto the furs. Ria scrambled across the large sleeping platform. His hand caught her by the ankle and dragged her back. Her caftan slid up to her waist.

Slapping her sweetly on the ass, he said, "That's more like it."

He shoved her thighs apart with a knee. Anchoring her waist by his forearm, he held her firmly. Pulling loose the drawstring of his pants, Gyrr freed his cock. Pressing Ria into the soft furs, he placed the tip between her nether lips and pushed into her moist center. He wanted her to experience the feel of the furs on her skin, on her breasts and against her pussy.

"Let my furs caress you."

Pushing the caftan up her back, Gyrr licked her skin. Later, he'd lick her pussy until she creamed. Gently, he pushed his cock deeper into her slick folds. When he had buried himself inside her, he removed her garment then his shirt.

"I'm not your slave. I am no man's slave."

"Then be my lifemate."

Every muscle in her body clenched including the ones surrounding his cock.

"Never!"

"Great Gods! You can hate me, but hold onto my cock."

"Do not play with me."

He drove into her, withdrew and plunged deeply. "I intend to spend my life, playing with you, loving you, fucking you. Accept me as your lifemate."

"I can't."

Thrusting harder, deeper, his heart thumping wildly, Gyrr drove inside her. Why did she deny him? Her pussy grew slicker, wetter with each stroke. They were perfect lovers, yet she refused him.

"You can. You will."

Cupping one breast, he fondled her, teasing her nipple with his fingertips while driving his cock relentlessly into her tight pussy, forcing her clit into the furs.

Faster, deeper, he plunged, until she cried out and her juices flooded her passage. Her climax triggered his. He stilled, spilling semen into her womb.

For several minutes, they lay upon the furs, his body draped over hers. Slowly, their harsh breathing settled into an easy rhythm. Gyrr kicked off the loose pants that had worked their way down his legs and remained wrapped about one ankle.

"I have to go back."

Pushing her hair to one side, Gyrr kissed her cheek. "Trust me, Ria. We are one."

Although he rolled onto his back, Ria didn't turn into the comfort of his arms. Instead, she curled into a fetal position and would not face him. "I can't. You don't know—"

Sy's sources were excellent. His heart heavy, Gyrr had listened to every painful detail of Ria's life. Perhaps, if she'd share the past with him, he could help her bear the hurt and pain. He reached out and briefly caressed her shoulder. "Test me. See if I stand by your side."

"My mother was a sex slave, trained as her mother was trained. My heritage."

Finally, she'd chosen to open her past, and hopefully her heart. "On Aktares sex is an art form."

"On Aktares, a woman is given a choice and she is not discriminated against for her profession. On Sark, a sex slave is forbidden to take a lifemate, but is allowed to birth one illegitimate child. A daughter must follow in her mother's footsteps. A son is forced into military service and may never become an officer. He is sterilized and is forbidden to take a lifemate."

Aware of the bitterness in her words, Gyrr remained silent. She needed to speak, to tell him what she perceived as the shame of her life in her own way. After a long moment, she spoke.

"At sixteen, she was assigned to the *Ultus*. Her job was to keep the officers, all ten of them, pleasured."

When she balled her hands into tight fists, Gyrr resisted the urge to pull her into his arms. He wanted to protect her from the painful memories, but Ria needed to talk and to heal.

"When the ship docked on the Merak skyport, she requested permission to take leave for several hours for shopping. Instead, she joined a group of settlers headed for Kochab. Security was lax and she escaped. I was born there."

Gyrr turned on his side. He didn't touch Ria, but he wanted her to know he lay within mere inches. "One of the officers was your father?"

"Yes. We moved often to avoid the authorities. No one knew I was the child of a sex slave. I didn't know until… Eventually, my father brought me to Sark.

"I wept when the Lord Chancellor convinced the council to abolish the practice. Not because of the sex slavery, but because women could finally join the military. I wanted to be a soldier."

"Your mother was finally freed."

"Death had freed her before the law changed."

He ached to drag her into his arms and hold her tight. Instead, he rested is hand on her upper arm. "I'm sorry, Ria. How did she die?"

"The time on Kochab destroyed her health. Some are severely affected by the dust from the mines. The particles of diamrrit float in the air."

"Do you have any ill effects?"

"I was born on Kochab. Particles remain in my lungs, but I am fine."

Gyrr made a mental note to have her examined at the first opportunity.

Sitting up, Gyrr balanced his weight on one arm. "Your mother was a brave woman. I owe you an apology, Ria."

She turned and looked up at him.

"I meant no disrespect when I told you I had captured you and intended to make you my sex slave."

He didn't tell her, he'd teased her deliberately, hoping to force open the door of the past. Once she realized her secrets would not, could not change his heart, perhaps she'd agree to becoming his lifemate.

"Did you know about my mother?"

He placed a hand on her hip. Now that she'd opened up to him, he dare not let her put any physical distance between them. "Yes."

"Why didn't you stop me?"

"I wanted you to tell me. We are one, Ria. There is no shame in your heritage."

She tried to move away. "You're part Sark. When your family, your friends learn the truth, you won't feel the same."

He tightened his grip. "My heart will not change. My family will support us. As for my friends, should they voice an objection, I will not longer value their companionship."

Although Ria ached to believe him, life had taught her the cruel lesson of reality. "You cannot give up your life for me. One day you will regret it."

"You don't know my heart."

She grasped his wrist, but he slid a thigh over hers.

"While we're alone, far from the social realities of life, accepting my past is easy. When you face the humiliation, the shame, things will change."

His gaze remained fast to hers.

"The day you see humiliation on my face or find shame in my heart, you'll be allowed to leave me."

He didn't understand. She did. "You can't force me to stay."

"Try leaving me, Ria. Try."

While on his ship, she had no choice. Convincing him to return to Zeon would be difficult, but no other solution made sense. They couldn't remain in the Odurh forever.

He kissed her on the forehead.

"I love you, Ria. I believe in you." His gaze met hers. "What will it take to make you believe in me?"

She slid her fingers into his hair and exposed the bump on his neck. "Teach me how to manipulate your pleasure node."

He rose to his knees. "Face me."

She kneeled before him. Remembering Doc's words, Ria changed her mind. "I can't. Doc warned me. I could hurt you."

A smile curled his lips. "You could also give me immense pleasure."

"Did — have others given you pleasure?"

"When I was young and living on Glacid, yes. There it is a normal and necessary part of the learning process. I've never taught a lover."

"Why?"

He picked up her hand. "Because the practice takes skill and trust must be absolute."

She tried to pull it back, but Gyrr held her hand firmly in his grasp. "Ria, your commitment must be total."

"Can you apply pressure to bring yourself to climax?"

He grinned. "Of course. When I began to reach puberty, I was sent to Glacid. Pleasuring oneself is the first part of the process."

"The women of Glacid are very fortunate. If the pleasure is so intense, why didn't you take a Glacidian female as your lifemate?"

Looking her in the eye, he pressed his lips to her palm. "Because I didn't fall in love until I saw you on Pyxis."

Despite logic, Ria had to admit something had happened on Pyxis. She'd broken a long-standing decision and had sex with a stranger. Some would call it fate. "I couldn't possibly give you as much pleasure as a Glad."

"Masturbating provides pleasurable release. Fucking is an incredible combination of the senses. Fucking the one you love is pure ecstasy. Having the one you love apply the pressure hold while making love is beyond measure."

"You've never..." Ria shivered at the thought of sharing something unique and special with this man who had touched her heart.

"I've never been in love before."

"Teach me."

Lifting her hand, Gyrr placed her fingertip beside the node. "Don't touch it yet. Move your fingertip around the nodule. Slowly. Don't press."

Ria began to move her fingertip then hesitated.

"Don't stop. Trust yourself."

Taking a deep breath, Ria began moving her fingertip over his skin. Using a circular motion she edged her fingertip closer to the node, until the pad settled over the small bump. When Gyrr cried out, Ria, fearing she'd hurt him, retracted her hand.

"I can't wait till you master the technique. Look at my cock.

Dropping her gaze, Ria saw that his cock was thick and hard. "It looks bigger. Is that possible?"

"Yes. Stimulation to the node pumps more blood into my cock. The desire to mate increases. I want to fuck you, Ria, badly, but if I entered you now, and you used even the slightest pressure, we could hurt one another."

"I wish I had a pleasure node."

"You do, my love. Do I not pleasure your clit with my tongue, lips, fingers and cock?"

"I can't die from it!"

"Then I'll improve my technique."

Ria smiled and touched her fingertip to his neck just below the node. "I want to make you come!"

"Gently move around it, then over it. No direct pressure."

Concentrating, Ria encircled the node. When her fingertip slid over it, Gyrr gasped. Around and over, she skimmed the small nodule.

Gyrr's breathing increased, but he held himself immobile. The muscles in his arms bunched and perspiration beaded across his forehead.

"Stop."

Ria carefully withdrew her fingertip. "I didn't hurt you?"

"It's difficult not to move when my heart is beating so fast, but until you are sure of your movements, we have to take it slow. I'm so hard, I feel ready to burst."

"Then let me relieve your pain."

Leaning down, Ria took him in her mouth. She caressed his thighs, loving the feel of his muscles beneath her palm. Cupping his balls, she gently massaged the tight sac. A groan, akin to a roar, tore from his throat. He thrust his hands into her hair and urged her to take him deeper.

"Suck me," he cried, between gasps. "Show me no mercy."

Working his hot flesh with her mouth, tongue and fingers, Ria felt him shudder. She'd brought him to the edge.

"Ria, I need you."

Barely, hearing the whispered words he uttered, Ria released him and straddled his thighs. Wet with need, eager to join, she guided his throbbing cock, covering the broad tip with her nether lips. Hips pumping, she accepted his rock-hard length. Although his muscles vibrated and his skin dewed with perspiration, he didn't move. Given total control, Ria rode him until her body screamed with joy.

His chest expanded as he gulped air. "Are you all right?"

"I'm fine. You're still hard as stone. Make love to me."

Repositioning her beneath him, Gyrr moved gently at first. Urging him, Ria grabbed at his cock, her flesh needing the feel of his hard length. He pushed, deeper, faster, she met him thrust for thrust. Her orgasm radiated from her center, consuming her like fingers of fire wrapping around her.

She opened her eyes to find Gyrr smiling down at her. His eyes glowed, pleased and sated. "That was intense. I feel like you sucked my balls through my cock, then strangled it with your pussy."

"Sounds painful."

"Believe me, it felt great. My legs…I don't think I can stand right now."

"Rest."

Gyrr rolled off and gathered her to him. "Will you sleep with me?"

"Can any woman resist a warrior offering the luxury of mank furs?"

A delightfully, sexy grin curled his lips.

Snuggled within the crook of his arm, Ria asked, "What will it be like when I can use the pressure hold while you're inside me?"

"We have to take it easy until you can sense the correct amount of pressure. Control is everything. When you know, our lovemaking will be extraordinary."

"How will I know?"

"Don't think about what you're doing. Know my body, learn my reactions, feel my response. Let your heart be your guide."

The next time Ria awoke, she'd reacted to the sudden lurch of Gyrr's body. Before she could sit up, he'd scramble from the furs and commanded the lights on. He snatched his discarded pants from the floor. "Get dressed. We've got company."

Climbing off the sleeping platform, Ria searched for her caftan. "Turn me over to them. Tell them I forced you into taking me. I'll go back to Zeon."

He shoved his arms into the sleeves of his shirt. "I doubt my brother will believe that."

She slid the caftan over her head. Had she heard him correctly? "Brother?"

"Did you expect the Outer Regiment?"

She had.

He pulled her into his arms and kissed her hard. He took her by the hand. "Come. It's time I started introducing you to the family."

Ria planted her feet. "I can't meet him like this. I have no shoes, no underwear."

His gaze slid over her. "You look...too beautiful...perhaps something more conservative would be better. Can't have my own brother lusting after my woman."

He pointed to the far wall opposite the meal alcove. "I think you'll find what you need in the closet. Choose what you like. Once Xxan's aboard, I'll bring him to meet you."

After Gyrr left, Ria used the cleansing unit. Hair braided, she searched the closet and found underwear, a bronze-colored caftan and brown slippers. Although the clothes were beautiful, the material soft and luxurious, and the slippers comfortable, Ria wished for her uniform and boots. At the very least, pants.

The feminine clothing made her feel vulnerable, aware she stood upon someone else's turf, without a job, without a home, without access to her credits, completely dependent. She wanted to stand on her own and not to lean on Gyrr or his family.

In Sarkian tradition, the man controlled the household and everything about his woman's life. Many in the younger generation had broken with tradition. Pol and Doc had a partnership of sorts. Still, Pol's needs and goals were primary. Although Gyrr wasn't raised on Sark, experience had taught her men expected their lifemates to share their lives on their terms. To keep her independence, she'd rather remain Gyrr's lover.

The idea that she worried over the issue of becoming Gyrr's lifemate, struck Ria with surprise. The man had a way of making her believe the impossible. She couldn't accept his proposal. She couldn't burden the man she loved with her past.

Gyrr had learned about her mother and he'd accepted that for now. But if Sy had told him about Natrh and the real reason she was dismissed from military service, and if he had learned about her father, the traitor, surely he would have prompted her when they had spoken of her mother.

No man could hold such knowledge private when he professed to be in love. Best she tell Gyrr the whole truth and given him reason to end it before his brother, or a family member, exposed her. She couldn't live through that again.

Ria should have expected Gyrr's brother would stand as tall, but the sheer size of the man introduced as Xxan gave her pause. He wore fitted trousers, belted to emphasize his flat stomach and narrow waist. His boots were trimmed with dark fur to match the vest adorning his bare chest. His golden skin was deeper in color, closer to her skin tone, than the lighter hue of his brother.

His brown hair was shot with streaks of deep gold and fell well below his shoulders. His eyes were golden with dark shards reminding her of the desert lynx. Despite his warrior-like appearance, Xxan's eyes held warmth and his smile reminded her of Gyrr. Even if Gyrr hadn't told her, she would have suspected Xxan was his brother.

He took her hand and lifted it to his lips. Calluses ridged his palm.

"I can see the reason you've defied our father, little brother. Welcome to the family, Ria Torr."

Unsure of how to respond, Ria smiled.

"You can let go of her hand now," Gyrr prompted.

Sighing dramatically, Xxan released her hand and winked at her. "Get used to it, brother. Your woman is exquisite."

Ignoring his teasing compliment, Ria asked, "What do you mean, he's defied your father?"

"Our father doesn't like us playing tag in the Odurh."

Tag?

"Don't listen to Xxan."

"We used to challenge each other to see who could race through the rings the fastest. I usually won."

"Did not."

Xxan merely smiled at Gyrr's protest. "Although we no longer race, it is the safest place if one is hiding. It seems my little brother has gotten himself into a bit of trouble. Angering General Sy is not wise."

"Because of me. Talk some sense into him, Xxan. I wish to return to Zeon and prove my innocence. I am more than willing to submit to a mind probe to do it."

Xxan's golden eyes narrowed. "I think I'm beginning to understand."

"I don't." Ria tried another approach. "He took me against my will and is holding me prisoner. As a Sarkian citizen, I demand to be returned to Zeon and face my accusers."

Xxan's left eyebrow raised a fraction. "Feisty?"

"Passionate."

"I rather prefer them that way."

"Will the two of you stop speaking as if I weren't present? I am no man's woman and no one's captive!"

"Ouch! If you wish to leave this lout, I'll take you on my ship."

"To Zeon?"

Gyrr snagged her braid with his hand and wrapped it about his palm. Within seconds her body slammed softly into his. His gaze bored into hers, holding her as surely as the iron muscles in his arms held her. "You are mine. If any man wishes to take you, he'll have to challenge me. Remember that."

"Sorry, Ria. I know he'll insist on ice blades, and I'm far too young and too handsome to die."

In that moment, logic died and Ria's heart pounded with pride. His passionate declaration, his determination to fight for her, touched her as no man had ever touched her. "I've seen him in action, your decision is wise."

"Now that's settled, how can I help you?"

"I need you to contact Sy and obtain an update on the situation. Also, you must tell Father not to come to Zeon. He must let me handle my own affairs. I will not allow my decisions to reflect upon him."

"I'll do my best to convince Father to leave this to us. I have spoken with Sy. She urged me to find you and convince you to return to Zeon."

"Until Ria is cleared, that's not an option."

Ria feared for Ania and Ula. "Has Sy performed the probe on my second officer or my com-tech?"

"I think Sy has eliminated your com-tech as a suspect."

"That's good. What of Second Officer Onacc?"

"I do not know. Sy has informed Councilman Onacc that Ania is a suspect. She awaits his answer concerning permission to perform the probe. I don't think the Councilman is as supportive of his granddaughter as she would have Sy believe. I understand he had arranged a marriage to a wealthy merchant nearly twice her age and her refusal caused him considerable embarrassment."

"I gathered that the relationship between Ania and her parents was strained," Ria offered. "But she said nothing of an arranged marriage. I always thought she had someone special on planet, but she was very private about her life and I respected that."

"Because of the women's rights law, her family couldn't force her into marriage." Xxan folded his arms before him. "When Ania refused, her father told her she was no longer welcomed in their home. None of her relatives will acknowledge her. I think her family expected her to give in and agree to the marriage. Instead, she took a position aboard the *Telum*. Do you think Officer Onacc is a traitor?"

If Gyrr's brother decided to help her, he had to believe in her innocence. "If you had asked me that before, I would have said no. Now, I'm not sure of anything. I'm not a traitor. I had no knowledge of those weapons. That leaves Ania as the logical candidate."

His penetrating gaze remained on Ria for several heartbeats. She realized Xxan evaluated her and weighed her words.

"If Sy gains permission to perform the probe, perhaps we will discover the truth and the traitors," Xxan said. "If Ania is guilty, she couldn't have acted alone. Someone in Arc headquarters and on Pyxis conspired to get those weapons aboard your ship."

He turned his attention his brother.

Gyrr released her hair, but continue to hold her close. "I regret dragging you into this, but I can't contact Sy and I dare not contact Father."

"I'll contact Father and Sy. You'll hear from me the moment I have any news, good or bad. In the meantime stay put and out of communication. Sy hasn't told anyone of Ria's escape or that she's aboard your ship. That's as much as Sy can give us, but time is running out."

"We'll wait to hear from you. If my decision displeases Father..."

The two brothers clasped hands. "I wondered why you insisted I come aboard." Xxan's gaze settled briefly on Ria. "I now know why. If anyone will understand your decision, your commitment, it would be Father."

Ria's fate depended on Gyrr and Xxan. Despite their confidence, Ria worried. All the evidence pointed to her as the traitor. She should tell them about her father. Before they defended her, she owed them the truth.

When Xxan started to leave, Ria spoke up.

"Before you go, I think I should tell you—"

Gyrr's arm tightened about her waist. "Nothing you will say will change my mind."

"Perhaps, but if are willing to support me, I owe you the truth."

"You're trembling."

Guiding her to the sleeping platform, Gyrr sat beside her. Xxan remained standing.

Looking into Gyrr's eyes, Ria told her darkest secret. Never had she told anyone about her father. "The officer aboard the *Ultus*, my father, he helped my mother escape. Like you, he deserted his duty."

"He loved her."

Tears welled in Ria's eyes. Would Gyrr doom himself to the same fate as her father had? "He paid a price for his love. An Elite does not choose anything over the regiment. He broke his word. He suffered greatly for his decision."

Xxan inhaled a quick breath. "Your father was an Elite?"

"He had to wear gloves in public, to hide his palms. He labored as a miner on Kolchab until my mother died in his arms."

Gyrr squeezed her shoulder, offering sympathy. "He brought you back to Sark?"

A tear slid down her cheek. She swiped it with the back of her hand. "Yes. We moved often. One day I came home to find our house surrounded by soldiers. We ran.

"He told me I couldn't stay with him any longer. Fearing I'd be with him when he was caught, he arranged for me to attend a school in Ferizz."

Be a good little soldier.

"The headmaster was an old friend. I lived in a dormitory. Father visited me every few months. The last time I saw him, he was being tried for treason, accused of selling information about the weapons system aboard the *Ultus* to an arms dealer from Vidar. That was the reason he was assigned to the ship, to test an experimental weapon.

"My father swore he did not sell the information. He admitted he had deserted. I couldn't speak to him or touch him. He was convicted, and executed as a traitor."

"Draa Ammar?"

Throughout her story, Gyrr's arm had remained firmly about her. As she revealed the truth, Ria had waited for his hand to slip from her shoulder, for his recoil. Even when he spoke her father's name, something forbidden to all in the Elite forces, he continued to hold her.

"You knew?"

Gyrr shook his head. "No. I remember hearing the story while training with the Elite."

"How did you come by the name of Torr?" Xxan asked.

"Torr was the name my parents married under on Kolchab."

"Thank you for telling us, " Xxan said. "It's time for me to leave."

Gyrr kissed her, a quick, sweet brush of his lips to hers. "I'll be right back."

Alone, Ria let the tears flow. For years she hadn't spoken of her parents. Not since that last night with Natrh. Grief shook her to the core. Her heart ached for her parents and for the past she'd thrust upon Gyrr's broad shoulders. She still had one horrible secret to tell.

Compared to treason, her parting with Natrh was a tawdry episode. Still, Gyrr deserved the naked truth.

Exhausted, Ria removed her clothing and slippers and burrowed into the comfort and warmth of Gyrr's furs. If it were possible and if the Gods would bless her, she would remain on his ship, forever. But Gyrr had a family on Aktares and responsibilities.

The tears came, for her parents, for herself, and for Gyrr.

When she awoke in Gyrr's arms, Ria smiled. Even her heart smiled. Despite her confession, he'd chosen her over family and duty. She prayed she would not bring harm upon this brave warrior who had convinced her he truly did love her.

Without speaking, he shifted his weight on his knees, between her thighs and probed her center with the tip of his hard cock. As he slid inside her, his lips covered hers.

His tongue slowly tasted her. His cock moved deeper, filling her. His slow, deliberate thrusts making her ache with need. His big hand, capable of handling a falx or finessing an ice blade, held her breast in a gentle caress.

Ria knew he was teaching her the difference between fucking and making love. His cock, his body, his lips were giving her comfort and with each sweet stroke Gyrr was pledging his heart as surely as if he were uttering the words.

His love soothed her pain and his heat drove the cold from her body. Wrapped in his warmth, Ria gasped as a thousand tiny tremors shook her. Gyrr stilled, his body shuddering. Holding him tight, Ria refused to let loose of him.

Understanding her need, Gyrr remained still.

When her hold eased, he kissed her. "I love you."

"I pray I never make you regret it."

"You won't. You can't. We are one."

She loved the feel of his big, strong body, covering hers. She felt safe, protected. Fear of discovery had driven her life. Her unwillingness to form close friendships had become so much a part of her emotional fabric only Doc and the man she knew as Aden had managed to penetrate the shield formed by her parent's legacy and Natrh's betrayal.

Aden the lover had transformed into Gyrr, the man of her dreams. "I wish we were."

"A Glad mates for life. It's beyond the thunder of the blood and the wildness of the heart. For a Sark or an Aktarian, love can fade or change with time. My Glacidian blood guides my heart. I have bonded."

"You mean you can't fuck anyone else?"

"Don't get cocky about it."

"Ohhhh, Gyrr, I want to get cocky about it." She stroked his hip. "I want to crow. Can this bond transfer to me? Am I bound to you?"

He didn't speak. She realized why. He'd feared she did not return his love or his commitment. As a Sark, could she bond?

"Since *we* are bonded, I have to tell you about Natrh."

"*We* are what is important. The past is not. I'd prefer to leave the past, both our pasts, in the past."

Ria caressed his cheek. "I do not want to know how many women have known you. I'm sure I cannot count that high. But what happened... I'd rather you learned my version of why I was dismissed from the military."

He didn't speak, but simply nodded. It took a moment for Ria to gather her courage.

"I met Natrh while in pilot training. For months, I ignored his advances. After graduation, we were assigned to different ships. Fate brought us back together again when I joined the crew of the *Isii*. The *Isii* ran supplies to the main docking stations for the Sarkian fleet. I preferred the long runs to the Outer Regiment, but my request was denied.

"One night while on station, I ran into Natrh. He bought me dinner. We had a few drinks. After that night, we began to contact each other on a weekly basis. Eventually, we became lovers."

Realizing she'd been staring at her hands, Ria looked up. She couldn't read Gyrr's expression, but she knew she had his undivided attention.

"After several months, he asked me to marry him. I refused. No one knew about my father and although I thought I loved Natrh, I couldn't take the chance his parents would probe into my background. Lineage is everything to Sarks and mine isn't the kind you present to the relatives.

"Although I had never accepted his proposal, he told his father of his intentions. Apparently, his father found out about my mother."

Gyrr reached out and covered her hand with his. She held onto him, tight.

"As was our custom, Natrh and I planned to meet in one of the recreation rooms used by sex-providers on station. He'd rent the room and pay the provider to disappear for a couple of hours so I could sneak in. We knew if we were caught, both of us could face disciplinary action.

"When I entered the room, Natrh hit me. He started screaming at me. I figured he'd learned about my father, but instead he told me my mother had been a sex slave."

Ria drew in a slow breath. "I denied it, but he had proof. His uncle was an officer in the records division. When Natrh told his family he wanted to marry me, his uncle checked into my background. He had access to records I had never seen. I also didn't realize that the military had been giving sex slaves special inhibitors for the last two hundred years to prevent them from infecting the troops they served with any sexual diseases. Those inhibitors are passed from mother to infant and appeared in my blood scans, but since the law had been changed, the military had sealed my records. Even my commanding officer did not know, but those records were presented in my hearing."

"I'm sorry, Ria. I'm sorry Natrh hurt you. But I'm glad you didn't marry him. Fate saved you for me."

Clutching his hand with all her strength, Ria continued. "That isn't the worst of it. Natrh believed I knew about my mother and he'd set up a surprise to punish me for embarrassing him.

"He drugged me with one of those stimulants used by the sex-providers, then he fucked me one last time. He wanted to hurt me and he did. But that wasn't his surprise. He told me I should have become a provider instead of a pilot and he would make sure I could never entrap another officer as I had him.

"There were six of them, all of them officers from his ship. He watched and taunted while they used me. Then he reported me to my commanding officer. The seven of them testified against me. I was discharged."

Wrapping his arms about her, Gyrr gathered her to him. He held her close and stroked her hair. When her sobs had ceased, he lifted her chin. Ria looked into his eyes. "I love you, Ria."

"You asked why I ignored the Sarkian officers on Pyxis. Now you know."

"Yet, given everything, you chose me."

"You're different. You were from the first. I don't know why, but you make me feel safe."

"You are my lifemate, I would give my life for you. Pray I never meet Natrh or any of his friends."

"I will remain with you, but not as your lifemate."

He cupped her cheek. His thumb caressed her temple. "Share my furs, Ria. Bear my children."

She kissed his palm, reminding him of his commitment to the Elite. "The daughter of a traitor? Can you dismiss the past, give up the life you have known?"

"Can you?"

"I will remain with you, as your woman, on this ship. A man is forgiven his choice of mistress, but his lifemate carries his name, represents him publicly. As an Elite, you cannot bring that shame upon your family or the regiment."

"Since the Sarkian Women's Rights Act, the heritage of sex slavery brings no shame."

"Changing the law doesn't change minds. When men know you are the daughter of a trained sex slave, they look at you differently and without respect."

"Any man who treats you thus, will face my challenge."

"You cannot fight the whole planet. I'll wager there are Aktarians who feel the same. I don't know why we're discussing the impossible. I'm a fugitive. I may not have a future."

"*We* have a future. If necessary, we'll make one elsewhere."

"You can't run from your past, you can only keep it hidden for a period of time. Believe me. I must prove my innocence. If I hide behind you, everyone will assume I am guilty and when the identities of my mother and father are exposed, your protection will be viewed by many as an act of treason."

He shook his head. "I love you too much."

"Love me enough to give me freedom. I cannot be condemned for something I did not do."

"You believe your father innocent, yet he went to his death."

"If he'd had the choice or the opportunity, I know my father would have chosen a mind probe to prove himself truthful, no matter what the cost."

"I will take you back on one condition. You will become my lifemate. You will agree to a public ceremony on Aktares with my family in attendance."

His determination to officially bind with her brought another onslaught of tears to Ria's eyes. If she did not agree to his terms, he'd remain on the run, defying his father, breaking his oath to the Elite. Should the probe leave her mindless, his condition wouldn't apply. If all went well, could she put off the ceremony long enough to convince Gyrr of the benefits of having a mistress?

"Agreed."

"Pledge your life to mine, on the hearts of your mother and father."

"I pledge."

"Accept me as thy husband, as protector and provider."

He'd proposed, formally, as was the custom of Sarks for over a thousand years. Ria's heart swelled. If they binded in a public ceremony, he would repeat those words.

His gaze narrowed.

"I accept."

His lips captured hers, moving tenderly as his tongue stroked hers. Ria expected another lusty session of lovemaking, but Gyrr lifted his head and rolled off of her. He slapped her smartly on the ass then cupped her flesh. His finger slid along the crease. He lifted his hand. "Out of my furs, my love, before I forget we have two missions to accomplish."

"Two?"

Picking up his trousers, he began to dress. "Proving your innocence and preparing for our binding ceremony."

After slipping his shirt over his head, he pulled on his boots. Climbing out of the furs, Ria stood before him. Although desire smoldered in his eyes, Gyrr did not touch her.

"The next time we make love, you'll be my lifemate."

"What?"

"You gave your word. I intend to hold you to it."

"But--"

He strode to the door. "If you want to fuck me, you'll have to marry me."

CHAPTER EIGHT

"Are you ready, Captain Torr?"

Isolated in a small room in the detention unit on Zeon, strapped to a narrow operating table much like the one Doc used in sick bay for examinations, her head supported by a collar surrounding her neck and the back of her skull, Ria sucked on the tube Sy had placed in the corner of her mouth. "I'm ready."

Leaning close, Sy's face filled her vision. The Siluko's penetrating eyes fastened on hers. The tube slipped from Ria's mouth.

"I feel like I had one too many blasters."

"Look deeply into my eyes until you see flickers of light."

Tiny fragments of white light flashed before Ria. Everything receded from her vision except the flashes, white to intense blue.

Sy's fingers touched her temples.

"Relax. Tell me what you see."

"Blue flashes."

"Good. Do not speak. Concentrate on the flashes."

Pain, nothing like she'd ever felt before, blanketed her skull. Then the intense pain subsided to a dull ache. When the blue flashes ceased, Ria opened her eyes.

"Captain Torr?"

"It's over?"

Appearing relaxed, Sy took a chair near the foot of the table. "It is, but I want you to remain as you are for a little while longer."

"You've documented my life in a few seconds?"

"It's been closer to an hour. I documented only those events relevant to this case. Nothing else. No one will learn your memories. You have my word. You have proven your innocence."

Relief swamped her. "I feel so tired."

"That's the usual reaction to a probe. I think you should let Gyrr know what is in your heart. He needs to hear the words, Ria. We all do."

Sy's use of her first name conveyed the importance of the Siluko's advice and Ria's position as a friend. The label of suspect no longer applied.

"You know my past, how can I burden him with the shame?"

The Siluko's wide lips curled into a smile. "Like his father, he has broad shoulders and a big heart."

"In good conscience, I cannot become his lifemate."

"You're a lucky woman, Ria Torr. You have a man who will stand at your side with pride no matter what events color your past."

"He claims he will challenge anyone to defend my honor."

"He will. The Lord Chancellor defended mine. To many I was thought of as nothing more than an animal. When he made me his personal bodyguard, he demonstrated his respect and his belief in me. He was criticized on both Sark and Aktares."

"You have proven them wrong."

"And so shall you."

Ria wanted to believe she and Gyrr could overcome the realities of her past. He wanted children. Could she protect her child from those realities?

"I must convince Gyrr to release me from my pledge."

"It's too late to change your mind. He's told his mother. Plans for your ceremony are underway."

"I must speak to her."

Sy purred. "I'll arrange it."

"How?"

"She's here on Zeon. Gyrr left a friend behind when he ran for the Oburh. His friend felt compelled to inform Gyrr's mother."

"I don't want Gyrr to know."

"He's waiting in the next room. After he sees you are well, I'll tell him you need to remain here with me so I can observe. If you think you're strong enough, I will bring her to you."

"I'm strong enough."

"I'm going to leave you restrained, otherwise he'll want to take you back to the consort's quarters."

"Thank you, Portmaster."

"You may call me Sy."

"Thank you, Sy."

When Sy rose from her chair, Ria remembered her crew. Before she administered the probe, Sy refused to answer any questions.

"How is my crew?"

"All, except Officer Onacc have been cleared. Gyrr has made arrangements for them. Soon they'll be on their way home with credits equal to the bonuses they would have received if the *Telum* had finished its mission."

"Ania?"

"I received permission from Councilman Onacc. I performed the probe hours ago."

"Did she know about the weapons?"

"She had fallen in love with a smuggler, a Sark called Jinn. Pyxis was the base for his operations. He convinced her his plan was foolproof. And it would have been if one of the rebels hadn't exposed the plot."

"Who hired Jinn?"

"Farll, an executive at Arc. He provided Ania with your code. The Sarkian authorities arrested Jinn and he exposed Farll who was a member of the Nejd. You've aided the Sarkian government in uncovering a plot to undermine the Lord Chancellor's efforts in Vidar. You've aided in the prevention of a civil war. I understand the Lord Chancellor intends to reward you."

"It was happening right under my nose, on my ship. I think the Lord Chancellor should reward Gyrr."

"He will."

"What will happen to Ania?"

"She'll be tried on Sark. Unless her family supports her, she'll be put to death."

Ria closed her eyes. Her head hurt and her heart ached. Although, she hadn't formed a close relationship with her second officer, Ria had respected her as a pilot and intended to recommend her for advancement. Ania's betrayal to Sark and the crew of the *Telum* would carry the ultimate penalty. She'd fallen in love with the wrong man.

Had Gyrr simply fallen in love with the wrong woman? His love for her would not have such dire consequences, but as an Elite, he couldn't accept her as his wife. Thanks to the probe, Sy had cleared her. Unlike her father, Ria had proved herself innocent, but her past still threatened Gyrr.

"I would like to see my crew before they leave Zeon."

"I'll have them brought to the consort's quarters."

"Could I see Ania?"

"I'm sorry. Since you'll be expected to testify, speaking to her before the trial is impossible."

When Sy opened the door, Gyrr rushed to her side. He'd changed into the black uniform common to the Elite. The Chancellor's insignia rode over his heart. He'd tied his long hair at the nape of his neck with a black ribbon and looked every inch an officer. His gaze filled with concern, he searched her face. "Ria?"

"She's fine. Ask her anything."

"I'm okay. Just a little tired. Sy tells me I'm cleared."

"You shouldn't have agreed to this. Ania's probe would have provided proof of your innocence."

"I'm glad I did. I wanted my named cleared, officially on the record."

Gyrr reached out and caressed her face. "Why is she still restrained?"

"I'd like to observe her for a little longer. She needs to rest. Come back in an hour."

"I'd prefer to stay."

"She'll be fine. In one hour, I'll release her to you."

Leaning forward, Gyrr kissed her lips and her forehead. "I'll be back."

His gaze remained on her all the way to the door. Before the procedure, Gyrr had held her in his arms and told her he loved her. She had whispered *I love you*, but Gyrr hadn't heard.

Ria ached to hold him. She'd come to need his strength, the feel of his arms about her. Safe. She hadn't felt safe since her father had left her at school, until now.

Sy released Ria from the restraints. "Don't sit up. Your mind will be clearer if you continue to remain still. Are you sure you want to speak with Gyrr's mother?"

"Yes."

"Close your eyes and rest. I'll return."

Tired, Ria followed Sy's orders.

Sensing a presence, Ria opened her eyes. She blinked, but the image leaning over her did not vanish. Short, spiky, silver-blonde hair framed the vision's delicate Glacidian features. Eyes, shimmering like ice crystals, stared into hers. Jeweled clasps decorated the left shoulder of her ice-blue skinsuit. The vision resembled...it wasn't possible.

The vision smiled.

"Hello, Ria, I'm Tayra, Gyrr's mother."

The vision spoke her language. *I'm dreaming.* "You're the Queen."

"On Glacid. But we're on Zeon, and I think my son owes both of us an explanation, don't you?"

The probe had affected her mind. Surely, this wasn't happening. "If you're the Queen, then Gyrr is..."

"Gyrr Thrane, Prince of Glacid, Commander of the Outer Regiment."

Thrane! Ria sat up. For a moment, she felt faint. "His father is... is the *Lord Chancellor*?"

The Queen smiled and nodded. "He should have told you."

"He's lost his mind."

"Excuse me?"

"Gyrr pretended to be Aden. It was all an act to find the weapons. He doesn't really want to marry me. I'm just a captain of a commercial freighter. Well, I used to be a captain. Now, I'm no one. You have to convince him to—"

"He loves you."

"Has he told you about my parents?"

"Yes. Your mother was a victim. Your father loved her enough to take her away from the *Ultus*. They were very brave to rebel against the injustice of slavery. You should be proud of them. It isn't easy to choose love over tradition."

Other than her father, no one had told her to be proud of the woman who had given her life. "But I would bring shame to your family."

The Queen picked up her hand and held it between hers. "Never. You have a family to protect you, Ria. If anyone speaks ill of you, they will face the wrath of the Thranes. We're quite formidable."

"I'm dreaming."

"I understand my son has asked you to share his furs."

Ria recalled Gyrr saying that to her before they made love. "Yes."

"He asked you to become his lifemate. On Glacid, our warriors propose by asking us to share their furs."

"He asked me to accept him as a husband. I only agreed so he would return me to Zeon so I could clear my name. I will not hold him to the proposal."

"You do not love him?"

"I love him very much, but my father is a convicted traitor."

"Gyrr told me you believed your father innocent."

"He would never betray Sark or the Elite."

"My husband has some influence with the Elite. He has promised to inquire into your father's case."

Ria fisted her right hand and placed it over her heart. "The Lord Chancellor."

"The Lord Chancellor is quite wonderful, isn't he?"

"My father loved him."

For a moment the Queen studied her. "I hope you don't mind, but my daughters have already begun to plan your ceremony. Gyrr is the first to marry, and his sisters are thrilled."

"But I can't marry him."

"Why not? The way I see it, you're the only one objecting."

The Queen placed her hands on Ria's shoulders and kissed her on both cheeks. Ria didn't know what to say or how to respond. One couldn't tell the Queen she'd lost her mind.

"Our time has passed. If I know Gyrr, he'll be here any moment. Marry him, Ria. Make my son happy."

Amazed, Ria watched the Queen of Glacid slip a matching blue cloak over her shoulders and walk out of the room.

Lying back on the table, Ria tried to deal with the knowledge that she'd picked up the Prince of Glacid in a relaxation bar and then fucked his brains out. What if the Veks hadn't attacked, would she have ever seen him again? Ria doubted it.

All this time, she'd been fucking a Prince. That accounted for his mixed heritage, but not for his lies.

Before she could count them all, the Prince strode into the room and stood at the foot of the table. "You know?"

"Why did you lie to me?"

"When we met, I was on my way to Zeon to meet with a Cheddian rebel leader. I couldn't meet with him in my official capacity, so I traveled under the idenity of Aden Conr."

"And if Veks hadn't attacked?"

"I intended to see you again, either here on Zeon, or on Vidar. I'm scheduled to attend a state dinner with the Vidarian Tetrarch. I was going to ask you to accompany me."

Ria pushed herself up and leaned on her hands. "You were going to ask a Capha2 pilot to attend a state dinner?"

"I was. As my lifemate, your attendance will be mandatory. Fittings for your new wardrobe will begin tomorrow."

"Why didn't you tell me? Even when you asked me to share your furs, you didn't tell me. Don't you think I should know exactly who I was agreeing to marry?"

"I wanted you to love me for myself, not because I'm a Thrane."

"But you *are* a Thrane, a Prince. You have to marry someone famous or sophisticated."

A smile curled his lips as he closed the short distance between them. "You'll be famous the moment our intentions are made public."

"Think about this, Gyrr."

"You gave me your pledge. Besides, I thought you and Mother had settled the matter."

"You lied to me."

"Never. I omitted certain details."

"Like my father works for the government?"

"He does."

"The guy who issues rover licenses and inspects outgoing cargo works for the government. Your father *is* the government."

"He'd disagree with that statement. The people are the government. We're merely the hired help."

"Some hired help."

Gyrr bent down, scooped her into his arms and marched out of the room.

"I can walk."

She wasn't sure if that was true, but he ignored her protest.

"I'm putting you to bed. No arguments."

Bed sounded good. Since he'd decided to bring her back to Zeon, he'd done no more then paste chaste kisses upon her face and lips.

He carried her down a long, narrow corridor before stopping before Sy's private lift. Within a few minutes, they were inside the consort's quarters. He lowered her onto the wide sleeping platform and proceeded to strip her naked.

After covering her with mank fur, he kissed her briefly on the lips.

"I brought my furs to keep you warm."

Ria reached out and slid her hand up his thigh and over his crotch. Beneath the material of his uniform trousers, his cock stretched beneath her palm.

He removed her hand. "After the ceremony."

"You can't be serious?"

"If you want to fuck me, marry me. That's the rule."

"And if I don't?"

"A contest of wills, my sweet?"

"You said you couldn't make love to anyone else," she said, reminding him of the last time they'd lain in each other's arms.

"I can't, but I want you for my lifemate, and I'll do anything necessary to accomplish my goal."

When he walked to the door, she called out. "You can't last!"

She'd managed to ignore her body's hungers for three years prior to meeting him. If necessary, she could hold out for days, or weeks.

* * * * *

For two days Ria did little more than sleep. Although Queen Tayra had visited her often before she'd left for Aktares, Ria still had to pinch herself to believe she wasn't dreaming. Despite Ria's protests, Gyrr's mother continued to treat her as a bride.

Now Ria paced before the massive permashield in Sy's quarters waiting for her crew.

Finally, the door slid open and Gyrr escorted the twins, Ula and Doc inside. Making a quick exit, Gyrr left them alone. The twins chattered, half in Sark, mostly in Aktarian. Ula gave her a quick hello and walked straight to the permashield commenting on the amazing view. Doc hugged her.

"You have any idea what they're talking about?"

Doc laughed. "What they have been talking about since finding out your Aden is Prince Gyrr, his cock. They saw it, touched it. He'll be their claim to fame until they are old."

"You touched it."

"Purely for professional reasons. At least he doesn't have to worry about me telling everyone I meet."

"I'm sorry, Doc."

"For what? Your Prince has granted me a full scholarship to medical school. He said he'd made an agreement with you to pay our bonuses. We're set, all of us. And we've quit our jobs with Arc. We're going home, all of us. We owe you, Ria."

After sharing a meal with her crew, the time came to say goodbye. Discussing the case against Ania was forbidden. Although none had mentioned her name, Ria knew she dwelled in their thoughts.

The four of them surrounded her, thanking her. Gyrr had kept his promise. Her crew wouldn't return home, broke and out of work. The twins and Ula departed, leaving Doc and Ria one final moment together.

"I'll miss you, Captain or should I say Princess?"

"No titles for me." Ria reached out and hugged Doc. "I love you, Cirrii. Thanks for being my friend."

"I love you too, Ria."

* * * * *

With Zeon a mere speck in space, the *Praesum* raced toward Aktares and the ceremony which would bind Gyrr and Ria together for eternity, but Ria wasn't cooperating. Pushing his chair back from the communications console, Gyrr dragged his hands through his hair.

"Is something wrong, your Highness?"

Nothing several hours in Ria's arms wouldn't cure.

The need for her thundering in his blood, Gyrr had slept little. Why did he have to fall for a stubborn female, when a number of docile, biddable women lined up on a regular basis to snag a royal?

"Why doesn't she want me for a lifemate? I can offer her protection."

"Lady Ria does not worry for herself."

Husi addressed Ria as if she were already his lifemate. Although Ria had corrected his aide several times, Husi politely ignored her. Despite her fears and resistance, one day, Ria would assume the title and the obligations.

"The investigation into her father's trial could take years before an official report is issued. I can't wait that long."

"The public ceremony surrounded by the family frightens her."

"I've seen Ria take on a pack of Veks, but she's scared to take vows."

"It isn't easy for someone with humble beginnings, especially those of Ria's, to step into the belly of the Thrane clan."

Pushing himself to his feet, Gyrr paced. "You make us sound worse than Veks."

"I think if you gave Lady Ria a choice, she'd rather take on Veks. They're known quantities. She can be herself. She doesn't know how to be a Thrane."

"You could teach her, Husi. You taught me."

"I would be honored. I think you should reconsider the public ceremony. Perhaps your father could perform the binding ceremony, here aboard this ship. The Queen and I would serve as witnesses."

Gyrr ceased pacing. The idea of a quiet ceremony suited him. "But my sisters are planning an event"

"Exactly. An event planned by your sisters scares me to the core."

Husi touched him on the shoulder. "Your Highness, Gyrr."

Whenever Husi wanted his full attention, Gyrr recalled the feel of his mentor's hand on his shoulder. "This isn't your sisters' binding ceremony. It's Ria's day. What would she want?"

Husi had guided him for most of his life. His words penetrated the chaos surrounding Gyrr since he'd told his mother of his intention to bind with Ria. "I think she'd prefer privacy. Any other suggestions?"

"Take her to Vidar. Let her first official act be the state dinner. With all the systems being represented, and most in attendance not of royal stature, she'll fit in. By the time you return to Aktares, she'll be comfortable as your lifemate and I will have had time to tutor her."

"What about my sisters and mother?"

"They can plan a great party for your return. As for your mother, we shall remind her of the young Glacidian Princess who in one short ceremony became the lifemate of the Supreme Ruler of Aktares and the Lord Commander of Sark and had to find her place on two planets she had never visited, and face your grandmother. She will understand."

"You came as part of her entourage?"

"It was difficult for all of us, at first. Now I am as comfortable on Aktares as I am on Glacid. As for Sark…"

Hope filled Gyrr's heart. "Do you think Lady Ria will agree?"

"She loves you. You could ask."

"I can't live without her. I experienced the binding, the elation and the physical change. It was like nothing I'd ever felt before. I performed the chant. I understood what every Gladcidian male accepts as his destiny."

A light glowed brightly on the communication console. "Answer it, Husi. I need to speak with Ria."

Gyrr started to leave the room, but Husi called him back. "It's Portmaster Sy. It's important she speak with you."

"Put her on screen."

Sy's face filled the console screen. "Your Highness. Commander."

"I prefer Gyrr."

"Officier Onacc is on her way to Sark. The authorities will advise you of her trial date. I thought Ria would want to know."

"Thank you."

"The authorities have questioned Jinn. The Vek attack, Ria was the target. He figured Ania would be promoted and getting rid of Ria would make it possible to move more weapons."

"Did Ania know about the attack?"

"Jinn had told her Ria would be kidnapped. Since she had no relatives or friends, her disappearance wouldn't be a high priority."

"For now, let's keep this information to ourselves. I don't want Ria to know. Later, when she had time to heal, I'll tell her."

Gyrr thanked Sy and closed the secure channel. He turned to Husi. "I thought Uyin had a traitor in his camp. Great Gods, the Veks were waiting for her to return to the *Telum*."

"How fortunate the two of you met. If Lady Ria had taken three darts, she would have died in the cargo bay."

"Ria was my destiny. Do you think the pymal used in the darts affected my ability to bind?"

"The pymal or the toxin-blocker you were given could have scrambled your chemistry. Perhaps we should let Dr. Iyra know about this."

Dr. Iyra headed the Glacidian School of Medicine. Her current project centered on the effects of Sarkian and Aktarian genes upon Glacidians. "Yes, perhaps my brothers and sisters should be warned to stay away from Veks. I wonder how Xxan will feel when he learns he could get stuck with one female partner for the rest of his life?"

"How do you feel about it?"

"I only want Ria."

* * * * *

By the time they'd left Zeon and had traveled halfway to Aktares on the *Praesum*, Ria was ready to shoot someone. But since she lost her position as a captain, she no longer carried a weapon.

True to his word, Gyrr had done nothing more than kiss her. He slept in separate quarters giving her the huge fur-strewn bed they'd shared before and left her to toss and turn, and curse him for hours.

She'd done everything she could think of to tempt him. She'd tried outright nakedness, but he tended not to linger, so Ria had refused his gifts, and resumed wearing trousers and boots and tight sleeveless tops that molded to her breasts. Although his gaze often strayed to her chest and at times lingered, Gyrr never touched her.

Other than sweet pecks on her lips and forehead, he treated her as a man would a chaste virgin.

How did a man with his appetites ignore the passion he knew awaited him in his own furs?

Her patience was wearing thinner with each hour. She tossed her hairbrush across the large room just as the door slid opened. The brush bounced off Gyrr's left shoulder and landed on the floor.

"We can't go on like this."

He strode across the room, picked her up and fell upon the furs. His weight landed on top of her. His lips tasted hers. Need rose, fast and hot. She met the thrust of his tongue, the delicious pressure of his groin, the feel of his hands on her breasts with mindless joy and reciprocating eagerness.

When his mouth covered her nipple and his hand slid beneath the waistband of her trousers to touch her, Ria nearly came. His not-so-gentle tugs sent heat racing through her middle to pool between her legs. His fingers pushed lustily inside her. Arching, she ached for release.

His fingers pumped inside her, making her wetter, hotter while his mouth suckled eagerly on one breast, then the other.

Her climax slammed into her, shattering every nerve ending. Before the last tremors had ceased, Ria tore at Gyrr's uniform. He ripped her shirt and yanked her trousers down to her knees and plunged his tongue into her sex.

A few licks to her pussy brought on another set of tremors. He massaged her ass with his hands. When he suckled her clit, she filled her fists with his hair and ground her sex into his face until she cried out his name and screamed, "I love you. You win, I love you."

"It's about time."

Ria opened her eyes. Gyrr kneeled before her bent knees grinning with the results of her climax glistening on his grin.

"Since you love me, you're going to marry me." He pulled off his boots and tossed them aside. "Here on the *Praesum*." He released the seam of his trousers, freeing his rigid cock. "As soon as my parents can get here."

He climbed off the platform and began removing his trousers. "My father will perform the binding ceremony." He stood, glorious, naked, with his cock pointing at her. He reached for her boots. "Then you," One boot followed the other over his shoulder. "...and I, will head for Vidar. When we arrive, you can pilot the rover to the state dinner. I'll even race you through the rings when we return to Aktares."

"No thanks, but I'd enjoy driving the rover."

His gaze met hers. "I'm ready for a long, deep run."

"So am I."

Removing her trousers in one quick motion, he climbed between her thighs. The thick head of his cock touched her. She shifted her hips. The broad tip slid inside. A gentle thrust of his hips and she held him deep inside.

"My furs are soft and waiting."

Without Gyrr's knowledge, Husi had visited her and taught her the response in Glacidian, if ever she chose to accept the Prince's proposal.

"Your furs will keep me warm for eternity."

∗ ∗ ∗ ∗ ∗

Ria's knees nearly gave way when she met Lord Commander Aaxis. Gyrr caught her by the arm, steadying her. Nearly as tall as Gyrr and similarly dressed, the Lord Commander was glorious in his black trousers and jacket. How could she not have seen the resemblance between father and son? In person, the Lord Commander was far more handsome than his photos and the news transmissions couldn't capture the golden shards of his eyes. Not a speck of gray touched his hair. His voice sent shivers down her spine. Great Gods, she stood before royalty.

His gaze flicked from her face to Gyrr's and back again. "Are you well?"

Gyrr's soft laughter joined that of Queen Tayra.

"She's overwhelmed by your presence."

"My husband still has a dazzling affect upon females."

Far too difficult for her mind to believe this hero, this god, really stood before her, the father of the man she loved, Ria latched onto the vision she'd had since hearing her father speak of the man he'd respected and served.

Revere him. The future of our world and the Federation lies with Lord Aaxis.

Managing to pull herself together, Ria realized she had forgotten her manners and her obligation. She fisted her hand over her heart. "Lord Commander, I am humbled."

He returned her salute. "I am delighted to meet you, Ria. Welcome to our family."

"Thank you, my Lord."

Picking up her hand, he held it between his. The Lord Commander's fingers were long, his palms ridged like those of his son's. She stared at them thinking how strong and capable they were, how powerful.

"You are to call me Aaxis, and a salute is not necessary."

Shaking her head, Ria glanced at Gyrr and looked up at the most powerful man in the galaxy. "I cannot, my Lord."

Smiling at her, Lord Aaxis released her hand. "With time, you will become accustomed to our family." He placed his arm about the Queen's shoulder. "And you will become our daughter."

After leaving Gyrr's parents in Husi's capable hands, Ria and Gyrr returned to his quarters. Ria apologized. "Your father must think you are marrying a woman without manners or decorum."

"My love, I've seen grown men stammer and stutter before my father. One man actually wet his trousers. My brothers and I had quite a laugh."

"You can't understand how we mortals feel. My father would have given his life for Lord Aaxis."

Gyrr settled her into a chair. "I am mortal, Ria. I am not the powerful man my father is. I will never serve as Supreme Ruler of Aktares or Lord Chancellor of Sark. Those roles will fall to my brothers. Although I have offical duties as a Prince on Glacid, I am simply a soldier."

"Thank the Gods."

He handed her a glass of water. "Drink this. The next time you feel like falling to your knees before a man, I'd like it to be me."

Looking up at him, Ria saw the sparkle in his eyes and the smile lines about his mouth. She smiled back at him.

"Soon you'll be my lifemate." Gyrr kneeled before her. "I want children. A houseful, if you're willing. Although I am an Elite, I will put my wife, my family first."

Ria knew if enemies threatened, as an Elite he would defend the Federation. And she would support him. Right now, becoming an official Thrane was scary enough.

* * * * *

Several hours later, Ria and Gyrr kneeled before Lord Aaxis. Dressed in a white caftan, her head draped in a delicate veil of gold, Ria trembled as Gyrr turned to her.

"Accept me as thy husband, as protector and provider," Gyrr said.

As Sarkian woman had done for centuries, Ria responded, "I accept."

Gyrr lifted the intricate veil and looked down at her, his amazing eyes glowing with joy. "You honor me."

Ria repeated the phrase in Glacidian as Husi had taught her.

Smiling, Gyrr clasped her hands with his.

Lord Aaxis bound their hands with golden cord in an ancient tradition of Aktares. "Bound by commitment to one another and by the laws of Aktares, you are now one, for eternity."

After the celebration meal, Lord Aaxis and Queen Tayra returned to their ship. Ria and Gyrr were alone in his quarters as the *Preasum* changed course toward Vidar.

"Your heart is beating faster than a saisi bird."

"It's been a remarkable day. Not only did I meet the Lord Commander, but I married the man I love."

He cupped her face in his hands. "You're so very beautiful. My father told me that he still feels his breath catch when he looks at my mother. It will be so with me."

"My husband has a dazzling affect upon me."

His kiss was brief, but potent. The heat in his gaze a promise for the hours ahead.

"Mother asked me if we wanted the entire ancient Aktarian ceremony. I assured her you'd prefer to wear a traditional Sarkian costume."

"What does the bride wear in the Aktarian ceremony?"

"Nothing. Neither does the groom. Only the golden binding cord."

Ria could feel heat flooding her cheeks. The idea of being naked before the Lord Commander…

Gyrr laughed and reached for the tiny gold clasps running down the front of her gown. "Although you are something to behold in your natural state, I'd prefer not to share your exquisite body with my father or my crew."

After opening the bodice, he slid the fine fabric from her shoulders. Beneath the gown, she wore nothing. Kneeling before her, Gyrr removed the gold sandals from her feet.

He rubbed his face against her belly. His tongue slid across her sex. "My receptors are aflame with your scent."

Ria skimmed her finger over his pleasure node.

He sucked in an audible breath. "You're ready?"

"Yes, my husband."

Gyrr rose and began to tear off his clothes.

Each time they made love, Ria grew more confident with giving him pleasure. She teased him that applying pressure to his pleasure node was similar to the delicate touch require to maneuver ships in docking bays.

Lowering her upon his soft furs, Gyrr climbed between her thighs. Slowly, his cock probed her sex and Ria lifted her hips to welcome his hot invasion. Although her husband was eager, his thrusts were gentle and measured as he filled her. Once joined, Ria touched her tongue to his pleasure node. His complete trust in her ability swelled her heart.

She flicked her tongue lightly against the node.

"Are you sure you don't have some Gladian blood?" he asked, his words thick with passion. His hand dug into the furs.

Answering with a lush lick, she teased the sensitive node. His thrusts were slow and deep as he drove into her and his skin dewed with perspiration. Ria's heart thundered in anticipation. When she fastened her lips over the node, his body went still and shuddered. She released him as her climax radiated through her middle. She clutched him tight as he thrust one final time.

"With practice, I'll last longer."

"Then we'll have to practice often."

Satisfied body and soul, Ria wrapped her arms about her husband and held him tight and close to her heart.

EPILOGUE

"Have you chosen a name?"

Gyrr's heart swelled with fatherly pride as his parents gazed proudly upon their new grandson swathed in a blanket of silver mank. His own gaze settled upon his lifemate's glowing face. Ria had insisted upon standing to greet the Lord Commander and the Princess, but Gyrr had managed to win this battle and she'd remained seated.

"Tell them, Ria."

Although, he had reassured her, Gyrr knew Ria feared his family would not approve of the name they had chosen for their child. She wished to honor her father, the man falsely accused and convicted of an act of treason. Ria had spent the two years following their binding ceremony researching her father's case. She had discovered the real traitor, a fellow officer serving on the *Ultus*.

Ria had proved her father's innocence and the Elite were now free to speak his name. Still, his lifemate hesitated. When she looked at him, Gyrr smiled and nodded, encouraging her to speak.

"Draa Ammar Thrane."

Gyrr waited for his father's response. Ria needed to feel the love and acceptance from the man she thought of as a living god.

Lord Aaxis reached down and gathered the babe into his arms. "An honorable name for my first born grandson."

Proud beyond words, Gyrr's heart pounded with joy as Draa's tiny fingers fisted about his grandfather's thumb.

"Draa, I am your Papa. Your wish is my command."

Princess Tayra held out her arms. "Aaxis, already you promise to spoil him."

His father relinquished Draa and winked at Tayra. "And you won't, my love?"

Leaning down, Aaxis kissed Ria briefly on the forehead. "Thank you, daughter, for this blessing to our family."

Gyrr kneeled beside Ria's chair. He kissed away the tears streaming down his lifemate's cheeks and whispered, "Like his mother, my son is something to behold."

The following is available from Ellora's Cave
Publishing, Inc. in eBook

www.ellorascave.com

SLUMBER PARTY

B.J. MCCALL

PREVIEW

"Tonight's the night. I can't believe it."

Jane Miller tossed a pair of lacy panties into her overnight bag. "Slumber Party was your idea."

Grinning from ear-to-ear, her best friend poured champagne.

"Oh no, Nina. Don't give me your scheming smile. Not now."

"I don't have a scheming smile."

"You do. You've had it since you were twelve. But now, I have a lot more to lose than my allowance. If Mom knew about this, she'd try to ground me."

"This isn't sneak-a-peek at Billy Adam's penis. This is Dr. Jane Miller, going for it." Grinning, Nina began to bump and grind to music only she could hear. Somewhere between a bump and a grind, she froze." You're really going to have sex with a complete stranger."

"That wasn't how your friend, Ellen, sold her exclusive service," Jane said, picking up a flute of champagne.

Omigod. *He* is a stranger, a total unknown quantity. Jane had fantasized about *him*, but hadn't laid eyes on him. "I wish Ellen would allow videos and photos."

"Ellen knows what she's doing." Nina picked up Slumber Party's printed rules. "Rule number one. Clients cannot preview, or prejudge, one another prior to the first rendezvous."

"I don't know a thing about him." Jane grimaced. "Nothing except, he wants sex."

"No preconceived ideas."

"You sound like Ellen." Jane locked gazes with her best friend. "You're not Ellen, are you?"

"Like I could hide anything from you."

"Tell me again, is this legal?"

"Slumber Party isn't an escort service. I vouched for you, otherwise she wouldn't have accepted you as a client."

Ellen, the convincing voice on the telephone. *You're not paying me for sex, just the opportunity to meet someone with similar tastes. I provide the time, the place, and the comforts. You must supply the enthusiasm.*

Think of it as being assigned a roommate. Tours and cruises do it all the time. Weren't you assigned a roomie your freshman year?

"Who is Ellen? Why is she so mysterious?"

"I wish I knew, I'd kiss her right on the lips for Joe."

"So would I," Jane confessed. "I've never seen you so happy. Joe's great."

Nina's brown eyes narrowed. "Don't even start thinking about Karl. Think about your mystery lover. Ellen has great taste."

Jane definitely didn't want to think about her ex. *Can I do this?*

"I can always back out. There is a clause." Jane gulped the champagne. "I have to show up, but I can change my mind. There are two bedrooms. What the hell am I doing?"

"You're living a fantasy. One you've had for years. He's been checked out. Thoroughly investigated and examined, just as you were."

"If he went through the same physical, I know he's healthy."

"Ellen's thorough. When she matched me with Joe, she hit a bull's-eye."

"What if we don't click?"

"What if you do?"

A thrill of hope and horniness zipped through Jane's middle. She drained her glass.

"You're supposed to sip the champagne in celebration. Not chug it down before you drive."

Jane could use two fingers of scotch. A stiff belt would keep her anxiety at bay, but a three-hour drive to the rendezvous in the redwoods demanded sobriety.

Nina picked up the bottle and poured a small portion of bubbly into Jane's glass. "Just enough for a toast, and stop frowning. You'll get wrinkles."

Despite her anxiety, Jane smiled. Pretty, petite Nina, always pushing Jane to step out of the box. Was this her fantasy or Nina's? Or some odd combination created by the two of them while sharing bottles of wine and boxes of chocolate?

"What if he's the worst blind date?"

The temptation to back out warred with the thrill of fulfilling her midnight dreams, but one night of uninhibited lovemaking with a sexy stranger prodded Jane onward. If a man didn't know you or what you did for a living, if he judged you only as a mutual partner in pleasure, one was totally free to explore one's sexuality completely. Ellen again.

That wicked smile touched Nina's lips. "What if he's handsome, hung, and the fuck of a lifetime?"

Jane lifted her glass. "To sex."

Nina gulped a large portion of her champagne and choked. Jane had to laugh. Nina was as nervous as she was.

"Have you chosen your name?"

"Beginning now, I am officially known as Summer."

Never in her thirty-two years had Jane done anything so outrageous. Studious, cautious, dependable, workaholic, no-nonsense described Jane. But Summer could be sexy, romantic, and uninhibited.

"It's been two years. I hope it's like riding a bike."

Nina laughed. "I hope it's more fun."

"Am I doing the right thing?"

"I've set you up with a dentist, a CPA and a CEO. What happened?"

"I mentioned oligonucleotide synthesis and was home by midnight, alone in my own bed."

"Exactly, and what is Slumber Party's rule number four?"

"No shop talk. Never tell your lover what you do for a living."

"What does Dr. Miller, workaholic, research chemist need?"

"An occasional lover. A man who wants what I want," Jane smiled. "Glorious sex with no complications."

About the author:

The youngest of seven sisters born in the hills of West Virginia, B.J. McCall lives beneath the redwoods of Northern California. Combining her love of romance and science fiction, she invites the reader to explore her universe.

B.J. McCall is the author of two contemporary novellas, Love Undercover, Secrets Volume 3, and Alias Smith and Jones, Secrets Volume 5.

B.J. welcomes mail from readers. You can write to her c/o Ellora's Cave Publishing at 1337 Commerce Drive, Suite 13, Stow OH 44224.

Also by B.J. McCall:

Slumber Party, Inc.

Why an electronic book?

We live in the Information Age — an exciting time in the history of human civilization in which technology rules supreme and continues to progress in leaps and bounds every minute of every hour of every day. For a multitude of reasons, more and more avid literary fans are opting to purchase e-books instead of paperbacks. The question to those not yet initiated to the world of electronic reading is simply: *why?*

1. *Price.* An electronic title at Ellora's Cave Publishing runs anywhere from 40-75% less than the cover price of the <u>exact same title</u> in paperback format. Why? Cold mathematics. It is less expensive to publish an e-book than it is to publish a paperback, so the savings are passed along to the consumer.

2. *Space.* Running out of room to house your paperback books? That is one worry you will never have with electronic novels. For a low one-time cost, you can purchase a handheld computer designed specifically for e-reading purposes. Many e-readers are larger than the average handheld, giving you plenty of screen room. Better yet, hundreds of titles can be stored within your new library — a single microchip. (Please note that Ellora's Cave does not endorse any specific brands. You can check our website at www.ellorascave.com for customer

recommendations we make available to new consumers.)

3. *Mobility.* Because your new library now consists of only a microchip, your entire cache of books can be taken with you wherever you go.

4. *Personal preferences are accounted for.* Are the words you are currently reading too small? Too large? Too...**ANNOYING**? Paperback books cannot be modified according to personal preferences, but e-books can.

5. *Innovation.* The way you read a book is not the only advancement the Information Age has gifted the literary community with. There is also the factor of what you can read. Ellora's Cave Publishing will be introducing a new line of interactive titles that are available in e-book format only.

6. *Instant gratification.* Is it the middle of the night and all the bookstores are closed? Are you tired of waiting days—sometimes weeks—for online and offline bookstores to ship the novels you bought? Ellora's Cave Publishing sells instantaneous downloads 24 hours a day, 7 days a week, 365 days a year. Our e-book delivery system is 100% automated, meaning your order is filled as soon as you pay for it.

Those are a few of the top reasons why electronic novels are displacing paperbacks for many an avid reader. As always, Ellora's Cave Publishing welcomes your questions and comments. We invite you to email us at service@ellorascave.com or write to us directly at: 1337 Commerce Drive, Suite 13, Stow OH 44224.

Printed in the United States
29164LVS00010B/124